RIDER OF
THE HIGH HILLS

RIDER OF
THE HIGH HILLS

Max Brand

DODD, MEAD & COMPANY
NEW YORK

1 2 3 4 5 6 7 8 9 10

Library of Congress Cataloging in Publication Data

Faust, Frederick, 1892–1944.
    Rider of the high hills.

    (Silver star western)
    I. Title.
PZ3.F2775Rh   1977   [PS3511.A87]   813'.5'2   77–14593
ISBN 0–396–07499–5

RIDER OF
THE HIGH HILLS

CHAPTER 1

Dave Bates had the outside job. Next to Gene Salvio, he was the best shot of the three, but they had matched for the choice position, and the turn of the coin insisted that Harry Quinn should go inside with Salvio.

The outside job was the easiest, because if the two inside men were both shot up without being able to complete the robbery of the bank, Bates could slide away undetected. But if the two came out with the stuff, he had his share of the trouble. Also, he had to watch the main door and see that, if a disturbance started inside the place, no sudden rescuers poured in from the street, no men with guns in their hands.

The day was still and very hot. It was ten in the morning, when there is just enough slant to the sun to give it a fuller whack at the body. There was not a horse, not a wagon, not a man, not a dog or even a chicken in the crooked little main street of Jumping Creek. The sun was making itself felt, and the wooden and canvas awnings bravely stretched out their arms and threw a gentle shadow down to the ground. The heat of that day was enough to make one want to sit still and trust time.

But Dave Bates could not trust time. He had to trust, instead, to his two partners inside the bank, to the two revolvers under his coat, and to the rifles which lay aslant in the saddle holsters under the right stirrup leathers of three of the saddles.

The other two horses would not be backed by men. They

were on hand to carry a heavy load, and the load would be gold, if all went well. A powerful canvas saddlebag hung on each side of both saddles.

When Dave Bates thought of the ponderous, unwieldy nature of such a metal as gold, he cursed the stuff and wondered why a bank had to be loaded down with that stuff instead of light, crisp, new, delightful bank notes? And his lean face, which looked as though it had been compressed in a mold to half of the proper width, twisted crookedly to the side. Then he glanced up toward the mountains that, in the distance, flowed away into the pallor of the skies. Of course, that was the answer, and out of the rocky sides of those mountains the gold was worked and the ore ground and washed, and so, in driblets, the precious stuff was brought down to Jumping Creek.

Well, as soon as the work had been finished, Dave Bates hoped that they would get out among those mountains. And he reached a hand under his coat and touched the handle of one of his Colts, already well warmed by his body. Then he drew himself up to the full of his five feet and five inches, and expanded his scrawny chest. The two guns were what made a man of him. People could laugh down a little fellow like Dave Bates, but they could not laugh down his guns.

What he prayed was that Gene Salvio would not be too hasty with his weapons. Guns are all very well, but they ought to be used with discretion. Otherwise a fellow had blood on his trail. Invisible blood, perhaps, but nevertheless damning. In a wide and careless country like the West, many crimes are forgotten. They wash away. But murder sticks worse than soot. Dave Bates knew all about it, and now he remembered the savage eyes of Gene Salvio and wished that he, not Harry Quinn, had walked into the bank with Salvio. He might be a stronger influence to keep Gene in check, if a pinch should happen to come.

In the meantime, the seconds went by, with gigantic strides, measured by the pounding of the heart of Bates.

2

And then it came, like the sudden first stroke on a booming bell—a gunshot in the bank. And then a voice screaming out. It might be a woman; it might be a man. Pain unsexed the sound. No, it was the scream of a man. No woman could cry out so loudly.

Words came babbling through the screeching. That was the voice of Gene Salvio, snarling, raging, threatening, and then came three more revolver shots in rapid succession—just the way Salvio knew how to fan them out of his gun!

The street had been empty, a moment before. Suddenly there was life in the shadows, here and there. Then some one shouted: "The bank! They're after it!"

Men came on the run. They came from up the street and down the street. They came with naked guns glittering in their hands.

Bates shouted: "Get back on your heels, all of you! Drop them guns and hold back. Watch lively now!"

And he fired a bullet just over the head of a chunky man with gray hair and a black mustache.

The advancing waves of armed humanity wavered, halted, and then swayed back and forth for a moment, uncertainly. If a single leader had sprung out now, to give the men new impetus, they would have closed over Dave Bates with a single rush, and he knew it. He even saw one about to act—a slender, tall youth with a ridiculously bright Mexican outfit on him. This fellow wavered less than the others. He began to crouch a little, with a wild look in his eyes.

Dave Bates drove a bullet into the ground at his feet and knocked dust over his boots as high as his knees.

"I'm watching you hombres. Back up!" he shouted. "I'm goin' to let a streak of light through some of you!"

The whole crowd gave back on either hand, and then Salvio and Harry Quinn came out, staggering with the weights they carried.

Gold—they were staggering under weights of gold!

3

Harry Quinn was a strong man, but he grunted as he heaved up a chamois sack and dumped it onto one of the empty saddlebags.

Some one in the crowd—well back toward the rear—yelled out: "Are we goin' to be bluffed out by three thugs? Come on, boys! All together. One rush and we got 'em! They're cleanin' us out of all our cash!"

The crowd was stirred by that appeal, but it was not stirred enough. The sight of Dave Bates, as he kept his body swinging a little from side to side, was too disheartening—the sight of him, and his lean hands that held the guns with such familiar ease, just a little above the height of the hip, his thumbs resting on the hammers. He could turn loose a torrent of lead from those weapons, and each man, as the little figure swayed, felt the dark muzzles of the guns draw across him like knives. The vast emptiness of death yawned at them from the little round barrels of the Colts.

So they hung there, in suspense, willing to be brave, but held back by the lack of a dashing leader. One man able to take one step forward would have loosed a double avalanche capable of smashing the life out of that band of three, but no man dared take the single step.

The two extra horses were loaded—well loaded. And more of those small chamois bags were dropped into the saddlebags on the horses which would have to carry riders, also.

"Ready!" snapped the voice of Gene Salvio.

"Ready!" said Harry Quinn.

Gene Salvio leaped into the saddle on his black horse. How beautiful all those horses were, well chosen for strength and for speed. But far better-looking was Gene Salvio, as he sat in the saddle with laughter on his lips and the devil in his eyes. Men shrank away from him. They looked down. They did not want those eyes to single them out, because they saw that this man was ready and willing and eager to kill.

Dave Bates and Quinn mounted in turn. Salvio was unencumbered on the black. Both Harry Quinn and Bates led one of the extra horses. They moved forward.

Gene Salvio said: "You fellows get on ahead. Go slow and steady. And keep looking into their eyes! Mind the windows and the doors, too, but mostly mind the windows! Go on ahead. I'll take care of these gents behind us!"

Admiration warmed the heart of Dave Bates. To be sure, Salvio might have been a little too ready with his guns, back there in the bank, but he was also the fellow to push them safely through the crisis that he had helped to bring on by his rash bloodthirstiness. Watching the windows—that was a good idea! Of course there might be men at any of those windows, and at the doors, too.

He heard Salvio shouting: "Stand back there. You in the black hat—don't move your hand like that ag'in! Give us room through here, or we're going to take room, and the room we take is going to be vacant for a hell of a while after we're gone!"

It was well expressed, thought Dave Bates. There was really a brain in the head of that fellow Gene Salvio.

The crowd, in fact, was bearing back. As the robbers went through the street, there was silence around them, but there was a shrill murmur ahead of them and a growling murmur behind them.

Men in that crowd began to shift their eyes from one face to another, trying to find that most needed thing—a leader, a man to cry out a single right word!

And still there was not a voice raised. Still there was only that helpless, groaning sound which only a crowd can make.

Then some of the cleverer heads, foreseeing that it would be hard to start the fight in that humor, broke away through the crowd and went for horses.

The end of the main street came under the eyes of Dave Bates. He looked out toward the foothills and the great mountains and felt that he was safe with his portion of the loot. Then he heard the beating of hoofs here and there on the outskirts

5

of the town, and then flying down the narrows of the streets; and he knew, with a grim pull at the corners of his mouth, that the trouble was only starting.

CHAPTER 2

That noise of the horses was almost enough to make Dave Bates call for action on his own part, but he knew well enough that it was best to leave decisions and commands to the outstanding man of the party, and that man was certainly the famous Gene Salvio. So Bates said nothing but, like his companions, kept two steady guns turned toward the crowd.

He had never done anything like this before. To face a gang in this manner was very much like facing a vast, a dangerous, but a witless monster. If it knew its strength, it would be heedless of the small harm that could happen to it and would instantly take revenge. For what would be the death of two or three of its members—to the rest of the crowd?

By a pretense, by a sham, they were holding back the others. And, in that way, they came to the cluster of trees around the bridge at the end of the main street of Jumping Creek. There Salvio at last gave the word and, with a rush, they galloped their horses around the curve, and thunder boomed from the planks as they rushed over the bridge.

A storm of bullets followed them. The bullets crackled like hail through the trees, whistled like invisible, incredible birds through the air. By the thickness with which they flew, the numbers of the crowd could be estimated, but already there was a rising shoulder of ground which gave the low-stooping fugitives shelter, and now they could sit erect, well down the winding road.

Dave Bates looked back at the saddlebags that jumped at the sides of the led horses. There must be five hundred pounds, or thereabouts, between the pair. And another hundred pounds of

6

the gold had been given to each rider. Say almost eight hundred pounds in all. Eight hundred pounds of gold nuggets and dust!

Well, it was not a very difficult bit of arithmetic to work the thing out. Somewhere around a hundred and eighty-five thousand dollars, at least. Split back one third to Pop Dickerman who had suggested the job and who had fixed the cashier in order to find out when the greatest available sum would be in the safe of the bank. That left about a hundred and twenty thousand. And this carved up into forty thousand bucks per man. Forty thousand dollars—and all in gold!

There was an ache in the head and a pull across the eyes of Dave Bates that had come there from facing out the crowd, so long. This ache began to pass away. He wanted to laugh. He saw that Gene Salvio and Harry Quinn were already laughing. They were good fellows, thought Bates. Quinn was something of a brute, at times, and Salvio was always something of a wildcat. But in a time of necessity you want a man who knows his job and can do it. This pair knew their work and they could do it. The heart of Bates swelled.

He did not even have to be troubled about the rather dim worry of having robbed poor men. The miners had been paid. There were only the great, million-headed corporations to consider, and to Dave Bates they were not worthy of consideration. He felt, almost, that he had honestly earned forty thousand dollars! Other men had found it and grubbed it. He had earned it by endangering his life!

As they pulled up the road, Salvio swung into the lead, from the rear, and when they came to a cross trail, Salvio without hesitation took the dimmer way, forcing his horse up steep rocks along the slope of a hill. This seemed a dubious policy to Dave Bates. The point of it, however, was clear. Far behind them could be heard the hoofs of many horses, rolling like the rolling of drums, and it was probable that the blind mob of riders from Jumping Creek would pour heedlessly up the wider road, looking for no sign, heads high to catch a glimpse, around a bend, of the three riders and the five horses that they wanted.

7

Therefore, instead of heading straight on toward the mountain wilderness which would give them sure covering, Gene Salvio intended to dodge the first rush of the pursuit, save the strength of the five horses, and angle off at a new direction, even though the mountains in this quarter were farther away.

In fact, when they got over the head of the hill, Salvio actually brought the horses back to a walk.

Considering the necessity which spurred them all forward, this seemed to Bates like standing still. He would not complain about it, however. To complain, in a time of need, of what is actually being commanded by the leader, is a foolish thing, as a rule. However, it was all right to ask questions about the past.

"Look here, Gene," he said. "What happened in there? You started the shooting?"

"Aw," said Salvio, "there was a fool of a red-headed kid hanging around. Kind of like a chore boy. And after I'd got the gun on the cashier, the redhead pulls a gat out of a drawer. I let him have it. A funny thing—I aimed for his head, because I wanted to put him out quick. It's better to put 'em out quick, in a time like that. Just a wound don't do so much good. They gotta flop and stay down, dead. That sort of discourages the rest of the boys a little. Well, redhead seen the trouble coming, and while he swings up his gun, he puts a hand out before him. Imagine trying to ward off a bullet, eh? Anyway, that slug of mine went right through his hand and his wrist.

"The funny thing was that it *did* seem to turn my bullet a little. It just ripped along the side of his head, and he falls down and starts moaning over his hand. And then he starts screeching. You could 'a' heard him in the street."

"You could 'a' heard him in hell," said Dave Bates sincerely. "He sure raised the hair on my head, and he raised a crowd, too."

"You handled that crowd fine," said Harry Quinn.

"Yeah, you done your job," remarked Gene Salvio, who rarely praised others.

"Then you turned loose three more," said Bates.

"That was for the cashier," said Salvio. "Pop Dickerman, you remember, said for us to cover him up pretty good, if we could manage it. So, since I'd already heard the crowd gathering, I thought that a little more noise wouldn't do any harm, and I turned loose on the cashier. Like I wanted to drop him. I put three bullets all around him in the air, and he curled up on the floor and died—he was scared to death, pretty near!"

Salvio began to laugh, rather guardedly.

Then, far behind them, on the other side of the hill, they heard the men of Jumping Creek go by like a storm. They listened, looked at one another, and then grinned.

"The gents that stay inside the law, they don't seem to have very good brains in their heads!" said Salvio. "Ever notice that? They're always wrong!"

"But when they're right, they hang a lot of gents from the trees," suggested Dave Bates.

For his own part, he did not like crowing until a job was well finished and the danger gone.

They came down off the slope and turned up through a pleasant valley that ran near the railroad line. In the distance, they could see the flash of the wheel-polished rails with the sunlight running on them like swift water, tinted blue. The trail was dim. They left it and took the straight way up the valley. This was still a longer way to the higher mountains, and security, but, again, it would save the horses. And Dave Bates knew the value of fresh horses in any pinch. His admiration for Salvio was growing every moment when, from behind, they heard a horse neigh.

"What could that be?" asked Harry Quinn, scowling. He stared back over his shoulder. Then, with a groan, he pointed.

Bates saw the picture that came out of the trees behind them. There were a dozen men, all with rifles, all riding hard, and at the head of them journeyed a tall man with a face so thin that his features stood out in a relief of highlights and shadows, even from this distance. He rode on a small, mouse-colored mustang, that looked more mule than horse. It took small strides, but so

9

many of them that it easily kept in the lead.

This man now turned and waved to his companions, and then pointed ahead where the robbers were in full flight.

Well, it was bad luck that somebody among the men of Jumping Creek had guessed that the fugitives might take the way over the short trail, uphill. However, this would be the point where freshness of horses would tell. Goodness of horses would tell, too, and the one thing on which Pop Dickerman never spared money was the sort of horseflesh with which he provided his missionaries of crime.

All five animals legged it valiantly, and in an instant it was clear that they had the wind and the foot of the pursuit.

They swerved along the edge of a marsh. They sped up a slope. They twisted through a denseness of trees. And then, suddenly, Salvio in the lead drew rein so hard that his horse stopped on braced legs, the hoofs plowing up the ground.

"There's somebody ahead!" he called softly.

Then Bates heard it, too. Right and left, as though spread out in a long line, he heard horses coming. He heard the shrill, penetrating squeak of saddle leather, and the far-off murmur of voices. He could see clearly what had happened. The men of Jumping Creek had divided. Half had taken the rear trail of the robbers; half had swung around the hill and blocked the robbers in their advance of the valley. Now they were blocked as neatly as though they had been cooped in a box!

CHAPTER 3

They could turn left—up the staggering face of a rocky hill, treeless, bare, open to a sweeping rifle fire. Or else they could turn right into the stench, the mud, the puzzling mists and vapors of the marsh. Gene Salvio took the only possible course. He swung the black horse to the side and struck right into the marsh; and as Bates followed, last of the three, a sudden crash of rifle fire told him that he had been seen.

That made their chances one point worse.

He liked to estimate chances. When the crowd gathered in the street of Jumping Creek, their chances of getting away had been about one in three.

After they cleared out of town and escaped the first rifle fire, they had chances of two to one in their favor. When they put the high hill behind them and swung up the easy grade of the valley that contained the railroad, they had chances of four to one in their favor. Even the sight of the pursuit in the rear only decreased their chances by a point. Then that encounter with the unseen line of riders, blocking their way, beat them down to the bottom. They had one chance in five, as they turned into the marsh. They were seen, and they had a chance in six.

Salvio called, with inimitable cheer: "We'll get to the railroad, and we'll gallop up the ties and laugh our heads off at those fools!"

Bates looked forward and saw Salvio riding his horse out of a depth of thick, green slime that mantled the fine creature from the ears down and altered its color completely.

The marsh was a horror. It was a horrible muddy wash through which the horses broke. But they floundered on, keeping right behind Gene Salvio—who had the knowing brain!

They held on. Presently the foulness of the marsh, the thickness of the trees that made a hot twilight, here, in the middle of the day, gave way to glimpses of light, and suddenly they were out on the side of the railroad grade, with Gene Salvio already cutting the wires of the big fence!

Two strands had hardly clanged apart and whipped back under the clippers of Salvio when voices shouted to the side, and Dave Bates had a sight of a tall man with a face as thin as starvation, riding a little mouse-colored mustang out from the edge of the marsh.

He had found a solid way across the marsh—there was hardly a bit of mud above the hocks of his mustang!

Bates, as he backed his horses violently, saw the stream of

11

armed men break out behind that leader. Bates snatched out his right-hand Colt and opened fire slowly, accurately, intent to kill.

He wanted to kill that tall man. He wanted to kill that mouse-colored horse. He had a strange feeling that if he could dispose of either of them, chance would swing back to the robbers.

He steadied his gun for the third shot when he saw something flash in the hand of that rider. The gun spoke. Bates's right-hand gun, his old favorite, was knocked out of his hand and into a pool of black, stagnant water.

He grabbed his bruised hand between his chin and his breast and rode back through the trees, spurring his horse deep. He uttered no complaint. He was not disheartened by pain. He simply knew, calmly, that the chances were suddenly a hundred to one against them. Some people might have the frankness to admit that they had no chance at all.

Salvio's gun was barking behind them. Voices shouted everywhere.

With his numb hand—it seemed otherwise uninjured—Dave Bates led the way. His horse seemed to know something, and he let it have its head. Presently, it plunged into water up to its belly. That water shoaled away to knee depth. The horse forced its way into a hedge of thorny brush, regardless of the stickers. Bates found himself on dry ground—a little ridge that stood up in the center of the marsh.

He was glad of that. If they had to die, it was better to die on good, clean ground. As he checked the horse, Harry Quinn came up beside him. Harry's face was gray, and his mouth was pulled back from his yellow teeth, as though he were lifting a great weight, every muscle dragging at it.

"You fool, what you stopping for?" asked Harry Quinn, and pushed his horse straight past. In a moment he stopped, however. He seemed to listen to the voices that shouted close at hand or murmured far off. "Yeah," he said. "I understand!"

He dismounted and sat down on a rock. He was still sitting

12

there, rolling a cigarette, when Salvio broke up out of the marsh.

Salvio said: "You rat, Quinn—jump up and stamp on that smoke. Get down there at the other end of the dry land. I'll take the middle. Dave, you take this end. Shoot at anything you see. They think they got us, but we're going to show them a few tricks! Shoot at anything—and shoot straight. Hey, Dave, did that hombre get you?"

"He lifted the gun out of my hand. That's all. I'm all right," said Dave Bates.

"Get off your hoss then, and stand watch," ordered Salvio.

Bates obeyed.

They put the horses—and the gold—in the central cluster of brush that covered the middle of the little island. Then each man sank away in a chosen place of concealment, waiting for the approach of the enemy.

But there was no approach. Bates could hear voices shouting close up, or muttering far away. But they never turned into visible humans among the trees of the marsh. For his own part, he had a nest of rocks out of which he could look to three sides; Salvio was taking charge of the center of the island, and his back.

Those voices to which Bates listened were bright with joy, ringing with the certainty of triumph. And Bates could understand. A hundred to one chance—for their lives.

The gold? Well, there was nothing to that! It was simply a weight. It was worthless. It was worse than lead, which could be shot out of a gun. Well, they could shoot gold out of their guns, too!

Bates grinned as he had the thought. Then he heard a high-pitched, nasal voice. It was not loud, but it prodded through the silence of the near-by marsh like a needle, and into the brain of Bates.

"Boys," said the voice, "we know that you're in there on the island. But it ain't any good. You're in there, and we got you. What we wanta know is: D'you wanta come out?"

13 P

There was no answer.

Want to come out? Of course—but there would be other things to hear.

The nasal voice went on: "We got enough men to fence in this whole marsh and keep it fenced. Why not come out now, the way you'll have to come out sooner or later? We'll give you a fair break. You didn't kill nobody. And if you march out of there now and turn in the stuff you stole, you'll have a better chance with the jury. That there jury is goin' to be made up of some of the men out of this party, most likely. And that jury will recommend you to the mercy of the judge. You been and done a good job, but you lost. Now pay, and pay quick, or we'll sure raise hell with you!"

He waited as he ended this speech. And Bates listened for the answer of Salvio.

Presently Salvio called out: "What's your name?"

"Steve Balen," called the nasal voice.

"Are you the gent that rode the measly little mouse-colored bronc?"

"That ain't a lookin' hoss; but it's a ridin' hoss, partner!" said the nasal voice. "Yeah, I'm the man you mean."

"Then, the devil with you!" called Salvio, and followed his words with a shot that flew crackling through the woods.

Very cheerfully the voice of Steve Balen replied: "I don't blame you, brother. If I was in your boots, I'd hope to hang on to the finish. I didn't want to come and yarn with you like this here, but I figgered it was my duty. What I aim to wanta do is to string you up by the neck, the three of you, and I reckon we'll have a chance to do that before the month is out!"

That ended the parley.

Dave Bates was still staggering under the impact of what he had heard, when he made out the muffled voice of Quinn, which was saying: "Hey, Gene, you ain't gone crazy, have you?"

The voice came closer, repeating: "Gene, you ain't gone nuts, have you?"

Bates went to join the conference. It took place in the central

14

cluster of shrubbery, near to the horses. "They're giving us a chance, and you go and chuck it away!" said Quinn.

Salvio was very calm and restrained. He merely said: "You boys can load your stuff onto your hosses, if you want, and go out and give yourselves up. I ain't doing it, that's all."

"Hey, Gene, what's the sense?" asked Quinn.

"You tell the dummy," said Salvio to Bates, after staring for a moment at Quinn.

"They got hanging stuff on Salvio," said Bates, nodding his head.

"They ain't got hanging stuff on me," said Quinn. "Come on, Dave. We'd better get out."

"Get where? Into jail for eight, ten years?" asked Bates.

"Better jail for eight, ten years than hell forever," said Harry Quinn.

"Sure," said Salvio. "Go on and get out."

He stood by the black horse, patting its wet shoulder, sneering at them both.

Well, perhaps it was better to go to hell—in brave company.

Bates said: "We started this job with three men. We're going to wind it up with three men, I guess, Harry."

Harry Quinn threw out a hand in an eloquent gesture and started to exclaim in protest. Then he checked himself suddenly. A realization came into his eyes.

"Oh, I see," said Quinn. "Sure, I didn't think of that. I didn't think of that at all!"

He seemed to be vastly relieved and said to Salvio: "What about a smoke, Gene?"

"Sure, kid," said Salvio, and smiled.

It was very hot. Sweat began to run on all their faces, and the smell of the marsh was heavy and sick in the air. Out of the distance they could hear more horses pounding up the valley, or down it. Reinforcements were coming.

Salvio was walking up and down slowly, his hands clasped behind his back, his head bent, and a little veil of mosquitoes trailing unheeded behind that head.

15

CHAPTER 4

The sun had been sliding slowly down the western sky until now it no longer struck the island with its direct light, which merely served to show the vapors that rose from the marsh so thickly that breathing seemed more difficult. Then Gene Salvio paused in his walking.

He said: "They're piling up more men around us all the time. They're waiting for three men and five horses to try to charge out through 'em. They'll be expecting us the middle of the night. Well, we'll beat 'em on all those counts. There'll be no horses with us, and we'll go now!"

"Wait a minute," protested Harry Quinn. "Can you carry about three hundred pounds through this kind of a marsh?"

"We're not carrying out the stuff," said Salvio.

"Hey! Leaving it with the hosses?" asked Dave Bates.

"Leaving it inside that tree," answered Salvio. "Shift it into that hollow trunk, boys!"

He set the example and started carrying the small chamois bags to a tree which grew two strides from the end of the island, thrust out of the black water of the marsh. It was almost dead. Only one branch showed green, and this was turning yellow. There was no gap in the side of the trunk to indicate that it was hollow, but when Salvio pulled himself up to the crotch, he was able to drop the bags he carried into the interior. They were actually heard to splash in the slime at the roots of the tree.

"How'd you know that it was holler?" asked Harry Quinn, admiring. "You got X-ray eyes, Gene?"

"I tapped agin' it when I was coming up to the island," said Salvio. "Rush the stuff inside the tree. It'll wait there for us, I guess."

"I dunno," said Harry Quinn. "It could wait there a long time, for all of me, the way I feel now. I been feeling my share of it hanging around my neck all this time!"

They got the stuff inside the tree. After the first few bags had

16

fallen, the others dropped without bringing out that splashing sound. There was simply a dull, heavy, thudding noise, and presently the last of the gold had been put out of sight.

"Let 'em try to guess where the stuff is now!" said Dave Bates, gloating. "Just let 'em try to guess! Why, Gene, that's the best idea you ever had. But how'll we get through those hombres all around the island? There's still daylight!"

For an answer, out of the distance a number of rifles suddenly opened fire. The bullets could be heard crackling through the woods; then the echoes rang for a moment, and there was the silence of the marsh again.

"There's a mite of daylight," agreed Salvio. "But it'd be hard to read fine print by it, and it'd be hard to see faces very clear. There's so much daylight that they're not going to expect us to try to come out, and there's not enough daylight to make them very sure of us if we do. They're shooting at shadows already! Come on, Dave. Come on, Harry. We'll see what we find."

"You remember that they all had a chance to have a good look at us," suggested Bates.

"Yeah. They had a good look at us in the bright of the sun, setting up there in the saddle on our hosses. They ain't going to see us the same way now."

He went down to the edge of the filthy water, deliberately picked up a film of slime, and trailed the ugly green of it over one side of his face.

"That ain't pretty," said Salvio, "but it'll make a difference."

Without a word, the others imitated him, smearing slime here and there on their clothes, on their faces. Then they followed Salvio across the island, and slowly through the slime and water which sometimes rose higher than their knees.

Salvio went very slowly to avoid making noise. The others came exactly in his wake, and presently he held up a hand. Before them rose a narrow ridge of brush.

"They're out there beyond the brush," said Salvio. "Lemme have a chance to talk to 'em, and then you fellows do what I

17

do. Understand? Lemme think for you, and you do what I do!"

"I'm ready," agreed Dave Bates, putting his life readily into the hands of the leader.

Salvio pushed through the brush, rather noisily. "Hey, hello!" he called.

"Who's that?" answered a voice in the near distance. "What fool is that callin' out so loud?"

"Maybe it's one of 'em," suggested another.

"Hey," called Salvio, "is Balen around anywhere?"

"Who wants him?"

"Pete Bennett. Me and Charlie and Chuck, we've found the easy way to the island that Balen wanted to get at."

"It's too late to go in there now. It'll be pitch dark before long."

"Lookat here," said Salvio angrily, "what 'a' we been wallering around in the slush for, if Balen ain't going to use what we've found out for him?"

"Shut up talking so loud and come out."

"Sure," said Salvio. "That's fine for you hombres that been staying on dry land all the time. But what about us that been wallering?"

He stalked forward through the brush, calling over his shoulder: "Come on, Chuck! Come on, Charlie!"

"Not so loud!" cautioned the other speaker.

"I'm pretty nigh fed up with the whole business," said Salvio, as Bates and Quinn came on behind him.

Beyond the bushes there was another bit of shallow marsh. They crossed this toward some trees under which a number of men were in plain view, except for the increasing dimness of the light and the intervening vapors of the marsh.

"I got half a mind to pull out of the business," Salvio was saying as he advanced into the group. "Doggone me if I ain't spent!"

And, to the amazement of Bates, Salvio threw himself right down among the others, on the grass.

Bates took that example and plumped himself down on a

stump, resting his face in his hands, as though exhausted. He saw Quinn settled with his back against a tree, his head also hanging. Then he could hear the man who seemed in charge of this section of the line saying: "Well, I didn't know that Balen sent anybody into the marsh."

"I wish I didn't know it," answered Salvio. "I sure had enough marsh. I'm going to have the smell of it in my nose the rest of my life. And I'm dead beat. Anybody got a drink on him? Anybody got a flask?"

There was no answer to this, and Salvio fell to muttering.

A fellow came up beside Bates and said: "Dirty work in there, eh?"

"Yeah, and damn it," said Bates.

"I wouldn't 'a' thought that Balen would 'a' sent nobody into the marsh," said the other.

Bates said nothing. He merely groaned as with fatigue.

Then he heard some one saying, "Here's Balen now."

Bates stood up. He saw that Quinn was rising, also, but that Salvio, strange to say, remained stretched on the ground, face down, arms flung wide, as though worn out with labor.

"I'm going to see if I can find me a drink of something," said Bates to the man beside him.

"Say," said the other, "you look like—"

He stopped his voice suddenly. Bates went on into the brush with cold snakes working up and down his spine.

What did he look like? In another moment he would show all those fellows what his back looked like when he was running as fast as his legs could carry him. Off to the side, he saw Quinn moving away, also.

"Here, Balen!" called a voice. "Here's a gent to make a report to you."

Bates paused on the farther side of the brush. He could look through and see Salvio rising. Not twenty steps away were a string of tethered horses, which might mean liberty for them; but Bates would not desert his leader, even though Harry Quinn was already striding toward that group of mustangs.

19

"Wait a minute," Salvio said, quite loudly. "I'll be back in a minute. I want to get something out of my saddlebag, and I'll be right back."

And there was Salvio, stepping unhurried toward the horses. Bates made haste to turn in the same direction. He only risked one glance behind him to see, in the half light, that the man with whom he had been talking was now seriously debating something with two other men, and pointing after him.

The same worms of ice began to work again in the spinal marrow of little Dave Bates. He walked right up to the first horse of the group as he heard Balen saying: "Find a way through the marsh? I never told any man to—"

A big fellow jumped out from nowhere and grabbed the arm of Dave Bates.

"Hey, watcha doin' with my hoss?" demanded the stranger.

Salvio stepped right up behind the big cowpuncher and clinked the barrel of a gun against the base of his skull. The man dropped like a falling sack.

"Fast, boys!" said Salvio.

They swept into the saddles, each of his chosen horse.

"Cut the other ropes. Cut the ropes and drive the broncs with us!" commanded Salvio.

"Stop 'em!" yelled the ringing voice of Steve Balen. "You day-blind owls, you've been and let the three of 'em walk right through you! Shoot! Get the hosses down—anything to stop 'em!"

But the knives of the three already had slashed right and left at the tethering ropes, and now with busy quirts they beat the horses into flight.

Guns began behind them.

Dave Bates distinctly heard the sound of a rifle bullet bang into the head of a horse running beside him. It was a noise like the impact of a club. The horse went down in a heap and turned a somersault. And then the whole covey of horses and the three riders crashed through the underbrush and stormed up the valley.

20

Behind them, men were still firing, but with every moment the fugitives sped farther away toward safety, and with every moment the night was thickening the air. Salvio had been right. It was the moment of the most treacherous light in all the twenty-four hours of the day. To look down the avenues of the trees was like looking into a deep water.

Life was being given back to the three of them, and Dave Bates felt that he was enjoying separately and specially every breath that he drew.

They drew out of the valley and up a steep hill, on the shoulder of which Salvio drew rein and let the horses breathe.

"Gene," said Dave Bates, "you done that as well as anybody in the world could 'a' done it! You sure saved our hides, that nobody else could 'a' done!"

"And what about Reata?" asked Gene Salvio angrily. "You're always sayin' that he can do anything. Could he 'a' done what we three just done?"

"He couldn't 'a' done no better. It was a great job, and you did it all the way through, Gene," said Bates.

And Harry Quinn heartily agreed.

CHAPTER 5

Later, the three heard the loud river of the pursuit turn aside out of the valley, heading back, no doubt, toward the main road, and that gave the fugitives a chance to jog softly on through the night.

Harry Quinn even suggested that they should turn back and try to get at the gold they had left behind them, but Salvio would not listen to that.

It was night now, he reminded them. Fires would be lighted here and there. By lantern light people would probably begin to search the marsh to look for the buried treasure, because every one must have known that the three fugitives could not possibly have taken away any great percentage of the stolen gold. Bates had two or three pounds in the twist of a bandanna in his pocket; that was all they had taken with them. Balen would be in there at the island, working hard to find the hiding place. No doubt it was because Balen was back there with part of his men that the rest of the crowd had taken the wrong trail. Be that as it might, the three had their skins whole and they could be grateful for that.

Salvio said: "But maybe we ain't through with a pile of trouble. That Steve Balen, he acted and he sounded to me like a gent that would stick tighter than a corn plaster! We'll get to Pop Dickerman. He's always got ideas."

"Yeah, he's always got ideas," said Dave Bates, "and we've always got the blood to bleed for 'em!"

All through that night they journeyed on patiently. And in the first thin gray of the dawn they raised the dim outlines of Rusty Gulch and, finally, of the high-backed barn in which Pop Dickerman lived, on the edge of the town.

They put up the horses in the shed behind the house barn. Then they went to the back door of the place, and Salvio knocked three times, paused, knocked twice again.

"Do it ag'in, louder," said Harry Quinn. "He can't hear that!"

"You don't wanta forget that he's a rat," said Salvio. "He can hear everything."

A moment later a voice said, behind the door: "Go around to the big room. I'll open up for you gents there."

"You see?" muttered Salvio to his companions, as they went around to the side of the old barn. "You gents can see Pop Dickerman every day of your lives, but you ain't never going to get used to him."

"Sure we ain't," agreed Bates. "Poison is hard to get used to, too."

There *was* a poison about the air of the place, to those who knew it well. Few people knew the junk peddler as well as did

22

these three henchmen of his. The knowledge of most was limited to the big piles of rubbish which rusted and slowly consumed in the outer yard, or to the more valuable stuff that was piled on the floor or hung from the rafters of the mow of the barn. They knew these things, and the skill of Pop Dickerman in driving bargains. But his three men could have talked out whole books of information concerning this practiced and consummate fence. They knew his far-spreading knowledge, the underground wires by which he kept in touch with numerous scenes and opportunities for crime which he farmed out, at a high price, to his favored few criminals. They knew scores of his personal idiosyncrasies. But also they were constantly aware of a wall which barred them from a great intimacy with the strange fellow.

The sliding door was noisily unlocked from the inside and pushed back. They saw the tall, stooping silhouette of Pop Dickerman and the whole room vaguely illumined by a single hanging lamp which was suspended from a central rafter of the mow and cast just enough light to make the nearer heaps of metalwork and crystal on the floor glow, and all those great bundles of assorted junk which hung down at the ends of ropes and chains. Some of them were always turning slowly, winding and unwinding. And before he went inside, Dave Bates looked up at the spectacle and muttered: "Like dead men hanging in rows, Pop. I always think of dead men hanging in rows!"

Pop Dickerman made that gesture of his, ten thousand times repeated and always in vain, that attempt to smooth down the fur of whiskers and hair that covered his long face almost to the eyes.

"Maybe it's a kind of a prophecy, Dave," he said. "Maybe it's kind of like a lot of mirrors, and you see what's goin' to happen to you."

The three of them gathered under the hanging lantern, and they threw themselves down on the various chairs and couches which were always standing at this point.

23

"So it was a bust for you, boys?" said Dickerman.

"What makes you think?" asked Harry Quinn, rather angrily.

"Not a bust? You got the goods, but you didn't bring 'em back with you?" said Dickerman.

"They run us down in the marsh, this side of Jumping Creek," said Salvio. "You know the place?"

"Yeah. I know," said Dickerman. "So you buried the stuff, and then you managed to wriggle through 'em and come away?"

"How d'you guess that?" asked Salvio curiously.

"Because you look beat, but not all beat. You missed the money, but you kept your hides for yourselves, eh?" said Dickerman.

His husky voice continued with other words, that were not quite intelligible. The sound of that voice made one expect to see the face of a very ancient man, a man dying with years, but the bright, rattly sparkling of the eyes was a continual denial of weakness.

"We got off with our hides, and lucky," said Dave Bates. "Lucky because we had Salvio along to bluff a way through for us. I never seen a cooler or a smarter thing, Pop!"

"Yeah, Gene is cool, and Gene is smart, but that ain't money in *my* pocket," answered Dickerman. "When you boys goin' to go back and get the stuff?"

Harry Quinn generally left the talking for his more clever companions, but now his heart was full, and speech overflowed. "Listen," he said, "there was seven, eight hundred pounds of gold dust, Pop. And the gents are going to be digging up that marsh for a thousand years till they find the money. And the whole town seen us when we was riding out of the place."

"The town didn't see you if you didn't do some shootin'," said Dickerman. "That time of day, you shouldn't 'a' had no trouble!"

"There was a red-headed fool in the place," said Salvio. "I had to plug him."

24

"Dead?" said Dickerman.

"No. Not dead. Just enough to make him holler."

"Good!" said Dickerman. "It's better not to have 'em dead. A death trail stays red for a long while. The other kinds, they blot out pretty quick. A wind and a rain and a coupla weeks, and they're blotted out. But you boys wouldn't want to go back into that neck of the woods to get at the stuff?"

"Why should we wanta be lynched?" asked Salvio.

"Seven, eight hundred pounds of gold," sighed Dickerman. "Then who else can we get to salvage the stuff?"

"There ain't nobody," said Salvio. "Anybody that was smart enough to get at the stuff, would be crooked enough to keep it for himself."

Bates said: "Nope. There's one man."

"Who?" challenged Salvio.

"Reata!" exclaimed Bates.

"Reata? Reata?" said Salvio, in a jealous anger. "You'd think that he was a tin god on a stick, the way you gents talk about him. He's as big a crook as anybody."

"He's big, but he ain't a crook," said Pop Dickerman. "It's fun to him. Bates is right. Reata might do the trick. But how would we get at Reata? I ain't a clean enough kind of a man, the way I live, to suit Reata. Besides, the gypsy gal has him."

"Are they married?" asked Bates.

"They ain't married, but they will be as soon as they get the house they're workin' on finished. They're a mighty happy pair, boys! They've raked together a little money. They got their cabin started, and they're goin' to have a little land and start a small herd of cattle chewin' the grass."

"How d'you know all these things?" asked Salvio. "Been up there?"

"I got wires stretched around," said Pop Dickerman. "They keep me in touch. Yeah, and I think a lot about Reata. There's a fine, useful sort of a gent. There's an edge on Reata that would cut through chilled steel like butter. I dunno another man that could do the job of getting that gold back for us. Them that

25

could do it, they'd keep the loot. But Reata, you could trust him with your blood."

"That's the kind of a fool he is," said Salvio, sneering.

"Wait a minute, Gene," said Harry Quinn, scowling. "You're a dog-gone smart gent, and you're a cool gent. But you and Dave and me, we all owe our skins to Reata."

Salvio's face darkened, but he said nothing.

Bates said: "It's the gypsy gal that hangs up Reata. Pry him loose from her, and we might get him back to us ag'in."

"Pry him loose?" said Dickerman. "Ay, and I been dreamin' about that, too. How would you pry him loose? Kidnap her? He'd find her if it took the rest of his life."

"Get *her* to give him the run," said Bates.

"Her? She loves the ground he walks on," said Dickerman. "A kind of a hard gal, she is, but she loves Reata."

"Suppose you made her think it was for his own good?" said Dave Bates.

"How could you make her think that?" asked Quinn.

"Wait a minute!" exclaimed Dickerman.

He raised a grimy hand, commandingly, for silence, and then he said: "Don't speak, nobody. Bates has give me an idea. Wait till it hatches out of the egg, and it's goin' to fly like an eagle!"

CHAPTER 6

Up in the Ginger Mountains, the three riders found their quarry. Reata had not picked out the site of his home very wisely. He had it at just the wrong distance from the town of Ginger Gulch. He had chosen a site where no wagon road passed into the town and therefore where all supplies would need expensive hauling. He had picked out a small valley with a small lake. There were pine forests on the march up and down the sides of the mountains as far as the bald summits above the timber line. And in fact, there was everything that the eye of the nature lover could ask for, but very little to please the wit of a good cattleman. That valley would be a hot furnace in summer and it would be an ice box in winter. Furthermore, there were plenty of trees and not enough grass.

The three men of Dickerman, perched like patient birds of prey on a lofty mountain shoulder and looking down, day by day, upon the center of the valley and the little cabin which was growing there, took careful heed of all of these things. They commented upon the picture to one another.

Dave Bates, who had prospected the scene closer than any of the others, said: "They done only one sensible thing. They built the horse shed before they started on the house. But dog-gone me, unless they get a hustle on them, they gotta live in the cattle shed instead of the house, this winter. They ain't got it finished, and they ain't going to have it finished, even if they keep on working all day. You take Reata, he never was made for a worker; you take a gypsy gal—was there ever one that ever was worth a hang, when it come to work? But I'll tell you what, that there Miriam does the licks of hard work, mostly, and Reata, he sets back and gives ideas."

"I was down there the other day," said Harry Quinn, "snaking up to the edge of the woods where I could watch. Each of them had hold on an adz and they was making the chips fly off of the bellies of a couple of logs. But after Reata had hit a few licks, he takes a stop and looks around him, and rolls a cigarette.

" 'Hey,' says the gal. 'Go on and work, loafer!'

"He lights his cigarette and shakes his head at her.

" 'You don't understand me, Miriam,' says he. 'I'll tell you what the facts are. I don't get ideas, when I'm swinging an ax all day long. But now and then, when I stop, things happen inside my head—I get good hunches.'

" 'What sort of hunches have you got now?' says Miriam.

" 'Well,' he said, 'just for a sample. I've thought of damming up that creek yonder, some day, and out of that we'll get the water power to work a sawmill, and then we'll be able to ship

27

out timber. There's a fortune in good, clear pine, right around here!'

" 'Sure there is,' says she, 'if you can ever get the mountains to open up so that we can ship the stuff out. It would cost the weight of those trees in gold, pretty near, to haul them from here to Ginger Gulch. And even after you got them there, what sort of a market is there for them? People can cut down enough timber in their back yards to build ten new houses apiece!'

" 'Miriam,' says Reata, 'I'm sorry to hear you talk like this. People that haven't a good faith in a thing, they're going to have the bottom drop out of whatever they're doing.' "

"Did Reata talk like that?" asked Dave Bates suddenly.

"Sure he did," answered Quinn. "And I heard him, and I saw him leaning on his adz, and the girl just standing back and sort of laughing at him with her eyes."

"If that's what's in the air," said Dave Bates, "then I've got the idea. Reata's going to make the trip into Ginger Gulch with the roan mare and a couple of mules. He'll be back tomorrow afternoon; and instead of going down to the village yonder, where she mostly spends the nights, Miriam is going to camp out at the new cabin and hold things down, you might say. Well, boys, listen to me talk. I got ideas. I need some help, but I don't need very much!"

In fact, they found that the idea of Dave Bates was so neat, that even Gene Salvio, who was apt to be critical of all ideas other than his own, readily admitted the possibilities in this scheme. That very afternoon, as soon as Reata was seen to ride out of the valley, the three criminals descended to their work. They began at the cattle and horse shed, and they worked there for some time, before Dave Bates took his horse back through the woods, and came singing along under the trees, and so out into the clearing beside the lake.

The girl was still making her ax ring against the log. The chips flew far as she wielded the broad blade of fine steel which gave out a bell-like note at every stroke. Even a strong man can

28

easily grow exhausted by such work, but the girl made rhythm take the place of muscle. She was in a sleeveless jacket of brown doeskin, and she was as brown as the soft leather.

She was still working, when a mite of a dog ran out, yipping, toward the horseman, a slender little thing with a body as sleek as that of a rat, and a fuzzy face like a duplicate, in the small, of the head of a wire-haired fox terrier. Dave Bates had almost forgotten Rags.

The barking made the girl turn. She was looking straight into the west, so that she had to shade her eyes to see Bates clearly. Then she stepped back to where a good new Winchester rifle leaned against a sawbuck.

"Why, if it isn't old Dave! Hullo, Dave!" called the girl. "Glad to see you, old scout. Get down and rest your feet and tell me how's things!"

"Hullo there, Miriam," said he. "Things was never better."

He swung down from the mustang and advanced with his hand stretched out. Little Rags, in a barking fury, planted himself in the path, with bared teeth ready to bite.

Bates, inwardly cursing the little dog, had to pause, while he saw the girl throw one fleeting glance at the rifle. After that fractional hesitation, she came straight up to him and shook his hand with a firm grip. She always dazzled him a little. In spite of the roughness of her clothes, she looked to him like the sort of a jewel that should be laid up in velvet. Perhaps, he thought, it was because of the deep blueness of her eyes under her black hair and lashes.

"How's every little thing with you?" she was repeating heartily. "Found any good fat beef to rustle lately, Dave? Any bank safes been open when you were passing by?"

The nearness of that hit made him stare at her a bit.

"You look right up to yourself," he told her. "Stop that dog yapping, will you?"

She snapped her fingers. Rags jumped back and sat down between her feet, but still he growled very softly at the stranger.

29

"You know me, Rags," said Dave Bates. "You know me, boy. I'm a bunky of your big boss, ain't I? Don't you know me, boy?"

"Keep your hand away from him, or he'll take a finger off," said Miriam. "Reata put him on guard over me, before he rode off to town. Rags doesn't trust anything until his boss comes back and calls him off the job."

Dave Bates laughed. He sat down on the white of the log at which she had been chipping.

"You look fine," said he, insisting on that pleasant theme.

"Sure I look fine. Why wouldn't I look fine? Three squares a day for the old girl, and plenty of exercise to keep up her appetite."

"And plenty of Reata for sauce," said Dave Bates. "He keeps the world turning pretty fast, I bet."

"Yeah. You'd bet that, wouldn't you?" said she. "Full of rope tricks and fun, you'd think, wouldn't you? Babbling all day long, and telling stories about places he's been."

"He's a great card," said Dave Bates.

"Sure he's a great card," agreed the girl. "The sort of a card that wins the trick in the poker game, all right. But up here in the mountains, he's more of a poet. He has his dreams by day, and don't you ever doubt it, Dave."

"Good old Reata," said Dave Bates. "There's nobody like him. Kind of pleased with this spot?"

"He likes it a lot," she agreed. "But as I say, he's getting the soul of a poet—or a promoter. He's built a great big hotel there in the meadow, right beside the lake, and he's filled it with high-class dudes, at ten dollars a day."

"I can see 'em down there taking the sun right now, can't I?" said Dave Bates, staring from under his lean little hand. "But outside of the hotel, and all of that, what are you and Reata going to live on?"

"I don't know," she answered. "And I don't care, what's more. If I can once get him to pass the old ring onto my finger and say, 'I do,' a couple of times in front of a preacher, I

30

don't care what happens, after that."

"You like that hombre, all right," said Dave Bates. "But when does the marriage come off?"

"As soon as the house is finished. He's proud, Reata is. Many a time he sits out here and looks at the cabin and shakes his head and says that he can't marry me till he has a home to take me to!"

"Maybe he says that many a time while he sits out here and watches you work?" suggested Bates.

"Many a time," she agreed. "But what brought you sashaying down the mountainside, singing so sweet, Dave?"

"I came up here to see Reata," said Dave.

"You're not going to, though. Reata's away in town. He won't be back till tomorrow. What's the matter, Dave? Has Pop Dickerman got another job too big for his boys to handle? Is he sending out a hurry call for Reata?"

Bates blinked at her shrewdness.

"This time it's a friendly turn to do Reata," he said. "You wouldn't think that that rat of a Dickerman, or three roughs like me and Gene and Harry Quinn would travel very far to do a fellow a good turn, would you?"

"Yes, you'd travel a ways," said the girl. "How good is the turn?"

"I see it's no good at all," said Bates. "You've got him nailed down, and he won't move."

"You want to move him, do you?"

"I want to keep him alive," said Bates calmly.

CHAPTER 7

The quiet of Dave Bates's voice gave his words the necessary solemnity. He saw the brightness of her eyes narrow at him.

"Go on, Dave," she invited presently. "It must be a big idea. Why not sell it to the weaker half of the family-to-be?"

"It's not any good talking to you, Miriam," he told her. "Sure, you're fond of Reata. You're so dog-gone fond that you've about anchored him. And the waves are going to tear hell out of him when the first storm comes up. And the storm is coming now!"

"What kind of a storm?" she asked.

Bates shrugged his shoulders as he answered: "They're going to get him, Miriam. They got him located, and they're working on him already. I've said too much already. But as long as you asked, I had to tell you."

"You think he ought to move away from here?"

"I do."

"Where?"

"Anywhere. Just keep moving, or the wave'll drown him sure."

"Who's in the storm?"

"What's the good of going on?" said Dave Bates. "You know how it is. Reata is a clean-bred one. There ain't a better fellow in the world. I owe my skin to him. I'd be two times dead, except for Reata. But while he was helping me and some of the others, he sure stepped hard on a lot of toes. There's gents been getting together that want his scalp, and they're going to have it if they can. But—Oh, well, what's the use?"

"I sort of think you mean what you say," answered the girl.

"Do I? You bet everything down to the spurs that I mean it," said Bates. "But what's the good of talking? Anyway, he's pretty smart; he may beat them, no matter how many they are."

"They're going to come up here and try to cut down Reata? Is that the story?" she asked.

"Quit it, will you?" said Bates. "I've talked too much. But —well, Reata means a whole lot to me! Well—show me around the place, will you?"

She hesitated, her face dark with thought, before she said: "All right, I'll show you. There's two things to see. The cabin and the shed. Take the cabin first. Those uprights are the cabin uprights, old son. Those beams are the cabin beams, and when we get the logs laid, we'll have walls around it, and when the roof goes on, we'll have a roof on our little old cabin. See?"

"Sure. It's a great idea." Bates chuckled. "Let's have a slant at the shed then."

She walked over with him.

"A sliding door, and everything," said Dave Bates, putting his hand on the finger slot, and pulling back.

The natural way would have been to lean a shoulder against the door and walk it back, but he had the best reason in the world for not doing that. As the door opened to the width of a yard, a gun roared, and a huge charge of shot whistled out through the gap.

Bates, with a yell, sprang back, a gun flashing out into each hand.

"Get back to the house!" he yelled at the girl, and raced promptly around to the rear of the shed.

But when he reached the spot, he found the girl turning the opposite corner, her face wild and set, and a lean, dangerous-looking .32 revolver in her grip. She could use that gun, and how efficiently she could use it, Bates knew perfectly well. She stared about her at the trees, which advanced right down to the rear of the long shed.

"They're inside! We got 'em!" shouted Bates.

"Wait a minute." said Miriam calmly. "There's the gun that did the trick."

She pointed at a single-barrel shotgun of large bore which was strongly propped up against a sapling, its muzzle projecting through the rear wall of the shed, having been pushed through a large knot hole.

"That's it," said Miriam. "And there's the string attached to it. You see?"

"I don't make it out? What do you mean?" asked Dave Bates.

She gave Bates one long, searching look, and then her doubt seemed to leave her.

33

"I guess it's news to you, all right," she said. "But coming right on top of what you've been telling me, I thought for a minute—"

She did not tell what her thought for a minute had been, but led the way around to the front of the shed. Bates grabbed her as she started to go through the door.

"You don't know what hellishness is fixed up inside!" he said.

"There won't be anything more," she declared. And she slipped away from him into the interior.

There was nothing to be seen except the long line that ran past the ends of the stalls and connected with the front door. The pull of the door traveled back to the trigger of the gun. It was the simplest death trap in the world.

"Now I get it," said Bates, muttering the words hardly aloud. "Suppose that somebody put his shoulder against the sliding door to walk it open, the way most folks would—But who would 'a' been the first one to open this door ordinarily, Miriam?"

"Reata," she said faintly. "Reata, when he comes back from town. He'd put Sue up in here and turn the mules loose to graze."

Bates left her, rounded the shed, and took the shotgun out of the brace. It had been his idea, but Gene Salvio and Quinn had executed it perfectly. He was proud of himself, and he was proud of them.

When he went back, he found the girl sitting on the log beside the lake, absently stroking Rags, who lay beside her. The great shadow of the biggest western mountain had fallen across the lake so that the waves made only a dull glimmering as they kept rushing in toward the shore.

The sound of them pleased Dave Bates. He saw that he was winning and he determined to say nothing more.

The girl looked up at him.

"Have you got the makings of a cigarette?" she asked.

He proffered them to her, and she twisted up a smoke in short

34

order, and accepted his light. Breathing the smoke deep, she blew it out again in wisps.

"It tastes good—but a little dizzy," she said. "First smoke I've had since Reata took control."

"He doesn't like to see a girl smoke. He's funny, that way," said Dave Bates. And he began to guess, grimly, what this breaking of the prohibition might mean to the future of the girl and Reata.

"Yeah. He's funny, that way."

She pointed toward the shed, without herself looking in that direction, and Dave Bates stared down at the perfect brown modeling of that arm.

"He wouldn't have looked so funny—with that load of buckshot through him."

"It was big. I heard it whistle," said Dave. "I guess it would 'a' tore a hole through a tree, all right. But maybe Reata wouldn't 'a' got it. Maybe something would 'a' happened—"

"Shut up, Dave!" she commanded.

She closed her eyes, smiling very faintly. He could see that she was sick with pain.

"I've got to cut him loose," she said finally.

"What you mean?" asked Dave Bates hastily.

"You know what I mean," she told him. "I've got to do what you came up here to make me do. I've got to cut Reata adrift."

"You can't," said Bates. "You can't tell him to leave the place. He's crazy about you, Miriam. He'd never give up marrying you."

"Wouldn't he?" she asked sourly. "You don't know me, partner. Oh, I'll cut him loose. I'll make a free man of him!"

She was silent again, with the same sick, grim smile on her face, and her hand always went gently over the sleek back of Rags.

"Now I guess I get what you mean," said Bates. "You mean you're going to pretend that you're tired of him, or something like that?"

She shrugged her shoulders.

"You can't do it," said Bates. "You love him. You couldn't live without him. You—"

"I'd soon be living without him if a pound of buckshot was socked into him," she said.

He bowed his head, as though to this convincing argument he could find no possible rejoinder.

"I'm sorry," said Bates at last. And, in fact, there really was a measure of regret in him. He needed Reata. Dickerman needed Reata. The whole crooked gang needed that fearless and cunning magician's touch in their affairs. And yet Bates was sorry for the girl. "You tell me how I can help. Tell me what to do," he pleaded.

"I'll tell you what to do. Get out of my sight!" she exclaimed.

CHAPTER 8

When Bates was gone, she went slowly about the place, all that evening. And in the middle of the night she sat up in the mountain cold and breathed the sweetness of the pine trees until the breath of them was like music to her, and the tears filled her eyes. The next day it was the same thing—and she went from spot to spot, staring, filling her eyes with the many pictures for the last time.

Reata would not be back until the middle of the afternoon. He would come down the last slope racing the roan mare, yelling like a happy wild Indian, and the mules would be left to wander slowly along at their own gait, behind him.

She wished that she could have a longer interim before he returned. She wanted to have longer to steady herself for the part which she had to play. However, when the time came, she was in the place and taking the part which she had decided on.

She had dug out some tobacco and wheat-straw papers from among the things of Reata, and when she heard the long, echoing whoop, and then the clatter of hoofbeats coming down the rough of the trail, she was posted beside the lake, seated on that log where she had been working when Dave Bates appeared and darkened the world for her.

She made her cigarette and was smoking it calmly when Reata came whooping into view from among the trees.

She usually met him, running. But today she turned, merely, and waved a hand at him.

She saw him check Sue abruptly. The long, ugly, unmatchable roan machine fell at once to a trot, then halted near by. Rags flew into a passion of delighted welcoming, so shrill that it darted needles through the brain.

Reata stopped that demonstration with one harsh word. And Rags slunk at the heels of his beloved master.

The girl kept herself smiling, calmly, impersonally. She tried to reduce that brown face of Reata to a mere picture in which she had little interest. She tried to forget that the gray eye could burn with yellow fire, and all the quick, electric nature of this man whose like was not in the world. A hand was gripping her heart, but she kept on smiling, and as she smoked, she blew the thin cloud into the air.

He leaned over her. She turned up her face, as one submitting to a kiss, but he stepped suddenly back again.

"Hell's broken loose, eh?" said he.

She shrugged her shoulders.

"Where?" he asked. "Around the place or just inside you?"

"Just inside me," she answered.

"Quiet hell?" he said.

"Yes."

"That's the worst kind," answered Reata.

He sat down on a stump opposite her. Even in his sitting and his rising he was not like other men, but there seemed to be in him springs of steel strength. She looked at the broad shoulders and the strong neck and the high, fine poise of the head. He was all strength above and all wiry speed below.

"Maybe it's the worst kind," she agreed, looking out over the lake.

37

"Stop smiling that way," commanded Reata.

"Yes, my lord," said she, and kept on smiling, though every bit of it hurt.

"Smoking, eh? Just to show that the rebellion goes deep?" he asked.

"Oh, you know," she answered. "Kind of got tired of things."

"What things?"

"Oh, everything."

She waved at the scene around her.

"And me?" he asked.

She shrugged her shoulders again. There was a frightful desire in her to fling herself at him and pour out words, and weep. For his own sake she had to go through with this efficiently.

"I see," said Reata, making his voice very bright and cheerful, so that she recognized the steel in him for the thousandth time. He could do it, of course. If she could smile at disaster, he could laugh at it. "You have the old hunger, eh? Want to go back with the gypsies again? Want to see old Queen Maggie and get the whiff of her big black cigars? All of that?"

"You know, when a fellow gets bored, there's not much to say about it, is there?"

"No, I don't suppose so," said Reata.

He kept sitting up straight on the stump, looking directly at her.

"Let's be logical. Let's go sashaying right through the details, if you don't mind."

"I don't mind," she answered.

"Take it like this. The mountains—they're lonely. If a girl is left up here—twenty-four long hours—she's bound to be lonely. You know, Miriam, I suggested that you should go back to the boarding house, down there in the village."

"I know. I thought I'd try the place out, though."

"You've been feeling it come up in you for a long time, eh?" he asked.

"Well—" she said.

"Don't mind me. I want to get at the inside of the truth, if you'll tell me."

"Talking won't be much good," she declared.

"I won't persuade you," said Reata. "Not a quarter of an inch. I'd rather burn my tongue out by the roots than say one word to persuade you."

"Thanks," said the girl flatly. And she hated the rude, ugly meanness of that single word. After all, though, she had to make him despise her. That was the only way to cut deep enough.

There was a bit of a pause, because that single word had hit him hard. But after a moment he went on: "The mountains are lonely, eh? Well, we could change that. We could go to a town, or to a city."

"And live in a dirty flat, eh? No, it's better to have shanty life in the open than shanty life in a town."

"Put it that way, then. The worst thing has been I. Is that it?"

"Oh, I don't know," said the girl.

"Try to speak it out. I'll take it."

"No, you wouldn't have a broken heart." She sneered. "There are a lot more girls in the world. I know that."

"Of course there are," said he, with that deadly good humor.

"And there's the other side of it," she went on, with careful brutality. "There are a lot of men, too."

"Yes, that's true. A lot more men. I think you've always looked over my head a bit."

At that, she laughed. It was a thing she had felt that she would be unable to do, but the exigencies of the rôle supplied, suddenly, the strength that she needed for the acting. She was able to laugh, and then to say: "Yes, quite a bit over your head."

After that he remarked: "Well, it's the finish, all right. Mind you, I'm not whining and I don't want to do any persuading. I'm just saying this—and I can be proud, too, even if it damns me—but I want to say that I'll do anything. Anything that'll help to put things back where they used to be."

"What could you do?" she demanded.

"I'm a lazy hound. I know that. I've sat around here and built castles in the air. I suppose you've even done more of the work around here than I've done. I'm sorry about that. I think I could change it. I really think that I could change myself for you."

"Sure you could. For a week. Then you'd be the same tramp that you've always been."

"I want to kill you, somehow, when you say that," said Reata softly.

"Do you?" asked Miriam sweetly, the devil in her eyes and her smile.

"Because I start thinking of a lot of things," said Reata. "I start thinking about all sorts of things such as—well, the hours we've had—good, clean hours—the cleanest in my life. I've been thinking that the world was all made of blue and gold, and you the middle of it. That's what I've been thinking. That's what—"

He jumped to his feet.

"Go on," said she. "Finish the speech."

"All right," said Reata. "I'll finish it. If you've been double-crossing all this time, playing a part like a sneaking little actress on a stage—why, it's high time for us to split up."

"All right, chief," said she.

She began to make another cigarette.

"But I can't believe it, Miriam," he said. "I feel as if you'd have to change, even if I touched you—and—"

"Try it, honey," said the girl.

And she put back her head and smiled lazily up at him.

"Miriam," said Reata, "you're only a—"

"Say it," said the girl.

"No, I won't say it. I won't think it. It makes me sick."

"Want me to say just one little thing?" she asked.

"Say whatever you please."

"All the way through I kept remembering, but only lately it's been beginning to grind on the bone. I mean, what *you* are."

"Say it, Miriam," he urged.

"A dirty little sneak thief and pickpocket," said the girl.

She looked down suddenly. The world was spinning. She knew that one touch, one breath, one word would shatter the last of her brittle strength. She had struck her last blow.

Well, it was enough.

"All right," said he. "I've been a sneak thief and a pickpocket. All right. You've a right to say that. It just seems sort of rotten—but that's all right, too. I'll sashay along. I'll take Sue. The rest of the stuff—oh, it may be worth something. The mules—the gypsies would like to have 'em, and you can load 'em down with the portable junk. So long, Miriam."

He stood over her. His voice remained clear and easy.

"You know," he said, "if you were what you look to me, I'd get down on my knees and eat dirt for you. I'm going to get out fast, so that I can keep a bit of what I thought you were in the back of my mind. I hope I never have to curse my soul with the sight of your face again.

CHAPTER 9

When Reata rode the roan mare over the trail, again, he was heading south, and he went by a clump of trees out of which three pairs of human eyes watched him with interest.

"White and smiling," said Dave Bates, as the rider passed. "Boys, didn't that gal do a good job on him? She turned his stomach and she slapped his face, and all he wants to do now is to find a nice little hot piece of hell so that he can break it apart and scatter it where it'll do the most people the most good."

"He's going to do that same thing, and he's going to do it quick," said Harry Quinn. "And what a lot of hell he *could* scatter around, if he made up his mind."

41

"Oh, I dunno," said Gene Salvio. "All he's likely to do is to get a slug of lead under his ribs. Don't forget that the fool won't never carry no gun."

"It's a pretty fast hand that can beat him with guns," said Quinn, "if he's in striking distance with that reata of his, and anything up to forty feet is his meat. Don't forget that. Don't forget all the tough gun fighters that have gone to hell account of Reata. Don't forget the damnedest man that was ever on this earth—I mean Bill Champion, if you got any doubts."

"He robbed me of my chance at Champion," growled Salvio.

"He robbed you of a chance to push daisies. Come on, boys," said Bates. "We better cut along behind him and see where he goes."

Reata went as far as the first town. It was not much of a place. Three roads ran together in a mountain valley, and that was enough excuse to make a bit of a village sprout up.

Reata went to the saloon and looked over the crowd.

They were big men, strong men, fierce men; they were true mountaineers, of the sort that swing axes in lumber camps, and fight with hands, or knives or guns for the fun of the thing. And there was a sprinkling of hardy cowpunchers in that lot, their Colts bulging under their coats.

He could not have picked out a better crowd for the purpose that he had in mind. He wanted hard rock on which to grind the hard, rough steel of his temper to a fine edge.

He took his rope out of his coat pocket, where the forty feet of that slender line of rawhide and mystery slumped into a not too bulky knot. He unraveled a knot or two with a gesture, and he began to make that rope perform for him.

The men at the bar turned and looked at him and grinned. The men at the tables along the wall grinned, also. Other men came from the back rooms, leaving their card games for a little time and staying till they forgot the course of their play.

For they saw that lithe reata jump snakelike into the air. They saw it tangle and untangle in the air, making swift, melting patterns that kept dissolving into one another.

42

"And look at here!" bawled a voice, over a round of brisk applause that came in the middle of the act. "What is that stuff all good for except to make the kids laugh?"

Reata smiled pleasantly on that big man with the big voice. This was no common lumberjack; this the pale face of a professional gambler and the wide, thick shoulders and brutal jaw of a prize fighter.

"It makes gentlemen take off their hats to the music," said Reata, and the next instant the snaky loop of his reata had jerked the hat from the head of the big man.

Once in the air, the good Stetson stayed there. It was sent spinning to the ceiling. It was caught before it reached the floor and driven whirling upward again. Finally it was deposited, once more, on the head of its owner, though a good deal awry.

At this feat of legerdemain, a loud roar of pleasure burst out of the chorus of those wide throats.

And beyond the window Harry Quinn muttered to Salvio: "Look at the yaller devil in the eyes of Reata! He's looking for trouble, and the big feller is going to give it to him!"

Reata, at the end of his "show," had taken off his hat, and now he was passing it, making a little bow to each man in turn. And a veritable shower of wealth poured into the hat. One man took a whole handful of silver out of his coat pocket and chucked it into the hat while the others cheered.

But when Reata came to the pale-faced man, that angry gentleman made his contribution by kicking the hat out of Reata's hand. The silver sprang high into the air and rained down in a wide, bright shower. And, at this jest, the big fellow laughed uproariously.

The others laughed, also. The rougher the jest, the better they were fitted to appreciate it.

Reata, however, laid the flat of his hand along the cheek of the chief jester. The noise of the blow was loud. The spatting sound of it wiped out the loud mirth instantly and left men staring, wide-eyed. It was apparent that the big fellow was a very well-known man.

He proved it now by whipping out a Colt and shouting: "Dance, you rat!"

He plowed one furrow in the floor with his first shot. Then the gun hand was gripped by the supple, iron-hard loop of the lariat. The fingers were crushed flat out by that pressure. The Colt itself was jerked into the air, caught by Reata, and flung out the window.

The gambler, with a low moan of exquisite rage, hurled himself straight at Reata.

"The poor fool!" said Harry Quinn, almost in sympathy.

But exactly what happened to the gambler, no eye in the room was swift enough to decipher. Certainly he missed the head of Reata with his long, driving punch, very scientifically delivered. And then he seemed to stumble even on the smoothness of the floor. He kept on stumbling, and as he went past Reata, his feet flew from beneath him, and he landed flat on his face.

There is nothing so discouraging as a belly flop even in the soft of water, but on a wooden floor it certainly shakes the spirits out of a man.

When the gambler got to his feet, there was a deafening yelling all around the room. So the big man charged again. More warily, this time, with the straight left jabbing in front of him to prepare his way. But if he moved more slowly, Reata sprang like a cat, and barely seemed to touch the gambler, who swerved once more, and fell again, flat on his face.

This time he sat up sick and dizzy, and he found the noose of that pencil-thin lariat around his throat.

"Get up," said the voice of Reata, "and pick up all that money you spilled a while ago. Hop to it, because from the look of you, stranger, I'd like to take you apart and see what's inside the case."

The gambler was disheartened.

It was plain that if he picked up that money, he would be shamed for the rest of his days. On the other hand, he felt that

44

he had been involved with a hurricane against which he was helpless.

But if he could not win with his own unaided hands, there were others who could help him. Three men had just come out of the gambling rooms at the back of the saloon. These three, the victim now picked up with his eyes, one by one.

Then he said: "I'd just like to see you make me do it."

That was to Reata, as the gambler tried to scramble to his feet. A flying loop of the lariat caught him and jerked him forward on his face once more. It was a massacre, and the crowd yelled, because massacres were what it liked.

But here a cold, snarling voice from the back of the room said: "Stranger, stick up your mitts and drop that rope of yours!"

Reata felt the presence of that leveled gun before he turned his head. He had wanted hot water, but perhaps this was a little higher temperature than he needed to find. And then, just behind him, through the open window of the saloon, two glittering pairs of Colts appeared, looking large as cannons to the startled eyes of the men inside.

"You fellers back up," said the voice of Harry Quinn. "Reata, come out through the front door. We got the skunks covered. Come on out. The three of us is all here waitin' for you!"

"Come out?" exclaimed Reata. "Like the devil I will. You fellows come inside, and the drinks are all on me!"

Gene Salvio went in first, stepping lightly, head high, a gun ready in each hand, and the gunman at the back of the room faded away, guiltily, softly, from view.

Harry Quinn followed. Dave Bates was the last, because he had kept watch from the window till the last minute.

A thick silence embraced the saloon, till Reata called out: "Set 'em up, bartender. There's plenty of money on the floor, and it's got to be turned into whisky before I get out of here. Open up your throats, boys, and pour the stuff down. My partner, there, on the end of the rope, he aims to get the money for us off the floor."

The gambler had tried three times and he had failed. Three times was enough for him. Therefore he went on his hands and knees, groaning, to gather the silver. The bartenders busily turned the money, as bidden, into whisky, so that the entire crowd was whooping and shouting long before Reata walked out of the place followed by his three companions.

When the cool air of the night struck his face, he found that whisky and excitement had not, after all, diminished the grim aching of his heart, and the world was as empty as it had been when he turned his back on that blue lake in the mountains.

However, a man must meet his obligations. And there was an obligation here.

He said to Salvio: "Gene, I owe something to all of you fellows. Just what am I going to do about it?"

"Owe us something?" said Salvio. "Not a thing. We owe our hides to you, partner!"

"Forget it," said Reata. "I want something to fill my hands. Any of the three of you know what I can do to put in my time?"

CHAPTER 10

The marshes along Jumping Creek belonged to the estate of Colonel Percival Lester, but even if they had not, he probably would have taken charge of the organized search for the stolen gold of the Decker and Dillon Bank, because Colonel Lester— though his title was entirely complimentary—liked to find himself at the head of large numbers of men. Nothing pleased him more than to be revealed in riding boots and breeches, extending his arm and pointing with a riding crop as with a sword.

The colonel did more than direct the labor. He supplied the mule teams and the wagons and the tools for the moving down of earth and broken rock until a road had been built across the shallows of the marsh to the island in the center of it. For it was obvious that the island was the place where the three robbers must have buried the gold. They had remained there for a number of hours. And certainly they would not simply have thrown the treasure into the oblivion of the mud and water of the marsh!

So the island was searched. That was a hard job, because it was chiefly rock and full of crevices, but the colonel supplied plenty of blasting powder and drills and double jacks, and the work went merrily on. Since everybody in the county could not be employed, the first fifty men were used, every morning—the first fifty to appear at dawn. The colonel arranged this, and every one admitted that this was eminently fair play. When the gold was found, the reward from the bank would be equitably divided among all the fifty. In addition, the colonel hired and paid from his own pocket two armed guards who kept watch on the island every night.

The whole range had to admit that the colonel was an extremely public-spirited man. When he went by with a severe preoccupation on his handsome face, the men would pause in their work, for a moment, and nod good-naturedly toward him before they spat on their hands and resumed their toil. For he was in fact as fine a looking fellow as you could wish to see, with his big forehead and regular features and neat mustache. His jowls hung a bit; that was all.

This afternoon his daughter Agnes, had come down to watch the work, and with her rode her fiancé, Thomas Wayland. If anything could have improved the good humor of the colonel, it was to have sight of this couple. He had faults to find with his daughter. To be sure, she was a very pretty blue and golden girl, but she lacked the poise, the dignity of mind and carriage which, he felt, should be inherent in every Lester. However, Tom Wayland more than made up for the defect. In lands and hard cash, the Waylands were to Rusty Gulch what Lester was to Jumping Creek. Tom Wayland was as tall as the colonel; he bore himself with an air of haughty aloofness which even the colonel could not have improved upon, and, like the colonel, he distinguished himself from the ordinary run of ranchmen by wearing, always, a very neat outfit of English riding togs. He was to marry Agnes Lester this same year and, as the colonel looked at the pair, he was reenforced by his conviction that a necessary aristocracy, a highly bred and highly educated leisure class, the brains and the culture of a nation, would soon be growing up in the West.

It was a little unfortunate that his daughter did not love Tom Wayland, but after all, children rarely know their own minds. How can they? He saw that it was, of course, far better for him to select her life mate, and he was glad that he had established, in his household, such a discipline that it would never enter her pretty little head to go against his will in any matter of importance.

So the colonel ranged slowly up and down the little island, overseeing the work, silently taking charge, occasionally extending his arm of authority and pointing out something with his riding crop. He had almost forgotten about the gold, to tell the truth, and he would have been rather shocked if he had known that one of the fellows who toiled here knew perfectly well where the treasure could be found.

That was Reata.

When he had asked Salvio and the rest to find something for him to do, Dave Bates had explained the thing very briefly. There *was* a thing for Reata to do. Down there in the marsh by Jumping Creek was a lot of gold which had been buried, a long time ago, in chamois sacks. Lately, people had begun to hunt for the stuff, but they were laboring at the hard rocks of an island in the marsh. As a matter of fact, that gold was hidden in the hollow trunk of an old tree situated near an end of the island. Why didn't the three of them go and get the stuff? Why, unfortunately their faces were all known to the people of Jumping Creek, and not known favorably. If they went down to the marsh while the hubbub of the hunt for treasure was on, they would be promptly nabbed and put in jail.

How had they come to know about the location of the treasure? They had just picked up a hint.

Why not wait until the present search had failed and the noise had died down? The trouble was that when the island definitely was proved not to be the hiding place, the search would extend farther, and the first man who tapped that tree would be aware that the trunk of it was hollow!

Afterward, Salvio had drawn Bates aside and told him that it was folly to let Reata go without revealing to him the entire truth. But Bates answered, with a snarl: "Yeah? You think that he'd touch the stuff if he knew that it was stolen money?"

"He'll hear about the robbery of the bank before he's been down there long," said Salvio.

"He'll have the stuff before he's had a chance to hear much," answered Bates.

That was why Reata was on the ground with nothing on his mind except the very difficult task of getting the treasure away, and he was glad of the difficulty, because it prevented him from letting his thoughts drift too often back to that valley among the Ginger Mountains and the picture of Miriam. She was back with Queen Maggie and the tribe, by this time, he told himself. She was happy to be free.

So Reata drew deeper breaths, and swung the big twelve-pound double jack in swifter, harder-striking circles, while his partner turned the drill slowly in the hole. There was no love of labor in Reata, and yet he persisted unwearyingly in his hammering, for the heaviness of the work acted as a cure to his mental sickness. He did not even look up, from time to time, to mark the passing of the colonel in charge, and never raised his head higher than the body of the huge brindled mastiff which stalked up and down behind his master. As for Rags, he lay curled up in the shadow of a rock near Reata.

And then, as the dull drill was jumped out of the hole and a sharp one was put in its place, Reata stood back to breathe more deeply and wipe the sweat from his face. And it was at that moment that he saw Agnes Lester. He saw her not dimly,

49

not vaguely and far off, as he told himself that he would always see women through the rest of his life, but she came intimately into his mind with the freshness of something never beheld before. She was a new point: she was a beginning. He did not compare her with the dark beauty of Miriam. They were not comparable. He thought that Agnes Lester was as beautiful as an angel. For angels are blue and golden in their loveliness, surely.

Perhaps Reata was a bit on the sentimental side. Certainly a fellow whose heart was broken by one girl should not be snatched up into a seventh heaven by the mere sight of another. Such changes are not heroic; they are not noble. As a matter of fact, Reata looked on Agnes Lester not as a woman at all, but as a divine being with just a taste, let us say, of sweet mortal femininity about her.

Then he remembered something else. He had seen that face before. He had seen it in the back of the watch which he had purloined from the vest pocket of big Tom Wayland, who rode yonder. Think of such a noble gentleman as Tom Wayland pasting the picture of "his girl" into the back of his watch! But that was what Wayland had done, and when Reata had opened the watch, he remembered how even the photograph of this girl had moved him to such a point that he had gone into the rodeo crowd once more and restored the watch to the pocket of Mr. Wayland. In that very act of restoration he had been caught; he had been chased; he had been jailed—

Well, that was long ago, and since then the hunting down of the notorious Bill Champion had made Reata free of the law and wiped out his past and made people willing to forgive a certain illegal lightness in his fingers. But it seemed to Reata that there had been a fate behind the whole thing. Otherwise, why should Wayland have put the picture in the watch case, except that fate intended Reata to see her image?

And now he was seeing her in the flesh!

"All right! All right!" said the man who held the drill, impatiently.

50

Reata missed the head of the drill entirely with the next blow, and his partner grunted.

"Hey, what's the matter with you, kid?"

Reata would have found it difficult to say what was the matter with him, unless he were able to burst at once into verse and music.

Music of another sort started, just then. For the big mastiff that haunted the steps of Colonel Percival Lester had just spotted Rags, and being without a sense of humor and trained for nothing but battle, the huge dog let out a growl that was like the harsh rumbling of thunder, and hurled himself at the little mongrel.

CHAPTER 11

Imagine a huge fist grasping at a floating bit of a feather, always so hard that the wind of its own motion knocks the feather away. It was like that when the mastiff charged at Rags. He came on with his mouth a great red gulf, but he kept champing his teeth on nothingness as Rags dodged from this side to that, letting the monster miss him by fractions of inches.

Work stopped. Men gathered around to shout with delight as the mastiff charged, missed, recovered, lunged again and again, wildly slashing at the air as he went by a target that he knew he could hardly get a tooth into. And always Rags waited for the charges with pricking ears, with little head cocked a bit to one side, and with bright eyes and wagging tail, as though he were sure that this was only a game out of which he could receive no harm. He waited until the red gulf was actually just upon him, and then he jerked himself to this side or to that, until the great mastiff, fairly baffled, stood back and howled out his rage.

Rags, at the same time, got behind his master's legs. He was a little tired of playing with death, perhaps, and therefore he went into the shadow of his god on earth. Having reached this shelter, little Rags stretched himself comfortably and turned a regardless eye upon the final charge of the great mastiff.

Colonel Percival Lester was not happy. Nothing in the world annoyed him so much as an attack upon his dignity. And the dignity of his very horses and dogs was a part and a portion of his own dignity. It was a personal reflection upon him, therefore, when the crowd bawled out its applause for the little dog and its mirth because of the mastiff's misses.

"Major takes the mongrel for a rat—no wonder he's trying to get hold of it! Take that mongrel off the island! Get it out of the way!" thundered the colonel.

Before any one could do this, however, the mastiff was charging. And when Reata saw that the little Rags no longer intended to continue the sport, but was serenely trusting everything to him, Reata took from around his hips, where it was hooked up like a belt, the many folds of his rope. As the big mastiff came gloriously in to make the kill, a double fold of a thin line, a jumping pair of noosed half hitches, as it were, dropped over the yawning muzzle of Major and jerked his jaws shut.

His charge he halted on skidding feet. He turned to tear to pieces this stranger—for Major was a guard dog in every sense of the word—but another swift loop of the reata caught about his legs and tumbled him on his side. He lay there, struggling, while the crowd shouted with delight.

The colonel was stifled with rage. But he knew that he had seen a very good exhibition of skill on the part of this sinewy young fellow with the brown face and the gray eyes. And there was nothing he could say. A man cannot be blamed from defending himself against the attacks of a huge and savage beast like Major!

The colonel, being silenced, was choking. If he could have commanded the lightnings of heaven, he would have brought down a special and a blazing vengeance upon the heads of Reata and Rags, at that moment. But he could only choke, and choke,

52

as Reata loosed the mastiff from those humiliating bonds, that sinuous bit of rope that looked no larger that twine, to the eye of the colonel.

Reata having loosed the great dog, Rags came around and sat down in *front* of the feet of his master, so assured was he of the defensive power that inhered in the very shadow of the great man. And at Rags—no, only at Reata, now, came Major, slavering with red-eyed rage. He was met by a dart of that rope as inescapably swift as the striking of a snake. The noose caught one forefoot and the neck of Major. It jerked his foreleg up against his throat and caused him once more to topple head over heels, while the crowd fairly howled with delight.

Agnes Lester, touching the arm of big, handsome Tom Wayland, said to him: "Tom, how can *any* man be so wonderful with a rope? I'd as soon have a bear at me, as Major in a rage."

Tom made no answer. She might as well have touched a stone. In fact, she saw that Tom Wayland was rigid with a pale-faced wrath which exceeded even the wrath of the great Colonel Lester.

The colonel was shouting out something, but it was a lost, a wordless sound in the great tumult of the happy crowd. Men forgot the heat of the sun in their ecstasy over this improvised entertainment, the more so when they saw Reata actually setting the formidable dog free for a second time!

But mastiffs, no matter how big they are, have brains. Major had an extra supply of them, which enabled him to see when he was licked. When he got to his feet this time, he went skulking off with his tail between his legs and took downheaded shelter in the shadow of the colonel's horse.

Could anything have been worse for the colonel than to see his favorite dog thus shamed and disheartened, publicly? And there stood little Rags, in perfect dog parlance laughing his small and silent laughter at the huge dog that was discomfited. If the colonel could have only the least shadow of an excuse, he would have seized upon it with rejoicings.

And behold, a good excuse was thrust into his hands!

53

For Tom Wayland, recovering from his pale-faced rage, now pushed his horse up beside that of Lester and exclaimed: "Colonel, why do you have such a man as that on the place? That's Reata! That's the rascal who was jailed in Rusty Gulch as a pickpocket. I caught him snaking my watch out of my pocket!"

These words were shouted out so loudly that every pair of ears was sure to hear it. But Reata cared nothing about what the rest might think. They were all men, and he knew the ways of winning their respect. However, before a woman he would be helpless, and that was why his glance went instantly to the face of the girl.

It was a very striking thing to her to see the head of the stranger suddenly turn, in this way, and to feel his gray eyes fixed upon her with a flush coming into his face.

No one noticed her. She was glad that all eyes were fixed on Reata. But even if her own father had been staring at her with a forbidding eye, she could not have helped smiling at Reata.

He could not smile back. Not at her, without impertinence that would be too public. But she saw him straighten. She saw him smile, in turn, at Colonel Lester himself.

The colonel was shouting: "Pickpocket? Why isn't he in jail? Isn't there an officer of the law around here? Where's Steve Balen? Steve is a deputy sheriff. Balen, come here and do your duty!"

Tall Steve Balen came slowly through the crowd. He was taller than the rest by a head, and only his hands were of the proper size, and those hands were specially fitted, on occasion, by the big handles of his pair of Colts. He wore a gun on either thigh, strapped low down, just under the grip of his dangling hands.

When Balen came into the inner circle, the colonel was repeating: "How does a rascally sneak thief come to be here among honest men, Balen?"

Steve Balen pushed back his hat and scratched his head.

"Are you Reata, partner?" he said.

He looked at the slender rope which was magically recoiling

54

in the slim fingers of Reata and saw his answer there. Then he added:

"Sure, Colonel Lester, they had something agin' Reata up there in Rusty Gulch. And they chased him, and when he was about to get away, he seen this here snipe of a dog in the river and rode in and saved that dog from drowning, and got himself in jail. And he sawed his way out of jail, and later on, it was him that trailed down Bill Champion, and got two bullets through himself. But he killed Bill Champion in that fight, colonel, and the governor thought it would be a good idea to pardon him. The law ain't got anything agin' Reata—not now!"

At that speech, Agnes Lester was so delighted that Reata saw her smile as a shipwrecked mariner might see the rising of the glorious sun.

The colonel was shouting: "Get off my place! Get off my land, Reata—if that's your name. I won't have scoundrelly pickpockets on my place. Get off, and take your rat of a dog along with you! Take him away, some of you. Tom, herd him off the land! An outrage—among honest men—a sneak thief!"

Tom Wayland was never given a job more to his liking than this one. He closed instantly on Reata, and with a gesture of his whip he exclaimed: "You heard the music. Get out, Reata! Move along there! Some of you fellows get hold of the man and hustle him along!"

None of "those fellows" chose to lift a hand. There was a range of mountains between Jumping Creek and Rusty Gulch and therefore they did not know a great deal about what happened around the other town. But every man jack of them had heard, vaguely, the terrible legend of Bill Champion.

And this was the man who had sent Bill Champion to the long account? This slender fellow whom half of them outmatched in size and in apparent strength?

They would sooner have hustled a tangle of rattlers with their bare hands. Only Tom Wayland, malice in his handsome face, crowded his horse close to Reata and urged him on his way.

Reata turned and faced him. A good many men were able to

55

see the yellow come into the eyes of the smaller man as he said: "Don't hurry me, Wayland. Don't come within twelve steps of me, in fact!"

That was all he said, but it was enough. Tom Wayland reined back his horse as though a wild beast had started up under its nose. And Reata, with happy little Rags leading the way before him, went on his way with a slow step.

He went straight toward the girl and stood beside the head of her horse and said: "Some day I'd like to come and do a little explaining. May I?"

"Yes!" she said. "I want to see you again!"

Reata walked on, and she saw Tom Wayland sitting motionless on his horse, at a distance, glaring at her with terrible eyes. He had not heard the words, but he had seen the smile with which they were uttered. Well, let him see. Let her father see. Let all men see whom she had favored.

She actually turned in the saddle, shamelessly, and looked after that retreating figure, and watched the light step as he rose on his toes like an Indian runner, and saw the little dog bobbing in front of him contentedly.

Well, thief or no thief, she knew that she had seen a man, this day.

CHAPTER 12

Reata, from the side of an overhanging hill, looked across the marsh as the day ended, and saw the thick mist rising from the wet ground, and saw it take on a ghost of the sunset color. His fingers idly pulled at the fuzzy ears of Rags, who lay asleep on his knees, and the awkward-looking roan mare he could hear plucking at the dried grasses among the tall brush behind him. But what he really saw was like a double photograph, one printed above the other—he saw dark Miriam, and this blue and golden girl. All that he knew was that the pain was gone from his heart and that, in its place, there was a strange excitement, and a stranger peace.

He saw the workers troop away from the island. He saw them get on horses or into buckboards and go rattling back toward Jumping Creek. He saw the proud colonel ride off, accompanied by big Tom Wayland and the girl. Then quiet and the twilight gathered over the marshes, and Reata called the mare with a whistle.

Her bridle hung from her saddle horn. He put the bridle over her head. A cheek strap seemed to tickle her, and she rubbed her head with fearless freedom against his shoulder. He swore at her gently and jerked up a hand as though to strike. She merely pricked up her ears at the gesture and then nibbled at the sleeve of the raised arm.

Reata laughed.

"Sure," he said, "I'm only a bluff!"

He walked down the slope, and the mare walked after him. When they came to the narrow roadway which the colonel had expensively built as far as the island, Reata took from a saddlebag a rather odd feature of his equipment, four moosehide, padded overshoes which he now tied over the hoofs of the mare, and with that gear on her, she went ahead as silently as a moccasined Indian.

This was a hunt. The half-bowed body of her master told her that, and she had been taught how to step with flexed knees, softly, when there was hunting at hand. Little Rags, also, sneaked on ahead. He was better than a searchlight, for showing danger in the way. His body was very, very tiny, but it seemed that his sense of hearing and sight and smell had been correspondingly enlarged to strike a balance between him and others of his race. His master trusted him implicitly, and when Rags stood still in the dimness of the starlight, Reata paused, also. Then he went stealthily ahead through the fringe of trees that shrouded the inner portions of the island.

Rags went with him cautiously. The mare, at a gesture, had been anchored behind them in the darkness. A whistle would

57

bring her in, when she was needed.

From between two tree trunks, Reata could see the fire which the guards had built. They had made it small. One of them was cooking. The other walked on guard very like a soldier, with his rifle over his right shoulder.

The darkness was thick. The rising mist gave the air almost the dinginess of heavy fog. No stars could be seen now. There were only the splintered, golden rays of the firelight, obscurely lighting the little island. And there, close to the farther end, Reata could barely see the outlines of the tree in which the treasure was actually planted.

Well, there were two armed guards between him and the taking—but neither of them was a Bill Champion. He unloosed the reata which still was around him like a belt of many strands.

The fellow who was cooking over the fire could be attended to later on. This one who walked on guard—well, he could be made the first victim and then the bait, perhaps.

The man came near, walking his round close to the covert of Reata. He walked briskly, a chosen man who was ready to do his part even if there were plenty of fighting involved in it. But with all his wits alert, how could he see the snaky line of the reata as it sprang into the air? There was the thin whistling sound near his ears, and then the invisible noose gripped him, jammed the rifle against his breast, crushed his arms to his sides.

He was jerked straight back against the trunk of a tree with an impact that knocked the breath out of him. And before he was thinking, before he was capable of movement again, a bit of strong twine had lashed his hands behind his back and around the tree trunk.

At his ear, he heard a voice whisper: "Call in your partner. Call him over here—or I'll slide a knife under your ribs!"

Reata could have laughed at the thought of using his knife in that way, but it was a device good enough to make the prisoner obey his will, no doubt. He shook out the noose of the reata again.

That silent weapon, why would not other men use its silent power instead of the fatal noise and the blundering inaccuracy of firearms?

"Harry!" shouted the prisoner.

The man bending by the fire jumped erect.

"Ay, Pete?" he called.

"The devils have got me! Give the signal—they've got me! Give—"

A jolting blow from the fist of Reata silenced him. Harry, by the fire, snatched a brand from the blaze and with it lighted a fuse that dangled by a tall, big-headed rod that stood by the fire. Then Harry ran for the roadway.

Reata went after him, running low and swift, his rope ready in his hands. But behind him he heard a loud explosion. From the corner of his eye he saw the heavy-headed rod shoot up from the ground, trailing a shower of crimson, bright sparks behind it. High up in the air flew the thing, and Reata, groaning, understood.

It was a signal rocket, and it would bring men to the rescue.

He no longer ran after the fleeing guard. A whistle served to bring Sue swiftly toward him. As for the second guard, he had done his mischief, and there was no need in bothering about him. With fear at his heels, he would run fast and far.

Reata looked up and saw a burst of wild red fire in the middle of the sky. It streamed downward almost to the tops of the trees before that fire went out. Then the report came dimly down out of the sky, and echoes spoke the same sound softly from the hillside.

It said to Reata, first loudly and then over and over again: "Hurry! Hurry! Hurry!"

He got to Sue, opened the narrow pack behind her saddle, and pulled out of it a strong ax. Then he waded into the water to the hollow tree. The first blow of the ax sheared through the thin rind of the tree. In a moment he had ripped the side open. Then he had to dive his hand into the cold muck and slime of the marsh inside the rind of the dead trunk. When his fingers touched the chamois leather, it seemed to him that he had grasped a water snake's slippery sides. He began to lift out the small sacks. There were twenty-two of them, according to Salvio and the others. And each one was indeed, a weighty little burden of treasure.

He called Sue and loaded the first lot into the saddlebags. She could carry three hundred pounds of that burden at a load, as well as himself. It was not fair to ask her to lug more through the treachery of the marsh where she might sink at any moment.

Eight of the bags he loaded her with. Then he mounted, put little Rags on the special place which he had arranged in front of the pommel, and waded the mare through the water.

To go back by the dry road seemed now the better solution to the problem, but he would have to make three trips. And before that, perhaps the rescuers would be pelting out from the town, out from the neighboring ranches. That fellow Lester, he would be sure to turn out, gallantly, at the head of all of his armed cow punchers.

Hurry, hurry, hurry!

He would follow his first idea! He would get out to the level of the railroad track. He would then hide two thirds of the treasure somewhere up the track. The remaining third he would carry away on Sue's shoulders and his own.

In the meantime, it was dirty work getting through the slime. Once the water rose to his knees, and Sue was almost submerged, but she was presently on better footing, and now she took him out to the back of the railroad fence, where the glimmering barbed wires stretched far away to either side.

His wire clippers rang on the strands. They flew back with a ringing sound, and he rode out onto railroad property. That was when he saw the tool that might make the rest of his work easier. Of course Colonel Lester had managed to borrow from the nearest station a handcar on which some of the supplies needed for the treasure hunt could be transported to the marsh.

And there it stood, derailed, at the bottom of the embankment.

Well, what had brought supplies could be made to carry gold away!

CHAPTER 13

He was out of the saddle at once, and hefted the thing from one side. It was murderously heavy. A heavy coiled chain on top of it did not decrease the weight any. He started to drag the chain off when it occurred to him that'here was a chance to use the power of Sue. Instantly he had the chain looped from the front axle of the hand car to the two stirrups of Sue. Those stirrup leathers were strong and they would hold. He himself put his shoulder to the rear of the hand car and called to the mare.

She walked the hand car straight up the embankment. The wheels clanged against the high rails and stopped her.

He found a stick and pried the wheels over the top of the rail. It took another minute of anxious sweating before he had the hand car settled properly on the tracks, and then, to his dismay, it began to roll slowly back!

He understood.

He had forgotten that there was a heavy grade here, that climbed as far as the throat of the pass which opened darkly, yonder, through the mountains. There it began to descend with even greater angles. Suppose, then, that he loaded the car and sent it shooting with the grade? Well, in that case he would have to whiz through the station yard at Jumping Creek and, as likely as not, he would find the way blocked, or else the light car would be switched off on a siding and come to a crashing stop. No, he had to labor up the grade, if he could manage it.

He blocked the sliding wheels of the hand car with the stick he had found, loaded the eight sacks onto the car, and hurried back through the marsh. Rags he left with the load.

Halfway back to the treasure tree, he wondered why he was there wading through the foulness of the marsh. Well, he had wanted something that would fill his hands, and of course his three friends had found something for him.

For the first time he asked himself how they could have known so surely where to find the stuff? There were a thousand questions that he should have asked, if his wits had been about him on that night. But, now that he had put his hand to the job, he would carry it through while there was still blood in his body.

He reached the tree. The voice of his prisoner sounded cheerfully from the island.

"You back there ag'in, brother? You sure knew where the stuff was, all right! Goin' to flag a train and load it all on?"

Reata said nothing. He was fishing up the dripping sacks, and with them he loaded the mare again, and made his second trip, to be greeted with a silent ecstasy by Rags. It had taken time to teach Rags when his voice was permitted to come shrilling out on the air of either day or night, but it was a lesson which the little dog never forgot.

For the third load—it should be the lightest of the lot—Reata returned to the end of the island, and again his prisoner was voluble.

"They're goin' to be along on your trail before long, brother," he said. "And maybe you're goin' to have a necktie party before the sun comes up. Maybe you're goin' to dance on air, after all!"

"Maybe," said Reata. He had fished the twenty-second bag out of the muck and loaded it into the saddlebag. He added: "You can tell 'em that I headed off toward the tracks with the stuff. Why shouldn't I rap you over the head before I go?"

"Why shouldn't you 'a' slid that knife between my ribs the way you promised?" responded Pete instantly and insolently.

"I don't know why," said Reata.

"I'll tell you why, brother," said Pete. "I dunno your name, and there ain't been light enough to see your make-up. But I know what you are—you got nerve enough to steal, but you

62

ain't got nerve enough to kill. I'm goin' to send 'em on your trail, and then—"

There was a picture in the mind of Reata of the gray stallion of Bill Champion leaping from the edge of the cliff into the empty air, and of the gigantic Champion drawn out beside the horse at the end of the lariat.

Well, he knew how to kill well enough, and he was almost tempted to put in practice a little of that art at the expense of Pete, who was bawling: "Listen! They're comin' now! They're comin' now!"

Reata, straining his ears, could hear it very well. It was not the rapid-fire pattering of his heart. It was the rattling of the hoofs of horses that were coming at a dead gallop over hard ground.

Reata turned the mare and urged her desperately through the marsh. To save himself, that was still easy enough with the speed of Sue at his command. But to save the treasure, also? That was the question!

He rode up to the hand car and fastened the saddle leathers once more to the double end of the chain. Then he mounted the hand car and gripped the handle to pump it forward.

From the raised position of the railway embankment, he could hear clearly the pounding of many hoofs that turned off the valley trail and took the narrow road which the colonel had built into the marsh. That self-assured scoundrel of a Pete would be telling them, in an instant, exactly the direction in which Reata had ridden through the marsh.

Reata called to the mare; she strained ahead, and he began pumping at the big handles where eight men could find a grip to sway up and down and shoot the car along the tracks, but up this grade there was no "shooting" to be done. There was only constant and heavy laboring to get the heavy machine rolling at all, with Sue taking most of the burden.

She walked; she jogged; she got into a shambling trot with her head down and her weight pulling steadily at the load behind her. She worked as faithfully as though she had been

63

trained at draft labor, or to the plow. So, very slowly, they worked up the grade with Reata straining like a giant at the reluctant pumping handles.

Now and again he turned his head and strained his eyes back toward that point where he had issued from the marsh, and far back there, most vaguely seen through the mist and the night, he saw the riders begin to spill out onto the railroad.

He could hear them better than he could see them. He could specially hear them when they began to whoop, and then came up the track after him like so many yelling devils!

There was no hurrying possible, for him. He was working his utmost and he was giving the mare all that she could do.

In the meantime, those shapes behind him grew out of the mist, grew taller, more distinct. Still he struggled with the pumping handles, and looking up at the great black mass of the mountains which drew back toward him, he told himself that he would never come to the top of the grade.

But at that moment he felt the speed of the mare increase to a full trot, while the handles began to swing up and down more rapidly and more freely in his grasp.

He understood, then. He had actually topped the rise, and now there was a down slope to aid him just as the up grade had been a frightful handicap to overcome.

The mare would be a hindrance now, instead of a help. He leaped forward off the hand car, uncoupled the dangling chain from the stirrup leathers, hurled the chain down beside the track, and sprang back onto the hand car.

Even without his work at the handles, the car was running along at a good pace. The mare was running now, at the foot of the embankment, keeping even with the car, and not far behind her came the shadowy troop of the men of Jumping Creek.

"Faster, men, faster!" shouted a voice which he recognized as that of the colonel. "Balen, open fire on the scoundrel! Balen, start shooting!"

A rifle clanged, and a bullet hummed with sickening speed

close to the head of Reata. And then he felt the swing of a curve take hold on the wheels of the car. The black shoulder of the first mountain gradually thrust out and shielded him, for an instant, from further attack. At the same time, the strength of the grade took stronger hold on the car. Moreover, there was suddenly cursing from the pursuers. They were finding rough going for their horses, no doubt, on the slanting foot of the embankment.

The car was shooting now at great speed. As the rails straightened out after the curve, it seemed to Reata that he was rushing down a long flume that narrowed in the distance before him. And the thin glimmer of the tracks diminished to a faint sparkling, probing the darkness of the pass.

More guns crackled behind him, but he did not hear the winged noise of the bullets. And off to the side, he saw even the roan mare losing in the race against him. How badly beaten the rest of the horses must be, if Sue was falling behind!

He was traveling now at such a round rate that the car rocked dizzily at every curve. The wind of that going hurt his eyes, dimmed them, so that the light which he saw far ahead was at first a dull thing that had no meaning to him.

Then he heard it, the faint roar thrown off the flat face of some distant cliff, the sound of a locomotive as it labored at the grade!

He could have laughed, when he thought of being trapped in this manner. Now, on the very verge of shooting away to freedom, his way was blocked not by intention but by chance!

He applied the brakes. A square-shouldered pile of ties not far ahead was his goal, and he worked the brake so that the hand car screamed to a halt beside the pile.

He leaped from the car, shouldered one of the heavy ties, and thrust the end of it under the front of the hand car. The ground was trembling, he thought, with the approaching vibration of the locomotive and its long train of cars, or was it only the humming sound of the rails that seemed to pass into the ground under his feet?

65

He heaved. The heavy car swayed. He heaved again, and the hand car lurched up, toppled, and rolled down the embankment.

CHAPTER 14

The broad glare of the headlight of the engine, as it pulled slowly around the curve below him, showed Reata the lay of the land. Up to his right there was the steep, erect mass of the black mountain. To his left, a hundred-foot cliff, or something more, dropped sheer down to the narrows of the valley beneath, and at the very foot of the cliff there was a little shanty.

Two or three of the gold sacks slipped over the edge of the height and dropped away from sight. Reata instantly thrust the rest of the bags in the trail of the first ones.

He could see, behind him, the flying form of Sue as she tore along the side of the track, but he could not use all her speed and her honest heart, now. He needed, rather, wings to get him off that height of land before the dim troop of shouting riders behind the mare came swarming up to the rock.

Instead of wings, he had the reata and he used it. As the full glare of the headlight of the train flashed out at him from around the curve, he was already fitting the open loop of the rope around a projecting point of rock.

Swinging over the ledge, he found himself hanging opposite a concave face of the cliff with a narrow ledge a dozen feet beneath him. Rags was curled on one of his shoulders, with teeth fixed into the collar of the master's coat. Above him, Reata heard the anxious whinny of the mare.

Well, she would find her way. It would be as hard to lose her in the mountains as to baffle a wolf, and she would discover some trail back to her old quarters at Rusty Gulch. He need not worry about her or fear that any other man would ever come close enough to daub a rope on her! He slipped down to the very end of the doubled rope, and found his feet resting on the ledge. A shake of the lariat loosed it from its hold above. By the same process he lowered himself from another crag, a dozen feet, and then found a short distance down which he could climb. But still again, at the very bottom of the rock, he had to use the rope for a last time across a sheer concavity of fifteen feet.

They had reached the edge of the cliff above him before he was down there on the safety of the level ground. He could hear their voices growing dim as they spoke behind the edge of the cliff, or booming loud and clear as they leaned out over nothingness, to wonder what had become of their quarry.

He heard the voice of Steve Balen calling: "Some of you ride up the track. You'll come to a place in half a mile or so where you can work back down into the valley. Go hell-bent, boys, and we'll try to get down this cliff while you're going that way!"

The roar of hoofs began again from the line of railroad track. Reata, pulling down his rope from the rock above him, stood on the level of the valley floor and saw a man come running out of the back of the shanty, carrying a lantern.

Reata ran forward through the bushes and encountered the stranger under the spread of a low tree, calling as he came: "Douse the light, partner!"

The man from the shanty knew how to obey orders quickly. He jerked up the chimney of the lantern and put out the light with a single breath. So in the thick of the darkness Reata came to him. Over their heads the high, nasal, penetrating voice of Steve Balen was calling: "You down there! Don't give no help to that feller! He's a thief and he's wanted by the law. Grab him and hold him for us!"

"Hey!" murmured the voice of the shanty man. "Looks like I got good company droppin' out of the sky tonight."

He was so perfectly calm that Reata instantly took heart. He said: "They're hounding me pretty close, partner. But if you can saddle up three or four of those horses in the corral for me, I'll pay you a forty-pound bag of gold for them and your time. Does that sound good to you?"

"Brother," said the man of the shanty in the same unemotional voice, "I'd sure sell my soul for five hundred dollars in hard cash. Come along, and we'll slam some saddles on them mustangs!"

In the shed they got the saddles, and in the corral they rapidly got saddles and bridles onto four horses. Then, on the run, they swept the mustangs to the foot of the cliff, where Reata rapidly loaded saddlebags with the loot.

Above him, he could hear the noise of the man hunters descending. He could hear them shout to one another. A revolver spoke three short, deep notes. The bullets thudded into the ground near by, but there was not even starlight, under the cliff, to show the hunters how to shoot at their quarry. They only knew that he was down there almost in touch of their hands, but still a chasm of dark distance kept them away.

Reata, as he worked, was saying quietly to the man of the shanty: "I pulled a gun on you. For fear of your life, you had to do what I told you to do. You had to saddle the horses. You had to ride away with me the minute the horses were saddled and loaded. Understand? Hop on that horse next to mine, and ride hard, because I can hear the other half of these lads from Jumping Creek coming down the valley."

Those other men from Jumping Creek came like mad, in fact, for out of the distance, from the face of the cliff where Steve Balen and his men were working out a perilous descent, they could hear occasional gun shots, and the loud, pealing voice of Balen himself urging them on. The tired horses from Jumping Creek charged valiantly to get to the vital place, but as they drew near, through the bushes, dim and shadowy, they saw two riders moving; they saw four fresh horses galloping, stretched out straight with speed.

For a few jumps the hunters kept up the pursuit. Then they pulled their guns and opened fire. But weary men with bodies and nerves shaken by long riding cannot shoot straight. And the trees that made a broken screen for Reata and his companion soon thickened between them and the pursuit. Rapidly they drew away. There was no sound of beating hoofs behind them. They were able to draw their horses back to a steady canter, and presently this gait got them into view of a single riderless horse that moved ahead through the night at a trot. Looking closely through the darkness, Reata made out a saddle on the back of the mustang.

A sudden hope made him whistle the call which Sue knew; instantly the horse ahead of them swung about and came at a gallop to him. It was Sue. He knew the long, low outline of her now, and even little Rags began to murmur a whining welcome.

"Hey!" said the man of the shanty. "How'd you learn to whistle hosses to you like bird dogs, stranger? You teach me that, and I'll lay off of working."

Reata, pulling up his horse and stopping the cavalcade, dismounted and took the saddle on Sue.

"What's your name, brother?" he asked.

"Pie Phelps," said the other. "What's yours?"

"You wouldn't want to know it, would you?" asked Reata.

"Nope. Sure I wouldn't. Come to think of it, knowing your name wouldn't do me no good."

"The night was so dark, and you were so scared," said Reata, "that you couldn't tell what I was like. Is that right?"

"You just looked sort of average to me," said Pie Phelps.

"Hide out this bag of stuff," said Reata. "It's not stolen. It was hidden away on the land of Colonel Lester, that's all. And he had the neighborhood under guard. But you have as good a right to it as the next fellow. However, you'd better hide the stuff and let it ripen for a while. I wouldn't go back to that shack again tonight, if I were you."

"I sort of hanker to sleep out under the open sky, anyway," said Pie Phelps.

He took the chamois sack and weighted it in his hands.

"All gold?" he asked in a low voice.

"All gold," said Reata. "So long, and good luck to you."

"Good luck? I've got it already in my hands," said Phelps. "I've got enough good luck to turn it into a ranch and a

69

cattle herd. So long, stranger!"

Reata headed up the narrows of the valley on Sue. Four loaded horses followed him, and he saw the standing form of Pie Phelps fade into the night to the rear.

CHAPTER 15

It was the next night, just when the dusk had faded into the complete darkness, before Reata came down out of the hills with his cavalcade. He had the twinkling lights of Rusty Gulch to guide him, but when he reached the high-backed house of Pop Dickerman, he halted his animals just inside the south gate of the junk yard and tied them to the hitch rack which stood there. Afterward he tapped at the kitchen door.

Beyond the shutters he could make out the dim glimmerings of a light, but it was some moments before the door was pulled a few inches ajar and the husky voice of Pop Dickerman asked who was there.

"Reata," he said.

The door instantly jerked wide.

"Come in, old son," said the rat-faced man. "It's all right, boys!" he added loudly.

A door on the other side of the room was opened by Harry Quinn, with Salvio and Dave Bates behind him. They waved gloomily at Reata.

"Had to give it up, Reata, did you?" asked Salvio. "I told these hombres that it wasn't no one-man's job. There was too much of it, even if you ever got a chance to lay your hands on it."

"He had his try, anyway," said Pop Dickerman. He was eying Reata keenly. "He had his try, by the look of him."

"What look?" demanded Salvio grimly, as Reata took a chair and built a cigarette swiftly.

"Like he'd had his fun," said Pop Dickerman. "What would

70

seven, eight hundred pounds of gold mean to Reata if he could have his fun, eh?"

This bitterness left Reata untouched.

"Did you even get a chance to lay a hand on that holler tree?" asked the gloomy Salvio.

"No one man could do it," said Dave Bates. "I told all you hombres that it was no one-man job."

"Well," said Pop Dickerman, "tell us about the story, Reata. What you been doin' to put the yaller in your eyes?"

A huge tomcat jumped down off a window sill and started stalking Rags. The little dog sat down between the feet of his master and watched that approach without the slightest concern.

Reata said: "I had a ride on the railroad track, boys. Went faster than a horse could gallop."

"On what?" asked Salvio.

"On a hand car," said Reata. "But I couldn't keep on the way as long as I wanted to. I was just working up a good breeze when the headlight of a train heaved around a corner and looked me in the eye, so I had to pry that old hand car off the tracks and roll it down the embankment, to let the train get by."

"Where was Sue?" asked Dickerman anxiously.

"She was following along."

"He's done something," said Harry Quinn suddenly. "Reata, what you been and done?"

"I picked up some loose horses," said Reata, "and brought 'em along. There's one for each of you fellows."

"You poor half-wit," groaned Salvio, "you ain't been stealing hosses, have you?"

"I bought 'em," said Reata, "but I bought 'em so cheap that you wouldn't believe what a bargain I got." He pointed toward the door. "Go out and look at those horses. You'll like 'em. One apiece for you."

He stood up and went to the stove, where a number of pots were simmering.

"What's in here worth eating, Pop?" he said.

"Look for yourself," growled Pop Dickerman. "Come on, boys. Let's see what kind of a fool Reata's been makin' of himself."

They trooped out through the rear door of the house, while Reata examined the pots and helped himself to some beans stewed in a hot Mexican sauce. He poured out a cup of coffee, cut off a large wedge of good bread, and sat down to his supper. From the outside he heard nothing, but presently all four men came in, loaded with burdens.

They piled small, much discolored chamois sacks on the table in front of Reata. He ate on, unheeding that pile of treasure. And the four men stood about the room silently, looking at the sacks, and then at one another, their eyes bright.

Pop Dickerman said: "Harry, you and Gene go out and get the saddles off of them hosses, and turn the mustangs out where they can roll in the south corral."

The two men hesitated. Harry Quinn said: "Can't that wait?"

Dickerman's lip curled till his yellow teeth showed.

"Wait till some gents ride up and spot them hosses. Sure, they can wait, I guess."

Quinn and Salvio, cursing under their breath, left the kitchen. Pop Dickerman moved softly around the room, with long strides. His furtive eyes kept traveling to the doors and the windows.

"There's only twenty-one of these here sacks, Reata," he said softly.

"One of 'em paid for the four horses. Cheap, weren't they?" asked Reata carelessly.

Dickerman extended his long arms above his head as though he were about to call down a curse, but he only groaned. Then he lowered his hands and stroked the discolored chamois. Strings and shreds of the marsh slime still clung to the leather.

That was Dickerman's occupation when Salvio and Quinn returned and came in with the breathless haste of men who fear

72

that something very important may have happened during their absence.

Now the four men were standing around the room.

"We'd better split the stuff and break away with it," said Bates.

"All right, boys. All right, boys," said Dickerman soothingly. "I'll take my third. I'll take my seven sacks, and then you can split up the rest any way you wish."

He began to pull some of the sacks to the end of the table.

Reata swallowed some coffee at the end of his meal and rolled a cigarette.

"You furnished the news about where the stuff could be found, Pop, is that it?" he said. "Well, you ought to get your share for that. But these three fellows saved my hide in a little saloon brawl up the line. The way I see it, we split the stuff into five equal lots."

Dickerman uttered a low moaning sound.

"Rob me of dog-gone nigh half my rightful share that was agreed on?" cried Dickerman. "What you thinkin' about, son? It ain't like you, Reata. I ain't goin' to believe my ears!"

Reata lighted his cigarette and blew out some smoke.

"Why do you argue, Pop?" he asked gently.

Dickerman stared about him. The other three with lowering brows met his glances. With another groan, Dickerman surrendered.

"All right, Reata," he whined. "If you're goin' to do it that way, I suppose that there ain't anything that I can say. Into five parts, you said? That leaves an extra sack over, and—"

"Take the extra sack then," said Reata, careless always.

The clutches of Dickerman were instantly on a fifth of the sacks.

"Get the stuff away—get it away quick. Up there in the attic in the corner. You know the place, Gene. Stow it all away up there. Here, I'll help you."

"Let them cart it away," said Reata. "What I want is a little more information about the gold, Pop. Sit down here and talk."

"Aye," said Pop. "But tell me first what happened?"

Quinn and the other two were instantly at work, burdening themselves with those ponderous little sacks, and their creaking footfalls went slowly up and down the stairs to the attic.

Reata simply answered: "I had to cart the stuff away from the hollow tree to the railroad track, and I loaded it on a hand car, got Sue to pull up the grade, and with half the men of Jumping Creek out behind us, like the tail of a kite, we sailed down the far grade. A train came for us. I had to pry the hand car off the tracks, and roll the sacks down a hundred-foot cliff. I climbed down after 'em, got hold of a fellow who was willing to sell me four horses and saddles for forty pounds of gold, and loaded the stuff on the new nags and rode away."

The other three returned from their work, and Dickerman, slowly, always staring fixedly at Reata as though hypnotized, repeated the tale as he had heard it.

At the conclusion, Harry Quinn was looking with a faint grin at Salvio, and Salvio made a sudden gesture of surrender. It was as though he had said suddenly: "Yes, he's the better man!"

"Now I want to find out from you," said Reata, "just where this gold hailed from."

"It's quite a yarn," said Dickerman. "Didn't you hear anything about it down there in Jumping Creek?"

"No. I was swinging a twelve-pound sledge on a drill head. I wasn't talking."

"The yarn goes back to a gent that found a rich strike up in the hills and worked it for pretty nigh fifteen years," lied Pop Dickerman. "And he ground his stuff out with a coffee mill, you might say, and then he loaded it away in sacks, but when he come to his last sickness, he didn't know where he could hide that money where it would be safe. So he—"

Here there was a sudden and loud rap at the rear door. Dickerman, when he heard this authoritative summons, waved suddenly to Quinn and Salvio and Bates.

74

"Out!" he whispered.

They faded silently through the opposite door of the room. Then Dickerman opened the outer door upon the stalwart figure of Sheriff Lowell Mason.

The sheriff came in with a frown, which disappeared when he saw Reata. He gripped his hand heartily, saying: "I'm glad to see you, Reata. I'm glad to see you, no matter where you happen to be!"

"Thanks," said Reata. "I'm not back in jail, sheriff."

"No," said Mason, darkening again. "And I hope that you never land there again. But bad company makes a lot of trouble in a man's life, Reata! A lot of trouble!"

He turned suddenly on Pop Dickerman.

"Dickerman," he said, "the time's come for you to move out of Rusty Gulch."

"Well," said Dickerman calmly, "that's kind of bad news. Who's goin' to move me?"

"*I'm* going to move you."

"You'll need a lot of drays, brother," said Dickerman.

"I'll need a warrant and a gun," said the sheriff. "I think there's enough stuff out to put you behind the bars, Dickerman, and I'm goin' to try to put you there. You've pulled the wool over the eyes of a lot of people, Pop, but I reckon you're more of a fence than you are a junk dealer."

That accusation made not the slightest change in the expression of Dickerman. "A high board fence is what I gotta have around my junk piles," he declared.

"You ain't as simple as you make out," said Lowell Mason. "Let me tell you this. You're a crook yourself, and you're a breeder of crooks. I've seen three of your men, from time to time—Quinn is the name of one of 'em—and they fit right into the descriptions of the three thugs who robbed the Decker and Dillon Bank in Jumping Creek and got away with eight hundred pounds of gold. I can't hang the thing on them just yet, but I know in my own mind that they were in it. I suppose they're over the border, by this time, but they'll come back, one day, and then I'll get 'em! As for you, I'd rather not handle the dirty job of collecting you for jail. I'm telling you to move on, and you'd better take my advice."

"Thanks," said Dickerman. "I always like to hear a gent talk even when he's wrong, if he talks pretty well. You been talkin' well enough to get yourself a pile of votes by election time, sheriff."

The sheriff turned his back on the furry face of Dickerman and confronted Reata.

"Old son," he said, "I hate to see you in this place. If you stay around Dickerman, you're going to get yourself into trouble. So long, Reata. It's great to see you, lad."

With this, and no further word to Dickerman, the sheriff walked out of the room and disappeared. The hoofbeats of his horse presently were trailing diminishingly toward the center of the town.

Reata and the junk dealer, in the meantime, faced one another silently.

"The old fellow that worked away at his rich strike, and ground out the stuff for fifteen years!" Reata sneered.

"It's this way, Reata," pleaded Dickerman. "What I wanta tell you is this—"

"It doesn't much matter what you tell me," said Reata. "Call the boys back in here, I want to talk to them."

When the three came in, in answer to Dickerman's call, Reata was standing near the door, with his Stetson on the back of his head, and little Rags on his shoulder.

He said: "Boys, the sheriff says that the three of you robbed the bank at Jumping Creek. You got eight hundred pounds of gold out of the safe. Well, I want to know if that's the gold I've just fetched out of a hollow stump in the Jumping Creek marsh."

"Why, no, Reata," began Dave.

"Shut up, Dave," said Salvio. "There ain't any use trying to pull the wool over his eyes now. He knows!"

"It's true then?" said Reata.

76

None of the three made answer. It was old Pop Dickerman who said: "Listen, Reata. The folks in Jumping Creek knew the three of 'em. They couldn't go back for the stuff. There was nobody else to trust except you!"

Harry Quinn looked at the grim, pale face of Reata and exclaimed: "Don't take it hard, Reata! Lookat. What else could we do?"

Reata closed his eyes.

"I thought I was pulling clear," he said slowly. "I thought that I'd washed my hands of the crooked work, but I see that I'm back in the dirt again."

"Go easy, Reata," urged Dickerman. "Don't say nothin' rash now."

"I'm not saying anything rash," said Reata. "I'm only seeing the truth!"

"The truth is," broke out Gene Salvio, "that you're a better man than the rest of us, Reata! We may 'a' done you wrong in this deal. We thought it was smart for us, and a way of putting a whole lot of money into your hands, too."

"Look here," said Harry Quinn, "you got enough money now to set yourself up right. If you think you wanta be a ranchman, you can do it now, and do it right!"

"That's correct," declared Dave Bates, with ardor.

"Set myself up with stolen money, eh?" said Reata. "Thanks a lot. I'm not doing that."

"Hold on!" cried Dickerman. "You mean that you're pulling out and leaving your share behind?"

"What can I do? I'd take the loot back to the Decker and Dillon Bank, if I could," said Reata. "But there are four of you to one of me. All I can do is to get as many miles between me and the rest of you as possible. And I'm going to put them between."

He took a half step toward them with rage and with hate in his face.

"I thought I was going clean, and you've made a swine of me again!"

77

That outburst of anger left him on tiptoe, but his rage vanished suddenly.

He added sadly: "There's been life and death between us. You've saved my hide, and I've saved yours. And now this is the wind-up. I'm getting out of the country, and I'm staying out. It's like tearing the heart out of my body, but I know what the thing will be like if I stay around here. One way or another, you'll get your hands on me again and drag me into some rotten business. I haven't the brains to handle crooks like you. Good-by!"

He turned and went suddenly out into the darkness.

When the door closed, Salvio slumped into a chair, his head in his hands.

Dickerman said: "Well, we had to lose him some day, boys. But he's left a nice little farewell present for the lot of us!"

Salvio jerked up his head suddenly.

"You fool!" he said. "You poor, rat-faced fool, don't you see that he was worth more than money to us?"

"Ay," put in Dave Bates slowly. "He was worth our blood!"

CHAPTER 16

Inside his roll of bedding, Pie Phelps had forty pounds of gold in a chamois bag. He had loosened the tie strings of the bag, worked the bag out into a sausage shape, more or less, retied the mouth of the sack securely, and then lashed it inside the blanket roll. He felt that he had lashed it very firmly, but in that he happened to be wrong, and that was why the shadow of the law fell across his path.

The nature of Pie Phelps was as large and liberal as his mouth, which divided his face almost from ear to ear, and though he knew perfectly well that the forty pounds of gold were part of the stolen money of the Decker and Dillon Bank in Jumping Creek, Pie almost honestly felt that it was now his own. So, as he rode across country, his mind was at rest. For one thing, it was Sunday, and if Sunday does not always produce good deeds, at least it is likely to cause a state of rather sleepy confidence. And when Pie Phelps came across the hills and saw the long, low bunk house of the Lester ranch, and when he heard the musical dingdong of the cook's bell and the cook's voice faintly and far away telling the boys to "Come and get it!" Pie saw no reason why he should not ride up to the house and sit down at the table.

It was true that Colonel Lester had taken a leading part in the search for the stolen money when that treasure was lodged in the Jumping Creek marsh. It was true that the colonel's formidable foreman, Steve Balen, had been the straw boss in handling the workers. But Pie Phelps did not feel that any considerable suspicion rested on him. All that people could know with any surety was that he, as he related, had been held up by a fugitive in the middle of the night, and forced by the stranger to help in the saddling of four horses, and then driven into accompanying the man in the first part of the other's flight.

The people at the ranch house would be sure to ask him a lot of questions about his strange adventure, and they might offer him some sympathy because he had been robbed of four horses.

He grinned a little as he thought of a ten-thousand-dollar payment for four ordinary range bronchos! He was on his way north, where he would settle down in a part of the country where people had never seen his face before. There he might change his name, and turn his gold into greenbacks, and then buy for himself just the sort of a small ranch which had always been his dream.

He was full of these comforting plans—unlucky Pie Phelps! —when he rode up to the side of the old ranch house, dismounted, and turned his mustang into a corral. He then carried his saddle and the heavy bedding roll and the bridle to the open shed which communicated between the kitchen–dining room and the bunk house. After that, listening greedily to the sound

79

of knives and forks against tin plates inside the kitchen, he retreated to the pump, filled a basin with water, and covered his face and hands with suds. His washing did not include neck and ears. Pie Phelps was only interested in presenting a good front.

As he dried his face and hands on an unsoiled section of the coarse yellow roller towel that hung beside the kitchen door, he looked at the trees which loomed on the other side of the hill. He could see, also, the red tip of the pyramidal roof of the house of Colonel Lester, a huge mansion with a Georgian porch of slender white pillars. To Pie Phelps, who had once stood in awe in front of that porch, it had seemed as impressive as any church façade or the front of any bank.

Now he rapped at the open door of the kitchen, and walked in. It was a big room, this end devoted to the uses of the cook and his big stove, the other end filled by the long table. That table was now surrounded by the men of the ranch, and at the farther end of it appeared the tall form of famous Steve Balen. He was one of the few men in the world who deserved the title of "two-gun man," because he could shoot straight with left or right; he was almost the only one of the two-gun men who was able to lay claim to a life of sterling honesty.

When Steve saw the stranger come in, it could not be said that his face lighted in the least. But having a load of string beans on his knife at that moment, he emptied the cargo into his mouth so that he could point more freely with the knife to the end of the table, opposite him. Around the beans, Steve Balen managed to say: "Lay another place, Doc."

The rest of the crowd gave Pie Phelps at least more attention if not a more rousing welcome. Some of the men half pushed back their chairs and turned sharply toward the newcomer. A little murmur ran around the table. Two or three waved their hands. One man said: "Hello, Pie."

And when Pie sat down, a grim-faced man on his right muttered: "How's things? Caught the gent that robbed you of them four hosses?"

"Ain't caught him yet," said Pie Phelps. "Goin' to get

80

the runt, one of these here days."

"Yeah? He was a runt, was he?" asked Steve Balen from far away.

"Well, I dunno," retracted Pie. "He wasn't so dog-gone big. Just about average, maybe."

"Yeah. That's what I heard you tell the judge," said Steve Balen, and there was no ring of conviction in his voice. "I guess the gun that he pulled on you must of been man-sized, though."

"Yes, it looked like a cannon to me, all right," agreed Pie.

He had started his meal when the others were half through. He was catching up nobly, toward the end, but he lingered to roll a cigarette and enjoy a fourth cup of acrid coffee before he went out to catch up and saddle his mustang, which by this time would have filled its belly with water and would have grazed on some of the sun-cured grasses which still grew around the edges of that capacious corral.

It was this final delay of Pie's that caused the trouble, because when the other men trooped out from the kitchen, shuffling as cowpunchers will, walking with their knees well apart, Steve Balen, who was a tidy man, as a straw boss or a foreman ought to be, picked up the narrow bedding roll which had fallen down from the horn of Pie's saddle, where it hung from a peg on the wall.

When he picked it up, his eyes opened a little. The extra forty pounds made him exclaim: "What's Phelps got in here? Half a dozen guns?"

And, with that, he gave the bedding roll a hard shake. This was where chance, and a bit of carelessness in the tying of a single knot, proved hard on Pie. For the weighty little bag of chamois leather broke loose from its fastenings and slid out onto the floor of the shed.

Two or three of the other men saw the thing and looked casually at it. But the teeth of the foreman were set hard as he picked it up. He deliberately untied the mouth of the bag, dipped his hand into the contents, and then allowed a sparkling

81

yellow shower of metal dust to pour back into the chamois sack.

"This here," said the grating voice of Steve Balen, "is sure the gun that robbed Pie Phelps of his four hosses, and a piece of his time."

Every one had seen it, by this time, that is, every one except Pie, who now came out with the fumes of tobacco sweetening his nostrils. And then he saw tall Steve Balen standing there with a gun in one hand and the bag of gold in the other.

"Well," said Balen, "it was sure a whale of a heavy weapon that that gent pulled on you, the other night. Dog-gone me if I hardly blame you for givin' right up and doin' what he wanted you to do."

Pie Phelps was no coward. He regarded the chamois sack with a calm eye, lifted his glance to Balen, and then inhaled heartily on his cigarette.

"Well, Steve," he said, "what about it?"

"Dog-gone me if I know," answered Balen. "What you think yourself?"

"Dog-gone me if I know what to think," said Pie Phelps. "I been wonderin'. Would you call it thievin'?"

This fine point caught the attention of all the cow punchers far more heartily than the more spectacular feat of the man's capture.

A puncher called Shorty said: "How would it be stealin'? The money was give to him, wasn't it?"

"Maybe you'd call it receivin' stolen goods?" said another.

"He might do a lot of suspectin', but when he took the sack, how would he *know* that they was stolen goods?" demanded Balen.

"That's right," said another. "Dog-gone me if lawyers don't have a pretty hard time figgerin' things out. I wouldn't be no judge for love nor money, says I. *Keepin'* the goods after he heard tell about the stealin' of them— that would be the worst thing agin' Pie, I reckon."

"We'll have to go up and see Colonel Lester," said Steve

Balen. "There ain't no doubt in my mind that you're as crooked as anything, Pie, and dog-gone me if I would want to take the blame for doin' nothin' about it!"

CHAPTER 17

There was plenty of trouble up there behind the white columns of Colonel Lester's house. It had started half an hour before when Agnes Lester, under the big trees south of the house, steeled herself to say to Tom Wayland. "We can't be married next month, Tom."

Tom Wayland was such a big fellow and such a handsome fellow, and the mirror had told him so often all about himself, that it required time before the full weight of this speech struck him. He fairly reeled under the impact, however, when the blow came home. And then he said to himself that the girl was a fool. But that, of course, was apparent. Otherwise she would never have been capable of saying such a thing to him. But even if she were a fool, she was the daughter and the only heir of Colonel Lesters' square miles of ranch. Therefore Tom merely said: "This is a terrible thing, Agnes."

"I don't think it's terrible," she answered. "You don't care about me, Tom."

"You haven't a right to say that," he declared.

"I don't suppose I have," she answered, "but I think I've been able to look a little way into you, Tom. I know that a lot of marriages are not romantic. And I know that it would be a very good thing, in a way, if the Wayland and the Lester properties were joined. I'm sure that father and your father and you have a lot of interest in that. But I'm selfish *and* I'm romantic. I want to be in the center of the stage when my marriage comes along."

He was so angry—because everything she said was true—that he turned quite white. He put a hand behind him and gripped it hard. Truthfully it must be admitted that he wanted to punch her pretty little face for her.

"Agnes," he said, "I've known for a good many days that you've been feeling differently about me. Ever since that day down on the island in the marsh—ever since the day that pickpocket, Reata, was run off your father's place—ever since that day, you've felt differently about me!"

"Yes," she said. "That was when I began to make up my mind."

This cool admission staggered him.

"One glance at a pickpocket, one look at a sneak thief, and you change your mind about what men should be? Agnes, is it because you wanted to see me pick up the little whippersnapper by the nape of the neck and throw him off the place? Great heavens, my dear, a fellow of my size could not touch a little rat like Reata."

She shook her head. Truth was in her like a cold poison and it had to out.

"That isn't the reason you wouldn't touch him, Tom," she said.

"You mean that I was afraid of him?" said Wayland.

"All the men were afraid of him, when they knew that he was the one who had killed that horrible monster, Bill Champion," she said.

He was fairly checkmated. There was no move open to him. He could feel that his face was working with his rage and with his open and discovered shame. That was why she looked a little away from him as she went on:

"Tom, I'm going to ask you to tell my father that our marriage can't go through. If I tell him, there will be a frightful scene. And after he's delivered a judgment, he's much too proud to change his mind. I want to beg you to go to him and tell him that we simply don't care for one another enough to marry."

"Well," said Tom Wayland, "I'll do it. I have to do it, if you ask me to."

She did not even say that she was sorry. She merely thanked him. And he went off with his head whirling. If he had been sure of anything in the world, he had been sure of her. If he had been sure of anything, he had been certain that she was just a sweet little clinging sort of a thing that a husband could pat on the head now and then while he went about his more important affairs.

And now she had turned into this soft-voiced, soft-eyed seer and bold speaker of the truth!

Suppose that a lamb should stand up and hit a lion between the eyes, and knock the lion stiff—yes, it was like that!

However, he was quite determined to play the part of a man. He went straight to Colonel Lester, who had just come in from his daily ride—or parade—across his range. And as the colonel pulled off his gloves in the hall, Tom Wayland said: "Colonel Lester, I've got to tell you something. The thing isn't going through. Between Agnes and me, I mean. It can't go through."

The colonel turned from him, placed his wide hat on the rack, laid his gloves on the table, and brushed some dust off his coat.

"You mean the marriage?" said the colonel gently.

Tom Wayland knew that a terrible river of anger was being dammed up behind the teeth of the colonel, but he blundered on: "It can't be worked. I'm sorry. I thought—"

"You're sorry, are you?" said the colonel. "When the plans that I have laid are to be shattered, when the fortune that—when the forethought of years is to be—when a young puppy dares to jilt my child!"

This speech was not exactly coherent, and yet the meaning of it was clear enough. And the last phrase came out with a good hard ring to it. The colonel wanted some good grounds for his rage, and he found a basis for it in his last words. Every man has a right to be wroth when his daughter is cheaply esteemed and treated.

The colonel took a breath to let out another terrible blast, but

Tom Wayland bowed to the blast. He forgot his good, manly intentions.

"*She* isn't the one who's being jilted," he said.

"The insufferable arrogance of the young fellows who can have the—" began the colonel. Then he saw that the last response of Wayland had altered the matter a good deal and required a refitting of words and measures. "Agnes?" said the colonel, panting a little because of the pressure of excess steam. "*Agnes* is the one who is not pleased?"

"Colonel Lester," said Tom Wayland, "I don't want you to let her knew that I've told you. I came here to take the full blame on my own shoulders. But then I saw—I felt—I knew, all at once, that it wouldn't be right for me to let you dream that I could never treat you or yours without the greatest respect, and affection, and esteem. I have to tell you the truth!"

Tom Wayland began to be noble, as he worked into this speech. He began to make a few of those fine, wide gestures that start with the hand on the heart. He was shocked when the colonel merely said: "You and your truth! Where's that ungrateful brat?"

"Agnes was outside under the trees," said Tom Wayland. "But please, Colonel Lester, please don't let her know that I've spoken to you in such a way as to—"

"I'll be the height of tact. She'll know nothing," said the colonel. "But I'm going to get to the root of this nonsense."

If there was one thing, above all else, upon which the colonel plumed himself, it was on his possession of the most exquisite tact. He walked slowly out of the house now, and gathered himself, and arranged his features. He presently produced a smile, but the smile furrowed a face that was half red and half white.

When he got beneath the trees, he found Agnes reading in a hammock. Yes, just lying there, stretched out, one hand under her head, reading—in a hammock!

The red cover of the book was to the colonel like a red rag

to a bull. Yet he constrained his voice to say gently: "What are you reading, my dear?"

"The cookbook, father," said Agnes, and she sat up dutifully in the hammock.

"The which?" said the colonel, going a trifle blank.

"The cook never has been able to bake real Boston beans," said the girl. "And I love 'em—on Saturday nights, don't you?"

"Humph," said the colonel.

"I mean," said Agnes, "that when you're hungry in the middle of the night, it's always nice to find some cold baked beans with bread and butter. Don't you think so?"

Baked beans? Bread and butter?

The colonel threw good nature and tact to the winds.

"You can bread and butter your beans when Tom Wayland is walking out of my house forever?" he shouted suddenly.

He raised his hand and shook his forefinger, also his entire fist, at the girl. She stood up.

"The plan which would affect the entire future of this county —the cultural future of the West—the whole effort toward which I have been pouring out—in short, the work of my life is what you're throwing over your shoulder for a pot of baked beans!" shouted the colonel.

She did not appear to notice the lack of sequence in these remarks. She merely said: "I thought that Tom would have to put the blame on me."

"Confound it," roared the colonel, "on whose shoulders *does* the blame belong?"

"On mine, I suppose," said the girl.

"Then march into that house this minute and beg Tom Wayland to forgive you for being a fool!" commanded the colonel. He wished for his riding whip to give his gesture more dignity; there was plenty of force in it, at that.

"Do you want me to ask Tom to consider that I haven't talked frankly to him?"

"Do what I tell you," said the colonel.

"A man who would let me do that—would you want me to

marry such a man?" she asked him.

She was neither pale nor red. She was simply steady. Something—just a trace—of this calm iron had been in her mother. The colonel felt as though a dreadful ghost had looked in upon his soul.

"Go—instantly!" he shouted.

"I can't go, Father," said she.

Colonel Lester swallowed the first ten words that rushed into his mind. At last he gasped: "Go—to your room—and stay there!"

She went, her head a little bowed, the red-backed cookbook tucked under her arm.

CHAPTER 18

The colonel stalked back toward the front door of his house in such a fury that his heels banged down on the ground in a sort of goose step that shook his entire body. And just as he was swinging in toward the steps of the porch, Steve Balen and half a dozen others came up with the big, loose form of Pie Phelps striding among them.

"Colonel," said Steve Balen, "here's the gent that passed the four hosses to the thief that stole the gold out of the marsh. And just now I shook down a forty-pound sack of gold dust out of his bedding roll. I guess the crook bought him, all right. But what we wonder is, what we oughta do with him?"

There are such things as sudden transferences of the passions. The colonel made a perfect one at this instant. The fury that was ripened and on tap under high pressure in him was instantly turned loose on Pie Phelps.

"The scoundrel!" shouted the colonel. "Put him down—down"—he was about to say "into the dungeon," but remembered himself in time—"into the sub-basement. Lock him up there. Tie his hands and feet. Leave him in the dark with a guard at his door—and—and—send for the sheriff. If there were *men* in this part of the world, they wouldn't ask me what to do with—with horse thieves and—and rascals—they'd hang them up to the first tree!"

He indicated the trees beside his own house and then strode through his front door.

Steve Balen said: "Well, dog-gone me, the chief is kind of upset. I guess we'd better take you down into a nice cool cellar and leave you there for a while, Pie. Stud, you and Bill take him down there and lock him up, and the pair of you take turn and turn about watchin' him till the sheriff sends out. Dog-gone me if I ain't sorry, Pie, but you heard what the boss said."

"Sure," said Pie, looking toward the tree, "I heard, all right. The cellar is good enough for me!"

"Tuck," said the foreman, "you sashay into Jumpin' Creek and get hold of the sheriff or somebody. I'm a deputy, all right, but I don't want to have that ride all the way in and back!"

That was why Pie Phelps sat in the darkness, close to the door of that dingy cellar room, and communed through the panels with his watcher.

"Supposin' that everything was to go wrong," said he. "What would happen in the court? I mean, suppose that they was to find me guilty of something?"

"Receivin' stolen goods?" said Bill, on the outside of the door.

"How would I know they was stolen?" queried Pie sadly.

"You wouldn't guess it?" said Bill. "Not with Steve Balen hollerin' off the top of the cliff to stop that thief, and the rest of us yappin' pretty loud?"

"I had a cold in the head and I wasn't hearin' very good," said Pie.

"I dunno that I'd tell a judge and a jury about havin' a cold in the head," said Bill thoughtfully.

"No, I dunno that I will," answered Pie, on second thought. "But supposin' that they socked me into jail, what you think it would be?"

"I dunno. Receivin' stolen goods is bein' a fence. A fence gets socked pretty hard. I dunno. Maybe ten or a dozen years."

"Ten or a dozen chunks of hell-fire!" howled Pie Phelps. "Lemme out of here!"

"Dog-gone me, I'd like to, but I can't," answered Bill.

"Lemme out!" shouted Pie Phelps. And then, realizing to the full his unhappy condition, his voice sank into the longest and the deepest of groans.

A good many events were being prepared by chance, at this moment. For one thing, when Tuck cantered into Jumping Creek, he intended to go straight to the office of the sheriff. And there was the sheriff waiting as a good sheriff should, with a goose-quill toothpick laboring earnestly to remove a bit of corn husk from between two molars. So that before the middle of the afternoon the sheriff in person should have arrived at Colonel Lester's ranch to receive Pie Phelps into his custody, and if he had done so, perhaps everything else would have been changed.

But when Tuck was cantering his mustang blithely down the main street of Jumping Creek, it just happened that he saw Sim Matthews come around a corner—good old Sim Matthews who had been away south of the Rio Grande for two years. And Sim ran out into the street and hailed his friend, and dragged him off his horse with big, happy hands, and pulled him into the Trotting Fool Saloon.

Those powerful hands restrained Tuck, who was quite weak with happiness at seeing his friend, and the pungent smell of whisky which flavored the air of the Trotting Fool.

Even by one hand, Sim Matthews was able to hold his friend, while he ordered and paid for drinks with the other. Together they hoisted the glasses and laughed in one another's eyes.

"I gotta go down the street and leave word with the sheriff and I'll be right back," said Tuck.

"Sure. I'll walk along down with you," said Sim, "soon as we've had one more drink."

Time, which had taken a good look at the pair who leaned at the bar of the Trotting Fool, promptly disappeared from the

90

place and did not return to lay a startling finger upon the conscience of Tuck until the dark of the night was spread over the town.

But just after twilight a rider came over the hills on the very trail which Pie Phelps had ridden. It was Reata, riding without song or whistle, down-headed, young no more in spirit. And the little dog Rags, who ran ahead of the trotting mare, did not need to hurry to keep ahead of the smoothly shuffling forehoofs of Sue.

Her head was down, like the head of her master, but for all her shuffling, she would not stumble, more than a mountain sheep. And for all the gauntness of her outline and the miles she had put behind her, there was a storm of tireless speed locked up in her tough body.

Reata, when he saw, at last, the glimmering lights of the ranch house, instead of continuing toward it swung to the side, and rounded the hill until he was close to the mansion of the colonel. He rode up among the trees, dismounted, and approached the house gloomily. For he was coming, as he had promised, to see Agnes Lester once more. He was going to say good-by before he left this part of the world forever; if need were, he was going to tell her why—that he had lived too long with thieves to escape from their influence now with ease.

Now, looking up toward the house, he saw that all the windows were dark, on that side of the place, except one in the second story. And at this open window sat a girl with the lamplight glowing on her golden hair.

To Reata, the thing was clear. Chance had placed her in his full view solely so that he would be able to see her with no trouble. For, if he presented himself at the door, he would very likely be ordered from the Lester place, as he had been ordered once before.

The thing was extremely simple—for Reata.

He stood under the window and whistled. The little dog, Rags, sat down at his master's feet and looked attentively up as though he knew what it was all about.

At the whistle, the girl leaned out over the window sill, holding a book in her hand.

"It's Reata," he called to her.

"I can't come down," she said.

"Then I'll come up," said Reata.

"You can't," said the guarded whisper. "Father won't let me see a soul."

"I'm not a soul. I'm only a Reata," said he. "May I come?"

"They won't let you into the house!"

"I'll walk up the wall then," said he.

At that, he pulled from his coat pocket the forty feet of his rope, sliding the leather round of it, pencil-thin and strong as steel cable, through his expert fingers until it was doubled strand. Then he threw, and with the end of the long noose thus made, he caught the projection of the wooden hooding above the window. He swayed back, putting his weight against the line, to make sure that it was strongly fixed. Then, as he had promised, he simply walked up the wall, handing himself along the rope with his powerful arms, and walking up the boards at the same time.

She was protesting all the way, though with the grip of both hands she steadied the lines, until suddenly he was seated on the sill of the window.

"Quick! Come in, or they'll see you against the light!" she commanded.

"Put out the light then," said Reata. "I can't come into the colonel's house till he invites me."

CHAPTER 19

When she went to the lamp and leaned over it, all her face and hair were lost in flame color. Then at a breath she was a part of the darkness. He could hear her coming toward him, but she was almost at the window again before he could make her out.

"This isn't all right," said he. "If somebody came in and found you talking to a tramp on your window sill, there would be trouble. But I promised to come back and here I am."

"I'm glad you came. I would have come down," she answered, "but you see I have to stay in my room."

"Ill?"

"No, I'm being punished."

"You?" said Reata. "Punished? Kept in your room? No, I don't believe that."

"It's the truth."

"Not for something you've done, but something you didn't do," said Reata.

There was a bit of silence in answer to this remark. It extended long enough to show that she did not want to continue the subject.

"I've come to say good-by," said Reata then. "I'm drifting out of this part of the country."

"How far?" she asked.

"A thousand miles or so."

"There's something wrong, then," said she.

"Not with the country," answered Reata. "It's my country. I know all this part of it. I've got all the mountains put down in my mind so that I can walk around 'em, and tell you what the back looks like when I see the front. I know where the rivers go and the way they run. I know the water holes in the desert. It's all my country and it's the best in the world. The trouble's with me."

He paused there, to gather his courage. She said nothing, but he felt that she was with him.

"Listen," said Reata, "I want to come clean to you."

"I want you to," said the girl.

"When I saw you the other day," said Reata, "I went off stargazing and day-dreaming. But now I want to tell you why I was down there in the marsh. I was looking for the gold. That night, I came back and got it."

"You were the one? Well, it had to be some one like you."

"I'm going to tell you another thing that'll be hard for you to believe. I didn't know that stuff was stolen from the Decker and Dillon Bank. The people who told me where to find the stuff in the tree let me think that it was cached there by an old miner. Can you believe that?"

There was a bit of waiting.

"I want to believe you," she said. "Pretty soon I shall."

"Anyway," said Reata, "when I found out that I'd been tricked, I didn't take any of the stuff. I got to thinking things over, and I saw that much as I liked this part of the world, it wasn't the place for me. The fact is, I've been what Tom Wayland called me. I've been a crook. I've been jailed for crookedness."

"That was all wiped out by the governor of the State," she answered, "after you got rid of Bill Champion."

"Not even the governor can wipe out such things," said Reata. "You know how it is. I can feel the crookedness in me. I'm a lazy fellow. I like to take the easiest way. And the easiest way is the crooked way, especially when you're around a lot of people who know how to give you wrong starts. Going straight ought to be a habit. I'm going to go away somewhere and try to get into the habit."

"I understand," said she.

"That's the whole story," said Reata. "I'll say good-by and get out of here before somebody walks in on you. Sometime I'm going to see you again, when I'm on my feet and standing straight."

"You've been frank with me and I'm going to be frank with you," she said suddenly. "When I saw you out there in the marsh, making that big mastiff helpless, and then freezing Tom Wayland cold with fear, it was like hearing good steel ring. I've kept on hearing it, ever since. That's why I hate to have you go away."

"I'm getting a bit dizzy," he told her.

"Don't!" said the girl. "But I've been trying to find the same ring in other men, and I haven't found it. That's why I'm confined to my room tonight. I told my father that I couldn't marry the man he wanted for me."

"Wayland!" exclaimed Reata suddenly. "It's Wayland that you mean!"

"Yes, it's Tom Wayland."

Reata said nothing. His heart was beating so high that speech would have been very difficult for him even if there had been words in his mind.

"What should I do?" he asked her at last.

"Follow your own way," she answered. "It may bring you back across my life, one of these days."

"If you say one word—"

"I don't want to say it," she replied. "There's no good in saying it. You're a free man, Reata, and I want you to stay free. Suppose that I tried to pull you into my sort of a life and suppose that you were willing to come. After a while, you'd be like the others. Just small and trifling."

"You know," said Reata, "a minute ago I thought this was turning into a regular love scene. I was about to reach out and get hold of your hand. But, by Jiminy, look how things have turned out!"

"Well," she said, chuckling, "you told me the truth about yourself, and I had to give you an even break, didn't I?"

"Thanks," said Reata. "I wish I had some light on this subject. I've thought that I could see you in my memory. But not the sort of a girl you've turned out to be."

"It isn't safe for you, if I light the lamp," she said. "Here's my hand, Reata."

"It's not a whale of a big hand," said he.

"It'll hold onto a friend very hard, though," said she.

"I'll bet it will," said Reata. "I'm saying good-by, and wishing Tom Wayland a lot of bad luck."

"Bad luck? It would be worse luck for him if he married me. Before long, he'd want to give away all the Lester acres and beef

95

to charity, if he could give me away along with the rest. There's another thing I ought to tell you. There was that fellow you hired the four horses from that night."

"Hired 'em?" said Reata. "Well, that's right. What about him?"

"Pie Phelps is here in the house. He came here for lunch today. Steve Balen found the sack of gold in Phelps's blanket roll. My father was in a fine fury, at about that time, and he had Phelps put down into the sub-basement, and a guard placed over him."

"Thanks," said Reata. "I suppose—confound it, I suppose I ought to do something about it!"

"I imagined that you'd think that," she answered.

"But why?" he argued. "I paid Pie a hundred times over for what he did for me. He's lost the pay and the horses. Why should I burn my fingers on his account just now?"

"There's no reason," she answered.

"Still, to lie there in the dark till the sheriff comes—I can't let him stay there. Am I a fool if I try to get him loose?"

"I suppose you are," said Agnes Lester. "Reata, there's a wide-awake armed man down there, every moment. Would you really go down there and risk your life for a fellow like Pie Phelps?"

"I'm a fool," said Reata. "You don't want me to go, then?"

"Oh, I want you to be your whole self."

He caught her suddenly, and drew her closely into his arms. She made no resistance, but she said: "Please don't, Reata."

"Why not, when I love you, and you half love me?" he demanded.

"Because I'm a silly thing," said she. "If you kiss me, I'll begin to belong to you from that moment. And that's no good, is it? If you follow your own life and your own way, as you ought to, maybe you'll never see me again; and I don't want to sit here the rest of my life with nothing but an aching in my heart."

96

He kissed her hand, instead, and kept his head bowed over it for a long moment, though he could not tell whether there were more love or awe or astonishment in his mind.

CHAPTER 20

Since the house was built on the side of a hill, there were plenty of cellar windows along the lower wall of the building. And when Reata had slipped down to the ground, he went straightway to that row of low, squat windows and began to try them. The very second one moved under his hand, and he slid into the damp darkness of an underground room.

He closed his eyes and made his outstretched hands serve him as guides until he was able to locate a door, which opened onto a narrow hallway that presently carried him to steps down which he descended to the sub-basement. A faint glimmer of light warned him to go slowly. While he was approaching the corner of the lower hall, he heard voices from near by, one that of a stranger, and one that of Pie Phelps, muffled by a partition. Reata could recognize the accents of the fellow from whom he had secured the four horses on the night of his flight.

This nearer speaker was saying: "Maybe he ain't in town at all."

"I wish he'd come," said the stifled tones of Pie Phelps. "I'd rather be in jail than layin' here where things are crawlin' all around me."

"When you get to jail, you're goin' to have a long rest, son."

"Yeah, I'll have to take what's comin' to me. I wonder if they'd really give me as much as ten years?"

"Sure they would, and laugh as they done it. Givin' sentences is a sort of exercise for a judge. It makes him feel good."

There was a deep groan from Pie Phelps.

"Look at here," said the guard. "Suppose that you was to

open up and do a little talkin'. They'd let you off if you turned State's evidence."

"What's that?" asked Pie Phelps.

"Why, it's where you take and spill everything you know about the gents in the game that are higher up than you are. Like the gent that come along that night and hired you and your hosses with the stolen gold. If you could spot him for the law, you'd be let right off, likely. You know who he was?"

Reata listened intently, and his heart sank as he heard Pie Phelps answer: "Sure, I know who he was, all right."

"Well, then, you don't have to be afraid of no jails nor no judges, neither. All you gotta do is open up and talk."

"Yeah, but how could I do that?"

"How couldn't you?"

"This hombre comes along, and I know that he's getting away with something, all right. And I take his money, and plenty of it. I sell him the hosses. So what call have I got to stab him in the back, afterwards?"

"Hold on. You'd spend your ten years in the pen instead of takin' a whack at a gent that don't mean nothin' to you?"

"I dunno," said Pie Phelps. "Somehow I can't hear myself standin' up and swearin' the law onto the trail of a gent that didn't do nothin' wrong to me. Maybe I'll weaken when the time comes, but I sure hope that I won't!"

"You got me beat," said the guard. "Listen to me—"

Reata heard the next words only faintly. He was venturing a glance around the corner of the wall, and now he saw, not twenty feet away, a tall cowpuncher who sat on a box, facing a door that closed up the end of the hallway.

The thin, weighted coils of the lariat that instant flew from Reata's hand. He had to make a difficult cast, for the ceiling was not much higher than the top of the peaked hat of the guard. But the noose slithered through the narrow space and dropped over the guard's arms. The jerk on the rope slammed the man flat on his back, and before he could shout, Reata, his bandanna pulled up to the bridge of his nose to serve as a mask, was

98

leaning over him with the guard's own gun in his hand.

"Just take it easy," said Reata. "I won't hurt you. I won't even gag you, if you'll take it easy."

He saw the face of the fallen man contort as he rolled the body on its side, then rapidly lashed hands and feet with lengths of twine.

"Me—done in like a washerwoman!" muttered the guard.

Suddenly Reata heard a quickly drawn breath. He realized what was coming, but before he could clap a hand over the parted lips of the cow-puncher, the wild yell of "Help! Help!" went pealing down the hall.

He was tempted to repay the guard with a tap over the head from the long-barreled Colt. But the mischief was done. He turned the key in the lock of the door and jerked it open, then leaned over the startled face of Pie Phelps, who sat agape on the floor of the dark room, his hands and feet lashed together.

Reata, as he slashed the bonds with the edge of his knife, said rapidly: "Want to take your chances with the law, or come with me?"

"Law? Damn the law!" said Pie Phelps, lurching to his feet. "I'll go with you."

And he went, on a dead run, behind Reata, down the length of the hall, while that bawling voice of the guard betrayed them from behind, yelling: "Help! Help! Pie Phelps is loose, and a gent with him! They're boltin' for upstairs! Help!"

Reata, still coiling the forty feet of his trailing lariat as he ran, reached the head of the steps. It was big Pie Phelps who carried the lantern that gave them light, for Pie had had wit enough to snatch the lantern from the peg on which it hung.

With that light they found the upper hall, then turned down to the door which stood open, and through which Reata had made his entrance.

But as they disappeared through it, more light flung toward them with the opening of still another door. Voices poured at

99

them. A revolver boomed like shaking thunder in the narrow confines of the hallway.

Reata slammed the door behind him, and locked it, hearing the voice of Steve Balen shout out: "Foller on here. Sam and Lefty, come on outside with me! We're goin' to get 'em!"

Pie Phelps was already through the window, and Reata slithered out after him, where little Rags began to leap up and down like the head of a shadowy fountain at his feet.

"Now, if they want me, they surely gotta pay for me!" gasped Pie Phelps.

He had taken not only the lantern, which he had dashed out in the last cellar room, but he had also snatched up one of the guard's Colts. Reata struck the edge of his palm across the fellow's wrist and made the gun drop to the ground.

"No shooting, you fool!" he whispered. "This way!"

He led him on the run through the trees to the place where Sue waited. Behind them, Steve Balen and the others were already rushing among the trees, and from the house came the heavy battering against the locked door in the cellar.

But Reata already had Pie Phelps in the saddle on Sue. He himself clung to one stirrup leather, and as the mare broke into a lope, Reata followed with gigantic strides at her side.

They cleared the trees. Behind them voices were shouting: "They're on hosses, already. Saddle up! Saddle up!"

Beyond the trees, the ground dipped into a hollow little valley, where some sleeping horses sprang up and scattered before them. But the noose of Reata's lariat was instantly over the head of one of them. A noose of the slender rope he then worked between the teeth of the mustang, and so could rule the animal by that grip on the lower jaw.

Onto the back of the half-wild horse Reata leaped. There were ten seconds of frantic bucking, and then, grunting at every stride, the broncho set sail after Sue, who was disappearing with Pie Phelps in the saddle and Rags in front of it, over the rim of the nearest hill.

Over that hill, in turn, the mustang carried Reata, and glancing back, he saw a stream of half a dozen riders come pouring out from the cloudlike shadows of the trees around the house of the colonel.

Before him, Pie Phelps, like the good fellow he was at heart, was reining in the speed of the roan mare until Reata ranged up beside him. Then the pair of them headed north for the broken ravines of the foothills. It would be very strange if even Steve Balen could catch them in that chopped and confused wilderness.

CHAPTER 21

Reata and Pie Phelps, by the time their horses had corkscrewed two or three miles and a hundred devious turns into the foothills, were safe enough, unless chances played against them. They simply pulled up and spent the night in a good camping place under big trees, with a trickle of water running down the side of the clearing. Pie Phelps was in high spirits. Concerning his misadventures of the day he said:

"It's all in a life. I been on the run before. I'm on the run ag'in now. And what's the odds? If I had had that forty pounds of gold on the horse, it would 'a' beat me, because I wouldn't 'a' had the nerve to chuck the stuff away. I'm forty pounds lighter without losin' no strength whatsoever, when you come to that!"

He added, after Reata had wrapped himself in a blanket with little Rags lying close to his head as a guard: "How about shovin' along through Chester Falls tomorrow? I got a coupla pals up there that would give us a hand-out and a change of hosses—because it's goin' to be my turn to ride bareback tomorrow!"

"Chester Falls?" said Reata. "I've heard that there was a gang of gypsies there recently."

"Sure there was," said Pie Phelps, yawning. "Had a letter from my friend up there, about seein' their show. They got a

101

strong man with a face like a cat, whiskers and everything. And the boss of the gang is a woman, dog-gone me if she ain't, and she smokes cigars all day long. But the prime number is the bareback rider. My friend writes that she's a gal worth seeing! Slim as a magpie and just as dog-gone pert and smart and dances on the back of a gallopin' hoss like it was a dance floor."

That thought held Reata as he closed his eyes for sleep. He had been thinking, since he first saw Agnes Lester, that all the other women of his life had been made dim and uncertain shadows, but the mere mention of the bareback rider made his blood bound. If they stood side by side, gypsy Miriam and golden-headed Agnes Lester, what man in the world would know how to choose?

He muttered aloud: "Wherever we go, we don't go to Chester Falls!"

"Hey, why not?" asked Pie Phelps.

But, receiving no reply, Pie was silent. He knew that he had fallen in with a leader, rather than a companion.

They were up with the dawn, and soon on the trail. Trouble hit them an hour later. It was as Reata asked Pie Phelps how he had been able to identify him on that other night, in the darkness and Pie answered without hesitation: "Well, as long as you keep that little snipe of a dog along with you, folks are sure going to recognize you every time, old son!"

And, right at the end of the words, Pie clapped his hand to his shoulder, and yelled. Into his yell chimed the ringing report of a rifle. As Reata twisted in the saddle, he saw riders come pouring out from a cloudy woodland up the slope, just as he had seen them issue, the night before, from the trees around the house of Colonel Lester.

Pie Phelps, groaning with pain on the bare back of the mustang, raced it behind the lead of Reata over rough and smooth for five heartbreaking miles, with the blood spreading constantly over his left side. Then they doubled back into a cool, shadowed ravine and heard the hunt go roaring past them.

In that ravine, Reata bandaged the shoulder of his companion. It was not a bad wound. The high-speed rifle bullet had clipped through the flesh without touching bone or tendon, but there had been a good deal of blood lost.

When they went on again, Pie Phelps was riding the roan mare, and Reata was bareback on the mustang. Reata had a silent groan deep in his own throat, for the only thing to be done, so far as he could see, was to get Pie Phelps at once into the upper country where they would have to spend ten days of isolation until the wound was well closed. It was another stroke of fate, he felt, to pin him down in this country.

Pie Phelps wanted to go straight on to Chester Falls, but Reata pointed out that if Pie had friends in that town, other people were apt to know it, and the man hunters would be fairly certain to look first of all inside those friendly houses. So they kept on straight for the higher mountains, and before they were an hour on the way, luck struck them again with a heavy fist.

In a great, broken country like this, where whole armies could have been lost without the slightest trouble, there was not one chance in ten thousand that Steve Balen and his men would be able to sight the fugitives a second time, but that was exactly what happened. A little dust cloud rolled up a valley, topped a ridge, and turned into half a dozen hard riders. Balen was after them again.

Well, let Balen push his men forward as hard as he pleased, they were not apt to catch Reata as he jockeyed the tough little mustang along. And certainly they would never get within hailing distance of Sue.

But two miles farther on, coming down a hillside, the mustang stepped on a loose stone—and went on with a dead lame right shoulder!

Pie Phelps, when he saw this, shouted: "There ain't any use. Everything's agin' us! Take your mare, Reata. She's goin' to run you out of sight over the edge of the sky in no time. I never sat on anything like her. And let Balen and the rest of 'em get me. I might 'a' knowed that Steve Balen would get me. There ain't ever a man he's started for that he ain't brought home!"

103

"Stay in that saddle!" commanded Reata. "Stay there till I tell you to leave it. If they haul you in, they're going to haul me in, too. Keep going, and we'll make luck come to us!"

They broke over the rim of a hill and, coming through a dense growth of trees, Reata saw a main road below them, a white streak winding through a broad-bottomed valley. Down that road moved a long train of covered wagons drawn by old horses and mules so thin with age or bad rations that their ribs stood out, skeletonwise. But here and there appeared men on prancing, sleek little mustangs, the very pick of an entire range; and the sun flashed on brilliant housings, and on gay scarfs that waved from the hips of the riders.

"Mexicans?" asked the pale-faced Pie Phelps.

"Gypsies," answered Reata. "It's Queen Maggie's gang. Those are her black mules in the lead. And there she is on the driver's seat. Ride fast, and maybe I'll be able to get 'em to put you up and hide you from Balen. Come on!"

He got the last strength and the last speed out of the crippled mustang, as they charged down the slope and up to the lead wagon of that procession.

There was a little rush of the gypsy men on their sleek, bright horses. They came swooping about the two fugitives and then split away, recoiling to each side, and shouting: "Reata! Reata!"

The women, putting their heads out of the wagons, and the little children, leaping down and running up the road, echoed in shrill choruses of fear and anger: "Reata! Reata!"

It was an ominous welcome for him, but he could not wonder at it. They had paid heavily for the two visits which he had made to the tribe and perhaps they were expecting to pay heavily again. It was not strange that the sun began to wink on drawn knives and guns.

Right up to the leading wagon rode Reata, and there he saw Queen Maggie close up, her face set in sullen lines, her big cigar tilting at a resolute angle between her teeth. She wore the same battered old man's hat, and a man's coat, and the look of her hands and her heavy jaw was mannish, also.

104

She stared straight before her, as though she could not see Reata as he wheeled his staggering mustang beside her. As though, above all, she could not hear him calling out: "Maggie, I'm down and out. This poor devil is drilled through the shoulder. Take him in. There's a posse after him. It'll come popping out of those trees yonder, any minute—and then it'll be too late to do anything. Take him in and hide him in the wagons, and I'll make it the best day in your life. Look here. I've got no money now, but you can trust me when I promise. You know that!"

She parted one side of her mouth, while she kept a firm lip and tooth hold on the cigar in the far corner.

"You never brought us nothin' but trouble, Reata," she said. "You've beat my men, and you've grabbed Miriam, and when she come back, she was never the same. I'll not lift a hand for you!"

"Hi!" shouted the gypsies, in a deep and angry chorus.

Up from the rear, on foot and running with a savage haste, came the cat-faced strong man, his hands reaching out before him in a significant way.

Someone also came past him at a swinging gallop, riding that sleek black stallion which Reata remembered so well. It was Miriam, with a twist of yellow silk around her head, and another of blue silk about her hips.

He called, with his hands out to her, for he knew that she could overrule even Queen Maggie, if she chose.

"You see me beaten, Miriam! Make them take in this friend of mine!"

He pointed back over his shoulder toward the trees that crowned the opposite slope.

Strangely enough, she did not look at Reata, but hard and earnestly into the face of Pie Phelps. Then, openly, she sneered, and shrugged her shoulders.

"Are you making friends of stuff like this, Reata?" she asked. "Have you dropped that far into the muck? Well, we'll take him in. Help him, there—"

She broke into a flood of the gypsy jargon. Queen Maggie,

105

slamming on the brakes so that the wagon after one groan and shudder stood still, sprang up from her place and began to shout back.

Two or three rattling repartees from the girl left her silenced. She threw up her hands and made a gesture of surrender. After that, things happened.

No matter how those gypsies might hate Reata, and for reason, they loved and followed their bareback rider with sufficient enthusiasm to forget that hatred now. She actually rode up to the strong man and grabbed him by the yellow striped neckcloth which he wore about his huge throat, and kept her grip, pouring out words at him, until he threw up both hands and groaned out an assent.

It was he who literally lifted Pie Phelps off the ground, as the wounded man dismounted, and carried him inside the third wagon of the caravan.

The girl went on shouting her orders. The gypsy men began to laugh.

"Now!" she called to Reata. "One minute and I'm with you!"

She darted into the wagon where Pie Phelps had disappeared and came out, a moment later, with Phelps's hat on her head and struggling her arms into a man's coat.

"Maggie!" she called to the queen. "When they come, tell 'em that Reata and his friend held us up. Don't name Reata! The men they're chasing held us up and made us give up our best horse to take the place of the lame mustang. That's why all our men have lined out chasing the crooks!"

"Reata!" called Queen Maggie.

"Aye?" he answered.

"Miriam comes back to us?"

"If I have to tie her hand and foot and bring her like a parcel!" he answered.

"Then go on—and luck with you, you wild fool!" shouted Maggie, and she began to laugh in her stentorian voice.

106

CHAPTER 22

It made the strangest picture of a rescue that Reata had ever seen. He and Miriam raced their horses across the road and over the wide field of grass beyond with the whole crowd of gypsy men streaming after them, firing, yelling in a tremendous chorus, and laughing between shots, between yells.

Looking back over his shoulder, Reata saw Steve Balen at the head of his men come storming down the slope. Would Maggie be able to send them on, or would wise Steve Balen pause for a time to search the caravan?

Reata had the answer for that, in another moment. He saw Balen, in a swirl of dust, halt his horse for an instant at Queen Maggie's side. Then Balen rushed his horse on in pursuit.

And Reata began to laugh in turn.

Catch him now—catch him when he was mounted on Sue with no wounded bulk of a man to encumber him? And neither would they overtake the black stallion with Miriam feathering him along like a jockey. Fresh as the stallion was, it was fairly matching, stride for stride, the tremendous rush of the mare. Afterward her long stroke might wear the stallion out, but by that time they would be well beyond the reach of Steve Balen.

Already the gypsies were lagging behind, though they had ridden as hard as though they were in earnest. And how could the horses of Balen and his men hold the pace?

They could not. From the top of a high slope, before dipping into the forest beyond, Reata saw the gypsies drawing rein. Behind them, Balen and all the rest pulled up, also, giving up the manifest absurdity of that chase.

Reata laughed as he looked down at them, and then swept the mare into the coolness beneath the trees. They came down into a long valley full of the voices of water, for innumerable little streams broke out from the rocks, here and there, and ran themselves white on their way down to the central creek. There was good, soft turf under foot to ease the steps of the horses, and stretches of burning bright sun, and places of quiet shadow.

This was his country at its best, with the big mountains on each side looking down and giving peace to the scene, but the exaltation ran suddenly out of the heart of Reata. When he glanced aside, he saw that the head of the girl was high, and she was smiling to herself.

He fell into gloomy thought.

"You might as well go back now," said he.

"Not yet," she answered calmly.

And a moment later she unsheathed with a whipping motion the rifle that was fitted into the long holster under her right leg. The butt of the weapon pitched into the hollow of her shoulder. Only then he saw a movement, a stir, a racing form through the dapplings of shadow in a grove. The rifle swung with it for an instant, then spoke. The deer which he had barely marked leaped into the air and fell lifeless.

"We'd better eat before we say good-by," she told him. "You look a little pinched and drawn, Reata. What's the matter with you, old boy? Struck a lean patch?"

He said nothing. He who had bent over the hand of Agnes Lester, only the night before, now to be finding the whole image of her turning dim, while music rang in his ears and quivered through his nerves as he looked at the gypsy girl—what was he to say of himself?

He went methodically about the hanging up of the deer but when that was done, the girl would let him do no more.

"You're going to be the big chief, for once," she told him. "You're going to sit still while the squaw works for you. Roll a cigarette, chief, and pull up your belt a notch. I'm going to do some venison steaks for you."

She kindled a small fire, breaking up a bit of dead brush with her gloved hands. Then she carved the meat she wanted in thick red slabs. A stack of it. After that, she let three pieces fairly burn over the coals.

"The outside pieces go to charcoal, Reata," she told him.

108

"The juicy inside piece is what the chief eats."

Out of his own small pack she had found the coffee and the coffeepot. With snow water from the creek she made the mixture and soon had it steaming on a fire of its own. She cut off a strip of clean bark and laid it before Reata. And then, for she had managed to have everything finished at once, she laid before him coffee, hard-tack, and that central thick slab of venison which had been protected from the fire by the burning of the two outer layers, and into which had run the juices of the wasted pieces.

"But what about you?" he asked.

"Ever hear of a squaw that ate when her man was eating?" she asked him cheerfully. "No. You never did. Besides, squaws don't have to eat. They look at the big chief feeding his face, and that's food enough for them!"

He knew her well enough not to argue the point. He simply said: "Not even smoking, Miriam?"

She shrugged her shoulders.

"The big chief doesn't like to see his squaws smoke," she said.

"Why d'you talk like this?" asked he. "Does it do you such a lot of good?"

"It doesn't hurt you," she answered.

"No? But it does."

He stared at her.

"Go and tackle that venison; it's getting cold," she advised him.

He fell to on the venison.

Well, here was another comment on his human nature, his too human nature. No matter how much he was hurt by the flippancies of this strange girl, his appetite became raging the instant he tasted the meat. And he was able to sit there and feast and almost forget his mental troubles. The very shame he had felt *because* those troubles could be so forgotten melted away from him. He finished the best meal he had had in many days. Then he sat back and rolled a cigarette and lighted it, and sipped the thick black coffee she had made.

109

"Tell me what you've been doing," she asked. "Where've you been? What devil have you been raising?"

He pondered this question for a time. It was very strange that, no matter how wild-headed she might be, no matter how well he knew that careless and flighty nature, he also knew that whatever he told her would be locked up as in a steel safe, a secret which all the forces in the world could never tear from her. He could talk to her freely, he felt.

He said: "You know there was a fellow who swiped the Decker and Dillon gold out of the Jumping Creek marsh?"

"I know," she said. "Everybody knows, by this time. Fellow who ran the gold up the track on a hand car and dumped it over a cliff, and flew down the cliff like a bird, and then got away safe and sound. Sounds like a fairy story. He a friend of yours?"

"That was my job," said Reata.

"Hi!" cried the girl. "Your job? I should have known it! Tying up one of the guards and not having the nerve to tap him on the head when he yelled. Why, Reata, whenever people run into a crook who's afraid to draw blood, they'll soon know that it's you!"

"You despise me for that, I suppose?" he asked.

"Don't bother about what I think. Gypsies have queer ways of thinking."

"You're not a gypsy," he told her. "Maggie told me you weren't. Your blue eyes tell me you're not."

"Blood doesn't matter," she answered. "It's the living that matters. I've lived gypsy, and I'm gypsy to the bone."

"All right," muttered Reata, frowning.

"So you're on the run because of that business?" she asked him.

"No, not because of that. This fellow Phelps—the one I left back there with the caravan. He was the one who gave me the horses that night I was getting clear with the gold. I gave him a bag of it. Well, they spotted the gold on him, the other day. He was locked up. And I had to get him free. They chased us. You saw the end of the chase."

110

"That sounds like Reata. But you're fixed up now, boy," she told him. "You got enough hard cash to last you the rest of your life."

"That stuff? It was stolen money, Miriam. Swiped out of the Decker and Dillon Bank in Jumping Creek."

"That makes it all the sweeter for old light-fingered Reata."

"I've changed that," he told her. "I'm not using stolen money, Miriam. The one thing I wish I could do before I get out of the country is to get that stuff back. Twenty-one more sacks of it. Get it back to Decker and Dillon. Then I'll be free to leave the country."

"You're wanting to leave the country?"

"Aye, and I'm leaving it."

"Look," she said. She pointed toward the shimmering green of the meadow, to the leap and shine of the creek, to the high, still rising of the mountains. "Leave this? This is what you love, Reata!"

"I'm getting out," he told her.

"The trail getting too hot even for Reata?" she asked.

His gray eyes had a glint of yellow in them, a quickening of light that she had seen before and that she knew very well. Men knew it better than she, and had learned to dread it. He had made trouble in this world, and he could make more trouble—very much more.

"Too many people know I've been a crook," he said. "Too many around this part of the world. I want to go straight, but I'm a fool. The first pull takes me down a dark alley—and hell starts popping."

"I know," she said.

He brooded on her more gloomily than ever.

"There's a better reason," he said. "I've found another girl who's too good for me."

He did not see, blank as his eyes were, the sudden gripping of her hands, but she kept on smiling.

"They're the little trouble-makers, eh?" said the girl. "She's a blond beauty this time, I suppose?"

111

"Golden. Blue. That sort of thing," said Reata.

"And a little dizzy aboout old Reata?"

"She could be," said Reata honestly. "But I'm getting out."

"Kind of tough on her?"

"She told me to go. She knows things. You know the quiet sort of a girl, Miriam? Quiet, very still, with a mind that keeps thinking? Too deep for me. I could see how much she was over my head. And she's another reason I'm getting out."

"Poor Reata—not worthy of her, eh?" asked the gypsy, her smile suddenly turning into a grimace.

"You know how far I'm unworthy of her?" he asked. "Let me tell you something. The last time I saw you, you were laughing at me. Not laughing. Worse than that. You were yawning. You were tired of me. You sent me off—you remember how!"

"I remember how," she said, rather faintly, looking down to the ground.

"It was sort of the end of everything. There wasn't any heart left in me. I was empty. You know—with you poured out, I was empty. Well, to show you the sort of a weak-headed fool I am —I run into this other girl, and pretty soon I almost forget you. You're glad of that, of course."

"I suppose so," said she.

"And then I leave her, the other evening, and come up here feeling that the world's at another end. I don't care such a lot about her at all. And I wish—

"You'll laugh at me. I wish I was back there in the valley whacking away at the cabin where you and I were going to live. See what I am? Fickle as a fool. Any way the wind blows is the way I travel. Now go ahead and laugh."

"Suppose you did settle down, how long would you last?" she asked him. "You've got plenty of enemies who want your blood."

"I don't know," said he gloomily.

"And every girl you know—that's another address where people can look you up. Quinn and Salvio and Dave Bates—

they ought to be friends of yours, but are they?"

"They pulled me in on the Decker and Dillon game. How am I to call them friends?" he asked her.

"They came up to the caravan today, all three of them. They thought that you might have looked me up."

"Quinn, Salvio, Bates—all three of 'em? That's strange!" he said.

"Is it? Well, they were all on the road together, with a lot of horses carrying loads. Not a lot. Half a dozen."

"With horses carrying loads?"

He jumped to his feet.

"Which way did they travel, Miriam?"

"Right down the road, but faster than the caravan was going. What about them? If they're not friends, what about them?"

"If I've got 'em in the open—" he said, through his teeth. "The double-crossing—"

He whistled, and Sue came swiftly toward him.

"You're off, are you?" asked the girl, her voice hard, her eyes still harder.

"I've got to start," he said. "I'll be going back towards the road. That's your way, in part."

"Never mind my way."

"What's the matter?" he asked. "All at once it looks as though you've started hating me. What's the matter? What have I done?"

"Nothing," she said. "Get going—and have luck, Reata."

"But it's true," he insisted. "You're practically hating me now."

"I'm only hoping that I never see you again," she told him, with a sudden outbreak of bitterness.

That pulled him up. He stared at her with blank, hurt eyes for a moment, and then mounted the mare.

"I'm sorry," he said. "I don't understand anything. I'm a dummy for fair. Tell Maggie that she won't lose by taking care of Pie Phelps. I'll pay up to the hilt. So long."

She merely waved a hand as she turned away. She would

113

have called out carelessly, cheerfully, but she was unable to speak. And she went blindly toward the black horse.

Well, he had been there, and with a gesture she might have brought him back to her—with a smile, even. She had chosen to let him go. It was true, as she had told him, that he had too many enemies in this world, and the happiness that he might try to find with a wife would not last long. They would find him —the manhunters.

But, in the meantime, as he drifted through the world, how many others would he find capable of making him forget her?

CHAPTER 23

That camp which Harry Quinn and Gene Salvio and Dave Bates had made, on this night, was securely hidden beyond a steep ridge, beyond the rushing of a creek, and in a tangle of profound darkness among the trees and the underbrush. They had the best of good reasons for secrecy as to their place, because they were carrying with them some seven hundred and fifty pounds of gold. They had the burden on three good, strong horses. And they had three other horses to carry them. They had three Winchester rifles, and at least one pair of Colts apiece, together with plenty of ammunition. But in spite of all of these safeguards they were ill at ease. For men with stolen treasure are bound to feel that danger may drop on them from the empty sky or rise among them out of the solid ground.

Danger, in fact, was coming toward them, slowly and surely. There was only one man, with a roan mare behind him, and in front of him the little wagging tail of Rags as the dog scented out the trail with the hair-trigger accuracy of his small nose. Up to the later part of the afternoon, Reata had been able to trail the cavalcade of six horses down the road. Then he overshot the mark and had to turn back with Rags who, by this time, had the proper scent well up his nose. It was Rags who had led his

114

master over steep and smooth until they crossed the creek on the huge, slippery stepping stones which the boulders offered. It was Rags who now worked furtively into the brush.

The roan mare, Reata left behind him when the brush grew so thick that even she, trained though she was to move almost as silently as a moose through thickets, was now apt to make a bit of a noise.

Then he went on.

He could not see Rags now. The blackness under the trees was so profound that he could hardly have seen his hand before his face. But the little dog knew how to lead his master in the dark, and waited, every moment or so, until the cautiously outstretched foot of Reata touched him. Then he went forward again, and step by step they proceeded in this fashion until the broken, golden rays of a fire pierced the undergrowth.

It was only a small fire and there were rocks which had been piled up to screen the light cast by the fire. But by the rays which escaped, Reata recognized the broad, rather good-natured face of Harry Quinn, the twisted, lean, half face of Dave Bates, and that beautiful and dangerous panther of a man, Gene Salvio.

Every one of the three had owed his life to Reata—Salvio only indirectly but nevertheless surely. And yet the three of them had combined to trap him.

Reata, leaning beside a tree, found his wrath a little tempered. According to the brains of these fellows, they had not actually been trapping him. They had merely given him a chance to make a fortune. A fortune in which they could share!

It was that thought which brought up his rage again. They had let him go single-handed to endure all the risks. And they had reaped the profits. All the profits, when he washed his hands of the stolen money.

He stepped out from the trees. One of the horses threw up its head suddenly and snorted. All three heads turned, and Harry Quinn shouted: "Reata! Here's Reata!"

They laid friendly hands on him and dragged him forward.

115

"Hi! It's Reata!" cried Dave Bates. "I'm goin' to sleep sound tonight for the first time since we hit the trail. Reata, you know what we've got in those packs yonder?"

"Decker and Dillon gold, eh?" said Reata.

"Decker and Dillon nothing!" said Salvio. "It's our stuff now. We sweated for it. So did you. The idea is that if you'll come back with us till we get the weight of it hidden out safely, somewhere, you get your split, the same as you always were due to get, Reata!"

"Is Pop Dickerman breaking up?" asked Reata.

"Him? They can't break him up," said Dave Bates. "But they've throwed the whip into him. Sheriff Lowell Mason ain't such a fool as we thought he was. He's searched that place from hide to hoof. But he didn't find our stuff. Why? Because Pop had the idea a day before and got us out with all the gold. *And* some other things. I tell you what we got in our hands, Reata. We got the whole savings of Pop Dickerman. We got 'em here. And if you seen 'em—"

"What that old gent had put away for the rainy season!" said Salvio. "Why, the gold's only a part of it all. It ain't the biggest part."

Reata said calmly: "Wonder to me that you fellows, now you've got your hands on all that loot, don't put the whole of it into your pockets and let Pop Dickerman go hang."

"Would we be that much fools?" asked Dave Bates, shrugging his lean shoulders at the suggestion. "Him? With lines laid out all over the country like a spider with a web? Why, son, which way would a man run to get clear of Pop Dickerman? No, no, Reata. You're dog-gone bright and mean, but you ain't bright and mean enough to talk turkey to Pop Dickerman!"

Reata, listening, felt a profound weight of truth in the words to which he had listened. There was no man in the world that he feared, hand to hand. Nature had given him a speed of hand that others could not match; training had equipped those hands with infinite cunning; but mere hands and ordinary wits were useless against Pop Dickerman. He was, in fact, like a spider couched in the center of a web, throwing out invisible meshes to entrap ordinary humanity.

"All right, boys," said Reata, "you're done in to Dickerman, but I'm not."

Salvio laughed. "I thought that, for a while. Lemme tell you a story. Go on with that cooking, Quinn! I'll tell you a yarn about what happened to me in the old days before I found out where I left off and Dickerman began. I'd picked up a good cut of hard coin by sticking up a stage—Dickerman had planted the job for me—and I figgered that I'd take that coin and get away from Dickerman, so far that he couldn't ever put a hand on me.

"I headed off in a straight line. I rode out my hoss gettin' to a railroad. I rode the beams on that railroad for fifteen hundred miles to New Orleans and stowed away on a ship for Cuba, and when that ship pulled into Havana, there was a big, long, lean, thin-faced hombre standing on the dock that walks by me, amblin', and he says behind his hand: 'Better go back to Dickerman, kid.'

"I looked after that gent. The view of his back didn't do me no good. I wanted to ask him a flock of questions, but I seen that it was no good. I got the next boat out of Havana and went straight back to Dickerman.

"From that day to this, he's never mentioned it, and I've never mentioned it. But I know that there ain't miles in the country enough to get me away from the reach of Dickerman's rope!"

As Salvio ended, Quinn said: "Yeah. That's all straight, too."

Reata stepped back from them a little.

"Boys," he said, "you're all mighty friendly to me, and I'm sorry to tell you what I've got in mind now. You think that I'm on your side, but I'm not. You think that I won't dare break with Dickerman, but I will. I was going straight when you fellows roped me in on a crooked job. There's only one way for me to clean my hands. And that's to get the gold you're carrying in those packs and bring it back to Decker and Dillon in Jumping Creek. I'm giving you a fair warning. We make an

117

even start now. But before I'm finished, I'm going to have that stuff in my hands. Watch yourselves!"

This speech had fairly stunned the three for an instant. It was Salvio who recovered first and shouted: "Take this where it'll do you the most good, then!"

He snatched out a gun as he spoke. In the frantic haste of his action the first bullet simply plowed up the ground at Reata's feet. The second one would have been through his heart, but he had leaped back behind a tree trunk into which the bullet spatted with a heavy impact.

"Get him!" yelled Salvio.

The three of them made a rush, but after they had gone a stride or two into the outer darkness, away from the reach of the rays of the fire, they halted.

"Get back to the light," said Dave Bates. "Reata can see like a cat in the dark. We got no chance, in here among the trees. Get back into the clearing!"

They backed up slowly. They stood in the clearing, each man facing out in a different direction, each with a gun in his hand. They looked like men making a desperate last stand against overwhelming numbers, resolved to sell their lives dear. But their single enemy leaned against the side of a tree trunk and studied them casually, calmly.

They were dangerous fellows, all of them; he could hardly have picked out three worse enemies. Yet there was fear in them in spite of their numbers.

He heard Harry Quinn say: "He don't carry no gun, or he'd pick us all off, one by one!"

"He'll get a posse on our trail," groaned Salvio.

But Dave Bates, wiser than the others, answered: "Reata works alone, mostly. He doesn't like the law much better than we do. We don't have to worry about him getting the sheriff after us. He'll give us enough trouble all by himself!"

"We've got to keep a guard posted all night and every night," said Quinn.

"Sure," said Salvio. "Talk soft. The devil may be hearin'

118

everything that we say, right now."

"The "devil" was, in fact, overhearing every word, but his mind was empty of ideas as to how he might be able to attack them. He saw that he would have to wait for time and new chances before he struck.

CHAPTER 24

All the next day, the three fugitives moved slowly on, not directly to the north now, but diverging to the northwest over open, rolling hills, and Reata, as he followed them from a distance, made sure that they never approached even small clusters of shrubbery or patches of woodland. He could guess the reason. They preferred to keep to the openest way, knowing that their guns could keep him off as long as they could see him.

He shook his head as he watched them, and began to regret the fair and open challenge which he had given to them. Trickery and murder were simply an ordinary part of the weapons of the men of Dickerman. Therefore why should he have acted as though they were honorable enemies?

Finally, at the end of the day's march, he saw them journey down into the strange phenomenon known as the Chester Draw —that great dry, flat-bottomed valley which runs for many miles in a loose semicircle until it comes close to Chester Falls. The flat of it is hardly ever crossed by a run of water. The grass is very sparse and poor. There is practically no game to be found on foot in it. And in every way it is about as unpleasant a road as men could wish to travel.

But this was the course that the three men had laid out for themselves, and Reata, setting his teeth grimly, could understand why. For over the unbroken flat of the draw, even starlight would be sufficient to show the men the approaching of any dangerous figure.

All that he gained, as he watched the stream of six horses

119

flow down the side of the draw into the bottom, was the definite knowledge that Chester Falls, or a place somewhere near Chester Falls, must be their ultimate goal.

That was why he turned the head of the roan mare and struck straight out in the direction of Chester Falls. On the way there he might learn something, or in the town itself something must appear to give him a clew. Otherwise he was beaten, and would have to admit it. It might be that he could pick up armed men enough to blot out even three such as Salvio and Quinn and Bates, but Bates knew that he would never adopt such tactics, and Bates was right. If he could regain the stolen gold from the trio, he would certainly do it only by some device, not by brutal murder.

That was the mind of Reata as he journeyed all that day back to the highway, and then down it toward the town of Chester Falls. He could see the town small in the distance, and it had grown to a good size when, in the end of the day, he came past a continual stir of dust that kept rising into the windless air from a wide flat of open ground where a herd of horses was being bedded down for the night.

There were hundreds and hundreds of the animals, guided by Mexicans. Even in the distance he could tell that the riders came from the south of the Rio Grande by the bigness of their hats and the thinness of their shoulders. He could tell, also, by something wonderfully light and graceful in the seat of these men.

Reata rode by very slowly.

A number of the mustangs broke loose and came pelting out of the herd, straight toward him. Two vaqueros went after them, helter-skelter, edging in on them little by little, little by little, gradually turning them into a circling flight that would bring them back to the herd they had just left. It was very neat work, perfectly done. Clumsy hands might have spurred wildly after those wild horses for a week, and never have brought them back.

As the mustangs came closer, Reata saw that they were the

true product of the Mexican desert—little horses hardly bigger than mountain sheep, sometimes with rather lumpish heads and roached-up backs, and all of them famine thin, but one and all with four wonderful legs and with hoofs of iron. As they flashed by, he saw the brands in the velvet of the hides, big scrawling brands, some of them still raw. And he grinned, quick and small, as he made this out.

If these were not stolen horses from south of the Rio Grande, he was a blind man, for certain. They were stolen, and these matchless riders, in their big sombreros and their gaudy outfits, were simply accomplished horse thieves. That was why Reata grinned without mirth. He saw the outbreak subdued, and the vagrant horses run back into the herd. Then he went on, jogging the roan mare, still looking toward the camp which the Mexicans were pitching. A wind of the road brought him close to it.

He saw three low wagons, a pair of old women working over a fire at the cooking of supper, a tall fellow with a handsome, savage, cruel face giving directions about everything, and a pretty Mexican girl sulking as she waited in the saddle. She turned her head toward the passing stranger and gave him a smile that even to a witless ancient would have been a thing of danger. But Reata laughed as he went on. He had been in Mexico. He had been far and deep in it and he had learned about the people a great many things that are not in books.

After he had left the stolen horse herd—he was certain that that was what it was—he found the windows of the town of Chester Falls not far away, glimmering toward the west, and in a few minutes more he was jogging through the town.

He knew it as he knew most of these towns in his country—the memory of it needed a little refreshing, but he knew that there was one place to put up the horse and one place to put up the man.

Over at the side of an alley that wound out of the main street there was a battered livery stable run by an old black man who knew good hay and oats, and kept them. That

121

was where Reata took the mare. The old man shook his head as he stared at the long, low lines of the mare.

"I recollect the last time you was here, mister," he said. "You had a mighty fine upstandin' geldin' then, that must 'a' cost you a whale of a lot of love or money, sir, but since that time, I see you been spending *real* money on your hossflesh!"

And he ran the tips of his fingers over the intertangling and flowing muscles of the shoulder of the roan.

He looked curiously, earnestly at Reata, and Reata stared back at him with interest. For he and the old man, as far as he knew, were the only two in the world who had been able to appreciate the lines of Sue at a glance. Yes, there was one other exception, and that was Dickerman, but he was more devil than man, of course!

CHAPTER 25

If that was the place for a horse to be put up in Chester Falls, the place for a man was in old Fort Chester. It had been a center for traders, in the old days, one of those outposts where the pioneers dauntlessly defended the frontier.

The fort was no longer a trading post, of course, but since it had been built very solidly in order to make it defensible, it was still standing intact, with thick walls and small windows, a loosely grouped range of buildings around a central court. Owls and rattlesnakes lived in part of the old place. The rest had been cleared out a little and was used, without payment of rent, by a very knowing Portuguese who was called Manuel. He might have a second name, but no one west of the Mississippi knew about it or cared.

What was important was to sit down at one of the little tables which were placed under the interior arcade of the patio of the fort and get hold of a large portion of brown-roasted kid, fresh from the spit, and with it Mexican beans adorned by many mysteries of green and red and yellow peppers. The cookery of Manuel was not all Portuguese or all American or all Mexican. But everything that came out of his kitchen was delicious, and afterward, one could spend the night sleeping on the mercurial softness of a deep feather bed.

So Reata went for this place of comfort as a cat goes for the coziest corner by the fire. He knew Manuel so well that the broad-faced old man, with a black, Mongolian mustache dripping down from the corners of his mouth, merely blinked and nodded imperceptibly by way of greeting. In the old days, he understood, most of the time Reata did not wish to be recognized or named. In the new days, also, it was much the same.

Reata got a table in a far corner and put out the lamp which lighted it. He preferred to dine in twilight which would leave him incognito while he used his own eyes. There was always something to see at Fort Chester when one ate in Manuel's place. People of all sorts would be dropping in.

Before Reata had sat ten minutes in his obscure corner, he had something to see. That splendid caballero who was in command at the horse camp, outside of the town, appeared in much finery, and with him came the pouting little beauty of a Mexican girl. She was not pouting now. The pleasure of a new place kept her head turning and her eyes brightening until the señor spoke to her. After that, she checked the motions of her head, but her eyes were busier than ever.

Reata, as he watched her, laughed to himself. There would be woman trouble on the hands of this proud Mexican before very many years were out!

There were perhaps a dozen other people at various tables when a larger party entered, and the loud, dignified voice of Colonel Lester at once rang deep in the ear of Reata. There was the colonel with his famous full-arm gestures directing his men to take their places at his table.

First and foremost of those men was Steve Balen, turning his grim face slowly, and looking deep into the shadows, here and there. There was the fellow who had been on guard over Pie

123

Phelps in the cellar of the colonel's house. Reata knew him well by his low and bulging forehead. And there was a man of fifty, with all his years printed in his face. He had a battered and beaten look as though he had not slept well for many and many a night.

In two minutes, Reata understood that he was no other than Decker, of the Decker and Dillon Bank in Jumping Creek. How he had managed to join so quickly the party which was on the trail of Pie Phelps, Reata could not tell. The colonel seemed not only in charge of the party but particularly in charge of Decker, and before the meal was five minutes old, he was reassuring the banker.

He said: "Time will have to help us, Mr. Decker. But with time and strong efforts, we shall apprehend the rascals. Certainly we shall bring them to justice!"

"For my part," said the banker, with a rather twisted smile, "I'd rather have the money back and let the justice go."

"A thing to say, but not to believe," answered the colonel. "I know, Mr. Decker, that the upholding of law and of order comes with you before your personal affairs. For my part, I assure you that I've put my hand to this work, and that my hand shall not be taken away until the work is finished."

With this, the colonel struck the table lightly with his fist. It would be remarkable if the rest of those people at the table did not see that the colonel was a good deal of an ass. But pomposity is usually forgiven when there is money enough behind it.

Decker said: "People think of a ruined bank without a great deal of sympathy. A bank is only a name. Hard-headed devils stand behind a steel fence and deal you out less money than you want. But behind every bank there are lives. When the bank goes smash, the people behind it go smash. Dillon's smashed. I don't know that he'll ever be a real man again, unless I manage to get my hands on some of that stuff that was stolen. I'm smashed, too. I can see it in myself."

The colonel waved a magnificent hand.

124

"We all have our ups and downs, my dear fellow," he said. "But—Hold on—here comes one of the ups, it looks to me!"

For, at that moment, a pair of Queen Maggie's gypsies, as gay as peacocks, came into the patio of the old fort with a flute and a violin and at once started rousing sweeter echoes than ever had flown from wall to wall of the court before.

Right between them came Miriam, the bareback rider, and behind her rode Georg, a slender nineteen-year-old whom Reata had seen long before among the gypsies.

CHAPTER 26

Reata had seen the show a good many times before, but never when the riding was the only part of it given. They went at it by turns. Georg led off. His black horse was perfectly trained and went through the tricky evolutions at a swift but exactly controlled gait while the rider had the abandon of a Cossack.

He got a good round of applause for that. Then Miriam came on with a few of her simplest tricks, and the colonel himself stood up and faced her, and clapped his dignified palms loudly and for a long time.

"Gypsies?" Reata heard the colonel say. "Well, gypsies or not, they're artists. What a world we have here in the West, my friends! What a world, indeed!"

Steve Balen, at this, gave the colonel a little side glance that might have caused his employer some uneasiness, but the colonel was flowing freely with good cheer, by this time. Miriam, in crimson and blue, was standing on her horse in a corner of the patio, breathing hard from the work, and then Georg cut in with his second round.

He had his big, wide-bladed saber out, and he turned it into glittering arcs of light as he slashed to this side and to that. He laughed with the joy of his work, as feline and beautiful a sight as ever a man could wish to see. He was under and over that

125

horse like a trapeze performer, and finally, with his feet locked in the saddle, he made the black stallion race in such small, swift circles that the body of the gypsy stretched straight out and, with his sword, he seemed reaching for the people at the tables.

How was he to come back to the saddle without a terrible fall?

The Mexican girl stood up, gasping with admiration and terrified excitement. But for Reata, far more than the antics of Georg was the picture of Miriam in the farther corner of the patio standing on her horse like a slim red candle flame which the wind blew and fluttered a bit from time to time.

And then, by a sudden miracle, Georg was again standing on the saddle and bowing right and left to the applause that came shouting to him.

He dismounted, bringing the stallion to a sudden halt in the middle of the court, and as he bowed, making a fine flourish with his saber, the stallion dropped to a knee, also; cunningly and invisibly compelled.

It was too much for the Mexican girl. She picked up a quantity of red wildflowers which Manuel had put in the center of her table, and then she ran out a step or two and threw them toward Georg with a little musical cry.

Her escort, tall, forbidding, strode after her and drew her back; but there was Georg picking up the flowers as though each of them were a gold coin, and bowing with his catlike, sinuous grace to the impulsive girl.

After that, he took an encore, as it were, making his horse go several times around the patio in various catchy steps. And on every round, the eyes of the rider found the Mexican girl, and there was such an electric intensity in his glances, that Reata saw her tremble with excitement. She was so far carried away, that she completely forgot the presence of her companion, it seemed. And the Mexican no longer made a protest of voice or of gesture. He simply sat erect, smiling, with a thousand cold devils in his face. The thunderhead was there above

126

the horizon, plainly to be seen. And Reata watched, and slowly fingered the lean, hard coils of the lariat in his pocket.

As Georg came to the end of this encore, he stopped the stallion directly in front of the two Mexicans, and dismounting, made his bow and the curtsy of the horse at the same moment. It was a very pointed little compliment. The Mexican girl was out of her chair in a moment, clapping, crying out her appreciation. And Georg was only human. How could he help forgetting that rigid, forbidding figure of the Mexican back there in the shadow? No, Georg was leaning over the girl, speaking, smiling, and what he said never came to the ears of Reata.

In fact, Reata was busily watching the tall Mexican. His hand, on the table, opened and closed once, convulsively. And suddenly the devil was up in him, and away. He got out of his chair with a speed that almost forestalled the lightning hand of Reata.

Plenty of people saw that tigerish spring and the flash of the raised knife in the hand of the Mexican, but there was not time for any one to cry out a warning. Certainly the blade would have been buried to the hilt in the back of Georg except that Reata acted with the flicking speed of an uncoiling spring. Out of his hand the noose of the lariat shot like a flat stone, cutting the air. It dropped over the shoulders and the two arms of the Mexican. The back pull jerked him down in a sitting posture.

The scream of rage and surprise that came out of his throat half paralyzed even Reata. It made Georg and the girl jump into the air. The Mexican tried to cut at the thin rope with his knife, but in a moment three more loops of the lariat had showered down over him, and he sat helpless. Only his face was eloquent, and the flash of his teeth beneath his curling lip.

Reata, now that the thing had been prevented, rapidly freed his lariat from the prisoner, and as the rope came free in his hand, he heard the sudden voice of the gypsy girl crying to him: "Reata! Look out!"

Instinctively he turned around and found, confronting him, the long, stern face and the tall, lean body of Steve

127

Balen, holding a gun in either hand.

"Stick 'em up, brother," said Balen. "Stick 'em up high."

"What's the matter?" said Reata. "Glad to see you, Balen. But what's the matter?"

"You ain't half as glad to see me as I am to see you, old son," said Balen. "Drop that rope and stick those hands up—grab a star with each of 'em and then hang on. If you bat an eye, I'll drill you, Reata!"

Reata did not bat an eye. He raised his hands above the level of his head and stood perfectly still. He would rather have had against him an armed crowd than this single man with his pair of steady guns.

"Now tell us what it's all about?" asked Reata.

He could hear the Mexican girl chattering rapid Spanish, weeping over her man, Pedro. He could hear Pedro snarling, irreconcilable, and then the quiet voice of Georg saying: "Reata, say when—"

"Don't budge. Don't lift a hand, Georg," said Reata. "Or I'm done for. This hombre likes to shoot, and he doesn't know how to shoot crooked. Just tell me what it's all about, will you, Balen?"

Colonel Lester had now appeared. There was a white spot in the center of either cheek, but he made his fine, full-arm gesture, pointing out Reata.

"There's the pickpocket of the Jumping Spring marsh, boys! Balen, good work that you spotted him! Very good work, indeed. Even if he did save the gypsy's hide for him."

"I'm kinda thinkin'," said Steve Balen, "that this here is the gent that roped old Bill, yonder, and took Pie Phelps away safe and sound! I got an idea that this here is the hombre that we're looking for on account of a whole lot of good reasons, colonel!"

Lester, as he heard this speech, immediately struck his hands together and agreed.

"You're probably right. You're rarely wrong! Probably this is the ringleader of the three scoundrels who robbed the bank in Jumping Springs. Get him, and we'll get everything else!"

Steve Balen said: "No, he don't match up with what descriptions we got of the three of 'em. He don't match at all. Bill, would you do me a favor, and tie Reata's hands behind his back?"

Georg came forward and said: "Look here. We know this man. This man is honest. You can't tie his hands!"

Balen merely muttered: "Back up, brother!"

But the colonel chuckled. "A gypsy telling us what honesty is, eh? A fine judge. I don't doubt that from *your* point of view this man is honest enough. But the law may have something else to say to him. Bill, can you recognize this fellow as the man who roped you?"

Bill, picking up the thin line of the lariat which Reata had been forced to drop, fingered it for a moment, his rounded forehead puckered.

Then he said: "Well, gents, I've heard this here Reata speak, and I heard the voice of the gent that nabbed me back there in the cellar of the house. But voices is hard to swear by. And when it comes to seein' other things, I was kind of dizzy, bein' grabbed and slammed down on my back, so hard."

"D'you mean to say that you didn't have a look at the man's face?" demanded the colonel angrily.

"Sure, I seen his face all right," said Bill. "But there was a bandanna drawed up over his nose, like a mask. Reata's got gray eyes, and those eyes that I seen was sort of yaller."

"Think, man, think!" said the colonel, urgently snapping his fingers, as though to urge on a child—or an animal. "You must have seen something else!"

"Sure I seen something else," said Bill, very slowly. "I seen Pie Phelps grab up one of my guns that had dropped to bash me over the head with it, so's I couldn't yell out and give the alarm while the pair of 'em was getting out. And I seen the gent in the mask knock that gun out of Pie's hand."

Bill rubbed his head, softly, tenderly.

"The second gent, the one that roped me, he'd rather 'a' took the chance that I wouldn't yell, anyway. He let me go, and

129

ran on—and I yelled all right, and because of my yellin', the pair of them was nearly caught."

He added: "I can remember that, all right." And suddenly he looked straight into the eyes of Reata, and Reata knew that he had been recognized from the first, if not by face, by voice, and by the thinness of that deadly little rope that Bill was still fingering so thoughtfully.

"What do we come to?" exclaimed the colonel. "What have we here that we can use, my friends? What is there that the law can use against this rascal?"

Georg had drawn back. The girl, Miriam, was whispering to him. Now the two went quickly away. There was some purpose in the mind of Miriam, and Reata could guess very shrewdly that he would have the benefit of it before long.

All around him, a crowd was packed, and he looked constantly down to the ground. For it is hard to remember the face of a man who is constantly looking down, and one of the things that Reata knew best is that it is well to be unknown to crowds.

"We can close him up in one of the rooms here," said Balen. "And while we got him there, maybe we can work up something agin' him. He's done some pretty fine things, but I reckon that the world would be a mighty sight quieter place if Reata was kept out of it for a spell."

"You want law for that!" said Reata.

For he thought of the three riders who were approaching Chester Falls by the long, roundabout way of the draw. If he were long detained, he would be helplessly out of the chase of them.

"Law?" said the colonel. "There's a higher law than law—there's the law of common sense!"

The sudden yellow flare burned in the eyes of Reata. He stared at Balen and murmured: "This'll be a thing to remember, Balen!"

"Aye," said Balen, "I wouldn't want you to forget it."

130

Steve Balen did another thing which, though it was inspired by caution, turned out to be a bad device. He took the slender reata from the hands of Bill and laid it at a distance on a table. After that, they took Reata himself up the stairs into the second story of the fort and put him into a room with thick walls. It had a window more fitted for rifle shooting than for the giving of light and air. That window was hardly a foot high and it certainly seemed less than two feet wide. It was placed, moreover, a good five feet from the floor, so that it would have needed a snake, and a long snake, to get out at that hole in the wall.

But, if one were actually through the window and in the deeps of the embrasure, the dull, rushing sound of the river that ran under the walls with a noise like that of a distant wind, or a coming storm, would have discouraged any but a winged thing.

When they got Reata up there in that room, with a bit of a wooden cot to serve him for a bed, and no bedding to put on it, they stood around for a time. There was the banker Decker, and the colonel, and Bill, and Steve Balen.

Only two of them counted, in the eyes of Reata. The first was Steve Balen, against whom he now had a grudge. The second was Decker, for whom he was genuinely sorry. As for Bill, he was a good fellow but he didn't matter. And Reata only wanted to forget that Colonel Lester was the father of Agnes Lester.

Of course the colonel did most of the talking.

He said: "Reata—if that's the name—you see where you are. You see what happens to you when you stand out against the law? Now, then, be sensible and tell us everything that you know."

Reata looked up at him with a sidelong smile.

"I know that Manuel is a good cook," he said.

Balen said, as the colonel exclaimed impatiently: "Look here.

131

The only way to get anything out of him is to throw in the steel."

Balen stood a little closer to Reata.

"We can get enough things on you," he said, "to throw you into jail. And we're goin' to do it, Reata. It's too bad, because you've done some mighty good things. But we've got to find out what you know. Will you talk?"

"The fact is, Balen," said Reata, "that I like you so well that talking isn't enough for me. I'd have to take a lot of time to handle you the way I intend to handle you some day."

"The whole of it is that you won't talk, eh?" said Balen.

"Of course I'll talk," said Reata. "I like to talk."

"Very well, then. Where's Phelps?"

"Phelps? I've no idea where he is." For in fact, he could not tell exactly where the gypsies were camped this night.

"Look here, Reata. How did you find out where Phelps was kept in the house of Colonel Lester?"

"I've never been inside the colonel's house." That was true, also. Unless the cellar were accurately considered a part of the house.

"Let's go back to the night you stole the gold from the Jumping Creek marsh."

Again Reata smiled.

"Balen," he said, "why do you think I'm such a fool? Even if I stole the stuff, would I be willing to tell you about it?"

"There's no good talking to the insolent puppy," exclaimed the colonel. "Let him go! We'll see what a competent judge can do about him in the morning. Is there any way he can get out that window? Or shall we tie him up?"

Balen said: "He might wriggle himself through that window. If he did, he'd have a hundred-foot drop down a sheer wall to the bottom of the creek. And there's a ten foot rise of wall above the window to the edge of the roof. He'd need to have a rope ladder lowered for him before he could get away. Close him up in this room, and I'll spend the rest of the night outside the

132

locked door. If he comes out through that, he'll kind of wish that he hadn't!"

There was about Balen the surety of a man who has had to trust himself through many a hard pinch, and who had rarely failed. But the eyes of Reata were glimmering with dangerous brightness as they searched the stern face of the foreman.

"That's all, then," said the colonel. "We'll let him think things over till morning. If we can connect him with that bank robbery, it'll mean the best part of his life in prison, I hope!"

The banker spoke for the first time, saying: "Well, to give pain to another man doesn't help an invalid!"

After the others went out, Reata kept thinking about that last remark. To give pain was no help to a sufferer. There was nothing in revenge, therefore. And still Reata wanted to get his hands on Steve Balen, particularly because Balen was the only man of the lot capable of really appreciating him. To be attacked by Balen with this persistence was a sort of treason.

Reata stretched himself on the cot. A cold wind struck in through the window and began to chill him, but if he were cold now, he would be far colder before the morning came, and the only thing for him to do was to harden himself against the discomfort and strive to forget his body.

That could be done. He had done it before on long desert marches. Now he made himself leave his body far behind while his mind dwelt on other things.

The gypsy girl was the chief problem. It seemed to him that the greatest mystery in the world was what went on behind her eyes. And if he could ever fathom that—

Something tapped at the wall outside his window. He sat up and listened for a moment. Then there was a light hissing sound in the air and a light noise as of a falling rope on the floor of his room.

He was off the cot in an instant, and his fingers touched the familiar hard, supple round of his own precious lariat!

He gathered it rapidly, and found the weight on an end of it,

133

by means of which it had been hurled through his window. With that slender bit of rope in his hands, he felt his strength renewed and remade.

There were only two ways out of the room. One was through the locked door beyond which were Balen and his guns. The other way was through the narrows of the window, which would lead to the impossible situation which Balen had described.

Who could have thrown him the rope? Old Manuel was fairly friendly, but he would not have risked such an interference. There remained Georg—who might be very grateful—and Miriam. One of the two, or both of them, must have purloined the reata.

He tapped on the door. Instantly the voice of Balen murmured: "Hello?"

"That you, Balen?" he asked.

"Aye, it's me."

"Why not come in and have a talk?"

"Are you ready to talk?" asked Balen eagerly.

"Why not?" said Reata. "Why should I stay in here and freeze?"

"I'll come in," said Balen. "But you back up across the room."

Reata obeyed.

"Sound off," said Balen.

"I'm here," said Reata.

"All right," said Balen, and when the sound of Reata's voice had assured him that his prisoner was at a distance, Balen turned the key and pushed the door open. He was revealed, then, holding a lantern in one hand, and a six-gun in the other. The gun followed his eyes across the room until it found Reata and settled upon him. "There you are, eh?" said Balen. "Glad to see you, Reata. It's cold in here, all right."

"A little talk would warm us both up," said Reata. "Take that chair over in the corner."

It was a little folding stool to which he pointed.

134

"All right," said Balen. "I wouldn't mind a chat with you, Reata."

He still kept the revolver pointed at the prisoner, but he turned away a little to get to the stool. And the instant his head had turned Reata struck. It was, in fact, like the striking of a snake, that swift underhand flick of the forearm that shot the noose of the lariat at Balen.

The noose gripped his arms, paralyzed him, and the resultant powerful jerk staggered him off balance. The first loop of the thin rope instantly gripped him about the throat, and Balen stood helpless to move or to yell. He could do nothing except pull the trigger of his Colt, but this was jammed right against his thigh by the grip of the lariat, and a bullet out of it would merely plow into his own leg.

"Any yelling?" asked Reata, as he twitched the gun away from those nerveless fingers.

Balen shook his head. He was rapidly being stifled.

"All right, then," answered Reata, and loosened the strangling pressure of the noose. "We'll tie you safe, Balen, and then we still might have a little talk together."

Balen said with some emotion: "Reata, I'd rather have ten bullets through me, than be found inside this here room in the morning, tied up."

"Brother," answered Reata, as he made fast the arms of Balen behind his back, "you asked for trouble, and you're going to get it."

"If you're a wise man," answered Steve Balen, "you're goin' to cut my throat now. Because if I live, I'm goin' to spend my life trailing you."

"Lie face down on that cot," said Reata.

Balen obeyed, and he was tied hand and foot to the wooden frame of the cot. With his own handkerchief, Reata gagged his victim.

Then he paused to make and light a cigarette. He smoked it out, sitting at the side of Balen, listening to his breathing to make sure that the gag would not stifle him. It was not the habit

135

of Reata to hurry when speed was not absolutely indicated. And he was still sitting beside his captive when he heard a man's voice call from down the hall: "Ho, Steve! Oh, Balen!"

CHAPTER 28

Reata ran to the door noiselessly. Already the outer hall was awash with swinging light and shadow as someone came down the corridor with a lantern. Reata took the key from the outside of the door, closed it gently, and locked it from the inside. He gritted his teeth with angry impatience, realizing that he had paused there in the room thirty seconds too long. Then he blew out the lantern and waited in the darkness.

He heard the footfall pause at the door.

"Hey, Steve!" called the other voice, which was that of Bill.

Of course there was no answer, and presently a hand rapped on the door.

"Well?" called Reata.

"You ain't got Steve in there, have you?" asked Bill.

"Look in and see for yourself," said Reata.

"Not me," said Bill. "I wouldn't trust myself that much. But I thought that I'd find Balen here. It ain't like him to sneak away from his place."

"Likely he's somewhere stretched out, and having a good rest," said Reata.

"That ain't like him, either. I'll wait here and see when he shows up."

The feet of a chair grated on the stone flooring, as Bill sat down to take up his part of the vigil.

"Hey, Reata!" he called presently.

"Leave me alone, will you?" said Reata. "It's time for me to get some sleep."

"Aye, and that's fair enough," answered Bill.

When his silence was assured, Reata tried the window. By standing on the cot, which was exactly under the embrasure, he was able to wriggle his head and one shoulder through. Gradually he worked his body deeper.

He could not yet reach the outside edge of the wall, but he managed to get a deep finger hold on a projecting edge of stone, and with this to pull on, he quickly wriggled his left shoulder through the opening.

He was now half through, and the hardest half, at that. Also, he was thoroughly wedged in his place. But little by little, expelling all the breath from his body and slowly, patiently contorting his muscles, he managed to get through to the hips. These followed, and now he was coiled up on the outer lip of the casement.

He sat on a deeply slanting shelf, as it were, which was canting down toward the darkness of the creek canyon. Soon his eyes were familiar with the starlight, until he was able to see the depth of the gorge, which was cut away far below the foundations of the fort. The opposite bank of the narrow ravine was higher than that on which the fort had been built, and there, under a tree, he made out two dim figures.

He waved his hand; after a moment, he made out that they were waving in return, and his surety increased that these must be Georg and the girl. If so, well, Steve Balen owed them something other than gratitude.

An occasional roughness of the stonework gave him foot and handhold so that he ventured to stand on the outer lip of the casement and look up. He could see, now, the edge of the roof above him, and a projecting drain a few feet to the side.

At the same time, danger exploded behind him in the room which he had just left. There was first a gasping sound, and then the voice of Balen, who must have worked the gag from between his teeth.

"Help! Bill! Help here! Reata's getting away!"

Reata, groaning, made a cast upward with his doubled lariat.

137

It barely missed the projecting drain.

"Hey, what you mean?" sounded the dim voice of Bill beyond the door.

"Break down the door, you fool!" yelled Balen. "Raise the place! Call the rest of the men. Reata—he's getting away, and I'm tied here hand and foot!"

Reata, making his second cast, dropped the end of his loop securely over the drain. Would it hold him?

He heard a great clamor from Bill, who was dashing his weight against that door. Well, it was oak and ought to hold out for a few moments!

Gradually increasing the pressure on the lariat, Reata finally swung free from the ledge of the casement. He was dangling, now, straight over that hundred feet of nothingness that extended between him and the bottom of the creek; and as he swung there, pendulous, he heard a faint cry from a girl's voice, beyond the stream.

After that, he handed himself up, cautiously, for the least jar or jerk might cause the lariat to slip from its precarious hold on the drain.

And now, one more arm haul and he would have his hold on the drain itself.

In the interior of the fort he could hear the calling of voices here and there, dimly behind walls.

Far louder and closer at hand, he heard the door of the prison room crash down as Bill forced his entrance at last. That meant that Steve Balen would soon be free. But Reata now had his grip on the drain and was swinging the weight of his body up onto the roof.

The slant of it was very mild, and it was covered with strong new shakes. Therefore he stood up and ran to the roof ridge and then down the farther side.

But there was no hope of getting down into the inner court. Already it was full of swinging lights and men who ran here and there. Instead, coiling his lariat as he ran, Reata sped down the side of the roof and crossed the ridge again to the outer side, and there he saw his chance.

The watchers had not yet come out to the open. There was a forty-foot drop, to be sure, but he had the length of the rope and a conveniently projecting drain, again, to fasten it to. He made the noose fast here, and was instantly on his way down. Two or three quick shakes and jerks, after his feet were on solid ground, served to free the noose from its grip above, and now, as he leaped back among some trees, he saw a quick current of men flow around the corner of the building.

The voice of Steve Balen led them on. His angry, snapping directions scattered them. Some he sent down the side of the wall. Others he told to fall back and scan the roof.

"He's somewhere not far off!" declared Balen. "He's most likely up there on that roof. And we want him, boys! I'm goin' to have the hide off of him for what he done to me, this here night, and I'm goin' to have the hide off of them that got the reata back to him! Scatter—and use your eyes!"

They used their eyes well on the old fort, but Reata was stepping without haste toward the old livery stable where the roan mare and Rags waited for him.

CHAPTER 29

When he got to the little livery stable, he found things in a bustle and a flurry, so that he almost thought, for a moment, that he would have to give up trying to go in and take Sue away with him tonight. He took refuge at the corner of the big-mouthed entrance until he made out the step and the face of Georg, and the voice of Miriam somewhere in the shadows.

Then he saw her coming toward the door, leading Sue, with Rags posted as usual in his special place in front of the saddle. Miriam had arranged the entire thing, Reata could be sure.

When he went up to her, she gave him hardly a word, except an injunction to hurry. It was Georg who gripped his hand so

139

warmly and said: "You see, Reata! Day or night while I live, if you call me, I shall be ready. But—death of my heart!—when I saw you dangling over the creek, I thought you were gone. And then Miriam dragged me, and reminded me, and we came galloping here as fast as we could!"

The girl stood a little back, smiling somewhat, nodding at Reata as though in approval. There was something matronly, or sisterly, in her attitude, and this troubled Reata.

He went up to her and took her hands. She let her head tilt back while she looked up at him with a surveying glance and a smile that seemed still full of a rather impersonal admiration, and also a mere touch of amusement.

"What did you do in there? What did you do to Steve Balen?" she asked him.

He noticed that her hands were cool and limp in his grasp. Her attitude put all the danger in the past.

"Steve is behind me," he said. "I'm not thinking about him."

"If you don't think about him, he'll get ahead of you again," said the girl, "and he's a dangerous fellow."

"Listen!" said Reata.

Out of the distance there was a muffled chattering of guns.

"Steve and the others have found a shadow, I guess," said the gypsy girl.

"I want to know what you're thinking of me just now," said Reata. "As a sort of distant cousin, or a brother, or a man who loves you?"

"I'm thinking of you as Reata," she answered.

"What shall I make of her, Georg?" asked Reata, for the gypsy had come close to them, urging Reata to be gone.

"Who can make anything of her?" said Georg.

Reata, with an exclamation, turned suddenly to the roan mare and threw himself into the saddle. Only for an instant he paused to grip the hand of Georg in a last farewell.

"I'd still be there in the fort, waiting for the daylight and jail," said Reata. "They would have cooked up an excuse to keep me there. I'll never forget, Georg!"

140

"Hi!" said Georg. "When it is I that must talk of never forgetting!" He added: "Besides, it was Miriam who stole back the reata from under their eyes. While she smiled, she stole it. It was she who planned everything. Now ride! Ride fast! I hear them just like hornets in the air!"

One last glance Reata had of the girl, still leaning a hand against the wall, aloof, smiling as if at an active child. Then he rattled over the wooden floor, and the roan mare went down the street with her long and flowing stride.

Behind him, he heard the sounds of confused riding hither and yon, growing dimmer and dimmer, which showed that the search was continuing busily for him in the streets and perhaps through all the rooms and damp cellars of the fort. What a fury the colonel would be in. And what a hot and festering rage would possess Balen!

To have been found locked and tied and gagged inside the room over the door of which he had been set to guard a prisoner —could there be a greater humiliation than this? The tale would grow in the telling; stories always do on the range. And Reata felt that his revenge on Balen was complete enough.

As the lights of the town died down and drew together behind him, Reata could turn his mind to another subject.

There was a moon yonder behind a river of clouds that seemed to be flowing up the long hill of heaven. Sometimes it whitened the high mists like flying spume, and again it was a vague light that showed mere rivulets of brightness. That same light, perhaps, was being watched by three riders, each with a loaded horse in tow, as they journeyed up the Chester Draw.

They could not have journeyed so rapidly as he had ridden that day. And they were coming almost twice as far by having to cover the long windings of the strange flat valley, between its cliffs. But, by this time, they must have come fairly close to the end of the draw.

It might be, now, that he had in mind the very agent which would blast them free from their loaded treasure horses. It might be that the thought which had come to him while he

141

watched the glimmering ranks and living coils of the horse herd of the Mexicans would be sufficient for the purpose which he had in mind.

At any rate, when he came close to the ground where the horses were under guard, he went more slowly, and found by a detour a place where he could come very close, through brush high enough to hide horse and rider. From the verge of it, he looked out on a strange and peaceful scene. That herd had been long enough on the road to learn road manners. It was lying down. There was not a horse up grazing. When the moon brightened through a gap in the clouds, it gave a blink and a dull glimmering across the confused bodies.

They seemed too small to be real horses. Seals on a rock might have looked something like this. Around and around and around them rode a single man on the night watch, a lone rider who, as he journeyed endlessly, kept singing a quiet, droning Mexican song. To be sure that herd must be well broken in, by this time, if the herders felt that they could trust all this mustang wildfire in the hands of a single guard!

Perhaps Reata could surprise them a little. He dismounted, and on foot left the brush when the guard was on the farthest side of the great circle. Little Rags went before him, and the roan mare trod stealthily behind.

CHAPTER 30

At the edge of the herd Reata with a single word brought Sue to her knees, and then she lopped over silently on her side, thereby melting into the fringe of the sleeping horses. To Rags, his master made a few quick gestures and whispered: "Get 'em, boy. Drive 'em! Drive 'em!"

Rags pranced ahead, looking gaily, fearlessly from the sleeping monsters toward his master. A final gesture of command started him going, and he flew in like a fury, running back and

142

forth and in and out, and every horse he passed received a cut from those needle-sharp teeth. A dozen horses were instantly on their feet, snorting. The noise of their commotion started another and a longer wave of horses rising before them. In an instant all the air was electric, and then into the dim brains of those wild beasts cut a hissing sound longer and more deadly than had ever come from a snake.

They were frozen to deadly attention. The entire herd was up in a flash.

Far away, Reata heard the Mexican guard lifting his voice and singing loudly, then calling: "Pedro! Pedro! The devil is loose in the air!"

At that moment, with another word, Reata made the roan mare spring to her feet, while he caught up Rags in his hand.

That was enough. The sight of horse and man rising suddenly out of the ground made the startled horses nearest at hand squeal with terror. A wild yell that burst out of the throat of Reata as he went in, waving his hat, was hardly needed. That whole herd sprang into movement as if at a magic signal, and raced away like mad through the dimness of the night.

Out of the dark silhouette of the Mexican camp other human voices now were raised. Men were calling out for horses, but the hobbled saddle horses of the herders were making the best of their way after their wild cousins, and it would be some time before the high-heeled vaqueros would be able to overtake them.

Reata had on his hands a fair start, and a herd running in a blind panic; by the grace of good fortune and the point at which he had supplied the proper stimulus, the whole body of horses was headed in the right direction, where two hills, a little separated, marked the beginning of the low ranges that opened, funnel-like, into the head of the Chester Draw.

Off to his left, he heard the voice of the night herder, poor devil. He looked back and saw the rider already dropping behind. His horse had probably been wearied by hours of going the monotonous rounds. In any case, it would not be capable

143

of carrying its rider along at a pace to match the unweighted, panic-swift career of the bronchos. Farther and farther behind fell the rider, and swifter went the herd, until even Sue had to stretch her long legs to keep pace.

How far would they go before they began to slacken?

Right and left, a few stragglers began to fall back, lamed horses or ones which were sore-footed from the long journey on the road. But the main body of the herd went at such a pace that rapidly the hills before them grew higher and blacker, and now the forefront of the mustang horde entered between the shoulders of the hills and beat up instantly a dull and rolling thunder.

It was music to the ears of Reata, who did not need to doubt that his horses would strike the mark now—if only Gene Salvio's impatient spirit had not urged on his companions to such a degree that already they were out of the draw and beyond the hills, somewhere on the plain and headed north. Perhaps, by a freak of chance, they were already in Chester Falls.

A very neat freak of chance if they appeared in that town and were recognized by the party of Colonel Lester!

Now the whole front of the herd dipped down a chute which angled sharply away to the left, with high walls rising on either side of it. It was the beginning of the Chester Draw. Reata, laughing with a reckless happiness, pulled Sue well over past the left-hand wall, riding along the fringe of the top of it, and letting the mare speed with all her might as the way grew level.

Even the speed of Sue, stretched and straining to her utmost, would never be able to bring her up to the head of that maddened herd before it was deep down the course of the draw. But it brought Reata far enough up to see, well ahead, the triple target at which he was striking.

For yonder, in a brightening of the moonlight, he saw three riders coming at a walk, with three led horses behind them. Now they halted, for the thundering of the herd must be in their ears. Now they checked in and turned their animals. Now, as

144

the forefront of the speeding mustangs swept around the nearest bend and poured in a frantic river down the draw, the three men were riding at full speed for the side of the ravine.

But they had not a hope! Their leg-weary horses could hardly raise a gallop to compare with the arrowy flight of that multitude. Through the high-flinging veil of dust that boiled up over the herd, Reata could see the three cutting loose their led horses. Ay, and with breaking hearts they might do that, but it was better so than to be dragged back by the laggards and knocked down and beaten underfoot by the savage, living torrent!

That was why Reata, as he galloped the mare along the edge of the draw, laughed long and loud.

As he came by, following dangerously close the lip of the ravine, he saw the three barely rush to safety in a small indentation in the wall. And past them stormed the dusty herd, rearing, plunging, kicking like so many devils.

Reata had one glimpse of them, and then swept on along the top of the cliff.

For a full hour, the good mare kept to her long-stroking gallop, and then Reata saw the speed of the mustang herd suddenly decrease. Far back among the lame and the halt stumbled the three loaded horses of Gene Salvio and the others. And as the herd slowed to a trot, then to a weary walk, Reata took Sue down the first easy slope that led into the bottom of the draw. There he caught the three burden bearers of the gold, easily, and tied them together by their own lead ropes, and then dragged them out of the Chester Draw and up to the ground above.

All the four horses needed a rest by that time, so Reata tethered the pack horses to Sue and let them graze at a short distance from the cliff, while he sprawled at ease on the edge of it and smoked cigarettes, and finally, out of the moon haze up the valley, thickened by the still unsettled dust, he saw three men on three tired horses which were barely able to trot.

They jogged on among the last of the herd. Gradually they

145

pulled around the next wide-sweeping curve of the draw. And so they passed away from the view of Reata.

He sat up, smiling.

There was no great hurry. He had dodged Colonel Lester and Steve Balen; he had left Pie Phelps safely in the hands of the gypsies; he had swept away from Gene Salvio and the others the stolen money of the Decker and Dillon Bank; and in accomplishing all of these things, he had not shed a single drop of blood.

Before him opened the way back to Jumping Creek. But it was more than an open way to a town. In restoring the money, he would wipe out the mark against his name.

The thought of Pop Dickerman slid through his mind as a cloud's shadow slides over the face of a hill. But he set his teeth and smiled at the danger. The honest road is always uphill. And on the top—well, it might be that he would find Agnes Lester there. It might be that the gypsy Miriam would be there, no longer smiling with amused, impersonal eyes.

CHAPTER 31

Dave Bates found the sign of four horses crossing a bit of almost green grass. He followed that sign because he was following anything. And he knew that Gene Salvio and Harry Quinn were slaving away in a similar manner perhaps miles away. Yes, necessarily they were miles away, since both sides of the Chester Draw had to be searched. A hundred and eighty thousand dollars in gold dust had been snatched away from them by a stampede of wild mustangs, and that might be considered merely chance, an unfortunate stroke of natural luck; but this luck no longer appeared merely natural when the three horses which had been laden with the treasure were not found among the weary, worn-out remnants of the horse herd.

So the three had scattered to search for the gold savagely.

146

Since they owned it by theft, the idea of losing it maddened them. Nothing seems so doubly ours as that which we have taken without right. And now and again, as one little clew after another petered out, Dave Bates turned his thin face toward the western horizon, hoping against hope that he would spy somewhere in it the wavering dimness of the two columns of smoke which he and his partners had agreed upon when they separated as the signal that one of them had discovered sign of at least one of the missing horses.

After the sign of the four horses crossed the grass, Dave Bates turned again to stare around the horizon, but the sunburned hills rolled in straw-colored waves far out of his view into one horizon, and toward the other there was the sudden lift of the mountains. There was no thin stain of smoke in between.

He resumed his trail, not hopefully, but attentively, and now the hoofmarks of all four horses crowded in between two boulders where many another animal had traveled, also; cattle and deer and sheep and beasts of prey having turned in this direction to take the natural gate through the fence of great stones, so that the grass was worn away, and the ground here was thinly padded with dust.

On that surface, faint as a gray chalk mark on an old gray slate, thinly traced among the tramplings of the horses, he saw a sign that made him jerk up his mustang and fling himself down on the ground.

The sun was barely up. The eastern light flooded aslant across the earth, and therefore helped to outline and imprint every ruffling of the dust. It helped to bring out the pattern of a fine tracery that caused Dave Bates to leap suddenly up into the air and shake his fist in the direction toward which the prints of the four horses and this other almost indiscernible trail vanished.

Then he hastily gathered two piles of brush, lighted them, threw on green boughs, and watched the columns rise high into the air until the wind struck them, slowly bowed them over, and caused the white heads to vanish in the sky. Then he pulled up his belt a notch, sat down, and lighted a cigarette.

Sitting down was no good. It never is to a man who has been long in the saddle; so Dave Bates stretched his lean little body on the grass and braced head and shoulders on a mound. He was weary, but his horse was so much wearier that the poor beast hung its head without desire to eat. There was a telltale quiver in the front knees of the mustang, and Dave Bates considered that tremor with perfect understanding, but with a cruel indifference. The pain of the horse did not trouble him, because he was on a trail of gold. The weakness of that mustang was a handicap, but other nags could be had not far away. He knew a ranch where there was always a plentiful supply of horseflesh, not pretty to look at, but good enough material to pass under the spur.

It was Harry Quinn who arrived first, spurring a staggering mustang into a gallop. He flung himself out of the saddle when he saw his companion.

"Hey, Dave!" he shouted. "I thought you found something! What the devil!"

"Yeah, and I found plenty," said Bates. He continued to smoke.

"Where?" cried Harry Quinn, his broad, red face wreathing into an expectant smile.

"What's the good of showing it twice?" asked Bates. "Wait till Salvio comes in, and I'll show you both at the same time."

Quinn glowered, then he flung himself down against the same mound that supported the head and shoulders of Bates. Both of them eyed the vast emptiness of the sky, and spoke about one another.

"You was always a sour kind of a hound!" said Harry Quinn.

"Aw, shut yer face," answered Bates.

Quinn raised himself on one elbow.

"Sometimes I got half a mind to—" he began.

His hands worked, but he would not let himself finish the sentence.

"What's the good of yapping?" asked Bates. "You know we

can't take a pass at each other so long as Dickerman's our boss."

"Yeah, and I know that," agreed Quinn. "Some day I'm goin' to be free from him."

"Sure. That's what the duck said when the fox had him by the throat," said Bates. "Hear anything?"

"No, nothing."

"Pull the cotton batting out of your ears," said Bates cheerfully. "There's sure a hoss coming this way, and it oughta be Gene Salvio."

It was. He topped the rise and came down toward them, his horse in better condition than either of the other two, partly because he was a finer horseman, and partly because he rode slightly better horseflesh.

When he came up and threw himself to the ground, he looked at the two of them in silence as they rose to their feet.

"It's him," said Quinn. "He spotted something here."

Bates went to the spot between the two boulders and there dropped to one knee. He pointed down at the ground.

"You two hombres come and see for yourself," he said.

They came. Salvio kneeled in turn. Quinn put his hands on his knees and leaned far over to examine the sign.

"Look at it," said Bates calmly.

Quinn, staring at the fine imprints, said suddenly: "It's a fox track. What about that?"

"No growed-up fox ever stepped as fine as that," said Bates.

"A young fox," said Quinn.

Gene Salvio ruled this out. "A young fox cub don't travel alone, and it has more fur on its feet. It wouldn't make a frog track like that."

"Like a toad had hopped along," agreed Quinn.

"Look again and use your brains," said Bates. "There ain't more'n one thing in the world that would make a sign like that."

"Well, you tell us, and maybe *we'll* have the laugh," growled Quinn.

149

"It's the trail of a dog, a dog so small that you could take him up and put him in your pocket. And that dog belongs to the gent that grabbed the three hosses out of the stampede!"

Salvio and Quinn, straightening, stared at one another.

"By the leaping thunder," groaned Quinn, "he means Rags! He means Reata's little sharp-nosed dog, Rags! Bates, you mean that Reata has got his hands on our pack hosses?"

Bates pointed to the ground again.

"There's the sign of four hosses in the dust," he said. "That would be the three hosses loaded with our stuff, and the fourth would be Sue, the roan mare. Look for yourselves and you'll see —here—and here—and here—where one of those hosses steps out longer than the others. And shuffles the feet kind of into the dust. Well, you all have seen the way that the roan mare steps, long, and kind of loose and sprawling!"

Quinn was groaning deep in his throat. Salvio said not a word and uttered not a sound, but his face was pale and tense as he bent over the sign which Bates pointed out.

Finally he straightened.

"It's true!" he said. "Reata told us that he'd get that stuff away from us—and he's got it. Then *he* is what sent that hoss stampede smashing down the Chester Draw?"

"Ain't it like him?" demanded Bates. "He never draws no blood, but he gets things done the way he wants 'em. Ain't it like him, I'm asking you?"

"It's like him, and it *is* him!" exclaimed Harry Quinn. "He's got the stuff, and he'll keep it."

"He won't," said Salvio. "No, the fool is going to take the gold back there to Jumping Creek to the Decker and Dillon Bank, where we got it in the first place!"

"It's true," groaned Harry Quinn. "He's going to try to go straight."

"Aye, and that's the only place that he's a fool!" declared Dave Bates.

"How come?" asked Salvio.

"Well, you've known Dickerman for a long time," said Bates.

"You tell me if any of Dickerman's men ever managed to break away from him? Come on, boys, this is the trail we ride down. Get on to the Hyman ranch and we'll have fresh horseflesh under us, and then—"

"Aye," put in Salvio gloomily, "but I'd rather be trailing a regiment than Reata all by himself. He ain't so much noise, but he's a lot more danger!"

CHAPTER 32

It was in the break of the dawn of this day that Reata had come in sight of the Hyman ranch. The house stood in the lee of a round-headed hill that would cut off the worst strength of the north wind. It wasn't a house; it was rather a mere shanty, but what mattered to Reata was not the look of the house, but the look of the horses in the fenced field near the house.

When he saw those horses he stopped the roan mare, loosened her cinches, and then went to the nearest of the three led horses. They had dropped their heads as low as their knees the instant they were halted. Visibly, they were badly done in, and could not go on much farther.

From a saddlebag of this first horse, Reata took out a small chamois bag. The leather was badly streaked with green stains here and there. The mouth of the bag he untied, then unstrapped his belt. Inside of it was a soft pouch, and into the pouch he poured from the sack a stream of glistening yellow dust and tiny nuggets. Three or four pounds of gold went into the pouch before it was filled. After that he sealed both the pouch and the bag, replaced the latter in its former receptacle, and then walked on.

Out of the grass, the tiny little dog jumped up and trotted ahead of its master, seeming to know exactly which way the man would go.

Reata was very tired. If the three pack horses were totally

151

spent, even the roan mare, ugly, wire-strung, tireless creature that she was, was now half spent; but her eyes remained bright, and so were the eyes of Reata. And his step was light and easy, the step of a man who has boundless resources of nerve energy when the strength of the body fails.

It was a half mile, nearly, to the door of the ranch house. But Reata walked that distance, because the instant he saw a prospect of getting fresh horseflesh, he would not put the burden of a single extra ounce on the saddle of the roan mare, though she stepped up freely behind him, never letting him get more than a pace ahead.

A great, tousle-headed, thumping fellow in his early twenties came out of the door of the shack as Reata approached. The youth was big from his feet to his hands. He was square built, and every inch of him rigged with muscle and that natural strength which some men have without training to develop it.

When he saw Reata, he merely stared.

"Morning, partner," said Reata.

"Hey; *you* been movin' pretty fast and far. What's been chasin' you?"

"I've been in a hurry," said Reata politely. "Is the boss around?"

"Why mightn't I be the boss?" asked the other.

Said a harsh, nasal voice inside the door of the shack: "Comin' right out, stranger!"

And then a tall man appeared in the doorway, a man with prematurely white hair and a sun-blackened face.

"Don't give no strangers none of your jaw, Rudy," said the older man. "How are you, partner?"

"Pretty fair," said Reata. "I'm all right, but my horses are done in. You've got plenty in the corral. How about three swaps and one buy?"

"Yeah," said Hyman, and he eyed the long, low lines of the roan mare and her ewe neck and her starved sides with perfect disfavor. "Yeah, I wouldn't swap nothing but a dead sheep for *that* one. But the others look like they're worth something. I'll

152

give you hosses for the three of 'em—with a little boot throwed in."

"How much boot, and what horses do I get in exchange?" asked Reata.

"In a hurry, ain't you?" asked the other.

"You can see that."

"You'll have to pay for the hurry," said Hyman. "What four do you want out of the corral?"

"There's two bay geldings, and a brown mare, and a thin-sided gray with a Roman nose. I'll take those," said Reata.

"Hey!" exclaimed the son. "Who told you about 'em?"

"Shut up, Rudy, and go and get them hosses for him," said the father. "As sure as my name's Joe Hyman, this gent's got an eye for hosses in his head. I wouldn't try to come nothin' over him in a trade, I wouldn't. Go catch up them hosses, and you come inside here, and we'll feed and talk about the boot."

"I'm not eating," said Reata. "We can talk just as well out here in the open."

"Sure, we can. That thin-sided gray you was talkin' about is a thumpin' good hoss, partner. Worth two hundred dollars of any man's money."

"Let it go at that," said Reata calmly.

Joe Hyman blinked as he saw how easily the asking price was accepted.

"About the others," he added gloomily, "I dunno. You got some bad-spent hosses here. That roan ain't worth nothin', for instance."

"She goes along with me," said Reata. "No, she doesn't stay. I'm talking about the others."

"She stays with you?" asked the rancher, staring. "Yeah, I can see something to her now. Well, partner, you sure know your business. What's your name?"

"Tom Graham."

"Graham, my name is Joe Hyman."

They shook hands.

"I sure like to deal with a man that knows his hosses," said

153

Hyman. "But, now, you take them other three, you can't tell about a hoss as hot and tired as them three until it's been cooled out. I wouldn't want to trade with you under—well, fifty dollars a head!"

He clicked his teeth on these words, for he knew that he was asking outrageous boot. To his amazement, Reata said: "That's pretty close to robbery. But I have to pay for being in a hurry, as you said before. Have you got a scales in the house?"

"I sure have. Why?"

"I'm going to pay you in gold," answered Reata. "Bring out the scales, will you?"

The tall man stared at him for a moment, then, without a word, strode into the house and came back carrying a small balance scales and several small iron weights.

"That's three hundred and fifty dollars," said Reata. "Call a pound of gold two hundred and forty dollars, and I'll owe you, say, a pound and a half."

"Hold on," said the rancher. "Gold, you know, it ain't the same as money."

"No, but it's much better," said Reata.

"It ain't so handy," said the rancher. "I'd have to have more'n a pound and a half."

"Two pounds," said Reata. And he looked Joe Hyman so straight in the eye that the rancher flushed a little.

"Well, all right," he answered, and placed a two-pound lump of molded iron in one side of the scales. Into the other side, from his money pouch, Reata turned a thin stream of shining gold dust. The little heap mounted. The breathing of Joe Hyman became very audible. The scales shuddered in his hands.

Only when the iron-weighted side of the scales began to rise did Reata pinch the mouth of the wallet shut, tie it carefully, and restore it to his belt.

Joe Hyman kept on staring. Then, looking down at the gleaming heap of gold, he murmured: "You went and struck it rich, eh?"

He turned and walked slowly into the house.

154

Rudy Hyman came up with the four horses on the lead at this point, and, giving the lead ropes into the hands of Reata, watched him tether the horses to the roan mare. He did not help in the shifting of the saddles, for Rudy was a person who detested work that was not demanded of him. Instead, he went inside the house, and there he found his father seated at the scarred, dirty little kitchen table with the double scales before him, and the yellow heap of wealth in one side of the scales.

Rudy felt a prickling go through his flesh and come out like electric rays at the roots of his hair.

"Hey!" he whispered.

His father looked up at him with burning eyes.

"He overpaid about half. In this. He's struck it rich somewheres."

"Gold!" said Rudy, and even out of his shapeless mouth the word issued with a sort of deep music.

"He's got more of it," said the father with another sudden glance at his son. "I dunno—maybe he's got a lot more of it on him—for the taking!"

The face of Rudy pulled all to one side. He grabbed at a rifle that leaned against the wall.

"Not that way, you fool!" said the father. "Blood's the only thing that weighs heavier than gold. Use them big hands of yours!"

ㅅ

CHAPTER 33

Rudy came out of that house bent on trouble, but when he looked at the slender body of Reata, a sort of sneering pity wakened in his heart.

His wrath he summoned up again as he saw Reata buckling on the fourth saddle, the one he had taken off the roan mare. This time he was cinching it on the back of the tall, thin-sided gray.

"Look here!" exploded big Rudy Hyman.

"Yes?" said Reata.

"Talkin' about the money, the old man tells me that he's gone and been a fool."

"He was overpaid. Is that being a fool?" asked Reata.

"That there gray—it's worth a pile of money. And you give us three wore-out old rags of horses besides, and think I'll take 'em?"

"I did the business with your father, Rudy," said Reata patiently.

"You're going to do it over ag'in with me!" shouted Rudy and reached out to collar the smaller man.

His hand gripped the empty air.

"Steady, old son," said Reata without alarm. "Don't get trouble started, because you're barking up the wrong tree this time."

"Barkin' up the wrong tree, am I?" said Rudy. "Then I'll take some of the bark off the right face!"

Suddenly he smashed a fist for the head of Reata. That head swerved aside at the last instant, and Rudy, in the full driving lurch of his punch, stumbled on nothingness, as it were, and then tipped sidewise and landed flat on his face.

Just what Reata had done to him, old Joe Hyman could not make out, but he opened his mouth and his eyes, and then he grinned.

After all, he thought, no matter how the fight went, he would be a winner. If Rudy won, they would make a handsome profit. If Rudy lost, he would have received a lesson which would make him a more endurable companion in the house.

As for Rudy, he came lunging in headlong this time, and found himself suddenly hoisted into the air. Yes, all the two hundred and odd pounds of him were suddenly floundering in the emptiness of space, and whirling. Then he dropped with an impact that knocked the breath whistling from his body.

Rudy knew, as he gulped back the lost wind, that he was beaten. But he felt that he would rather die now than live to be shamed, so he snatched out a revolver to finish the battle while he lay on the ground.

What happened then was most mysterious of all. The hand of the stranger had disappeared into his coat pocket as Rudy reached for the gun, but it was not a revolver that Reata produced. It was merely a length of coiling line that appeared to Joe Hyman, studiously looking on, no bigger than very large twine. But it flew from the hand of Reata as though it were heavy wire. It caught not the body, but only the gun hand of Rudy, and the tightening strands of the noose squeezed his fingers flat together and made the gun drop on the ground.

Reata picked that gun up and tossed it to a distance.

"That was a bad play, brother," he said. "When you get out among rough men, one of these days, you'll be killed first and talked to afterward, if you try one of those little tricks of yours. So long, Rudy. You're big enough now, and you'll know better later on."

With that he mounted the thinsided gray. The lead ropes tightened, and one after the other, with a lurch, the horses broke into a trot and then into a canter. But the roan mare followed her master uncompelled, shuffling over the ground at a gliding trot that made the canter of the other horses look futile.

Joe Hyman stepped out of the door and stared at the departing stranger, not at his son, who was rising from the ground slowly, nursing his crushed and skinned hand. And as Hyman stared, he made sure that the gallop of those three led horses was not free, as it should be under the weight of saddles only. It was labored and stiff, and shortpaced. They were weighted down, but where?

Why, the weight must be in the strong saddlebags. It could not be elsewhere. And what could it be, of small compass and so much bulk, heavy as lead itself?

The answer stunned Joe Hyman as his brain stumbled on it.

Gold! It was gold that the three led horses labored under! No wonder that this stranger was willing to pay a price and a half,

157

or two prices, for the horses he wanted.

A frantic impulse came to the rancher to saddle a horse and fly in pursuit, but he checked that impulse. He had seen too well how the stranger had been able to handle big Rudy, his son.

It was a good bit later in that morning that Joe Hyman had a chance to see three more very tired horses. They were ridden by three grim-looking men who swept down the slope and up to the door of the shack, into which Hyman himself stepped to view them more closely.

He knew one of them. That chunky fellow with the thick chest and shoulders and the bulldog jaw—that was Harry Quinn.

Quinn, waving at him, shouted: "You seen a gent go by here with three hosses on the lead and a little mite of a dog along with him?"

"Sure, I seen him," said the rancher.

"You didn't give him no hosses, did you?" demanded Quinn.

"I didn't give him none. But I sold him three," said Hyman. "What's the matter? Ain't he a friend of yours?"

"You sold him three hosses?" groaned Dave Bates.

"Four, now I come to think of it. But he took the roan mare along with him, though there wasn't no saddle on top of her. That makes five hosses, all added up in his party, now."

"There!" said Salvio, pointing. "That sorrel gelding is one of our three!"

"One of *your* three!" shouted Joe Hyman, his hair fairly lifting. "You mean to say that them was stolen hosses that he traded in to me?"

"They was stole, and stole from us," answered Quinn. "What you mean, doin' business with every bum that comes down the road? There's seven, eight hundred dollars' worth of hossflesh that you owe us, Hyman!"

The rancher stared, agape.

"Don't be a fool, Harry," said Gene Salvio. "We want new horses, and we don't want a lot of argument. Hyman, show us the best three horses you have in that corral and we'll leave the

158

three we've got under us with you. They're better than your stuff, but we won't charge you any boot. Hop to it, and get 'em out here fast."

The three best horses in the corral were promptly brought to them by a very subdued Joe Hyman and a frightened son, to whom he had merely whispered: "One of them gents is Harry Quinn. And Harry Quinn is hitched up to the queerest and the strongest gang in this neck of the woods. Yeah, or any other neck. Talk small and look smart when you're around these hombres! You might hear something."

They did hear something before Salvio and the other two went cantering away.

"You going to remember that hoss thief the next time you see him?" demanded Harry Quinn.

"I'm goin' to salt him down with lead and keep him for you to look at!" vowed the rancher.

"I'll tell you a name so's you can label him," said Quinn. "He's Reata!"

"Hi!" shouted Rudy. "Him that killed Bill Champion?"

And when the three galloped their horses down the hill, Rudy was grinning.

"Look! I was all busted up," he said. "And now I ain't nothin' but proud that I was throwed around by the gent that killed Bill Champion."

CHAPTER 34

Salvio and the rest kept no direct or headlong course. As Bates said to Salvio, they were engaged in a stern chase, and one that was always sure to be hard. It was apparent that Reata was driving southeast toward Jumping Creek. And the town of Rusty Gulch lay almost due south. The thing for them to do was to get word to Dickerman, and Dickerman could send out men to intercept the flight of Reata.

"Send word? You'd think we had telegraph wires strung up between us and Rusty Gulch!" exclaimed Salvio. "Even if we did, wouldn't a message like that be pretty fine? Think it over, partner! 'Reata running for Jumping Creek to pay back the stolen gold. Send out armed men to stop him.' That would look pretty good, coming in over the wire, wouldn't it?"

"Sometimes you kind of beat me, Salvio," said Dave Bates. "You've clean forgot that we have the heliograph. Right there on the shoulder of Mount Passion there's one of Dickerman's men. And I know how to write out the code."

"Do you?" said Salvio. "Doggoned if I can ever get the thing memorized. That place on Mount Passion ain't more'n five miles out of the way. And you're the lightest in the saddle. You ride down there and send in the message. If you don't find our trail, I'll call you in before night with a couple of columns of smoke."

Diverging on a long slant from the trail which Salvio and Harry Quinn held to, Bates aimed his course at a mountain with a cleft head that stood at a considerable distance to the south, just far enough away for its rolling sides to be a thin mauve between the brown of nearness and the blue of far away. When he reached the up slope of the mountain, he pressed his mustang hard. It did not matter, perhaps, how quickly he used up horseflesh on this part of the trail, because if his message went through, perhaps the major part of the work in the stopping of Reata would be done by other agents of Dickerman. So the horse rapidly climbed into a thick pine wood, slipping and stumbling over the uncertain floor of thickly laid needles, and so came out on the flat western shoulder of the mountain.

A shack leaned here against a tall boulder, and in front of the shack sat a very old man stretching a coyote skin on a light frame. He looked up silently at the stranger and waited. Dave Bates sprang down from the saddle, threw the reins, and waved his hand to the trapper.

"I've been looking for you," he announced.

"You have, have you?" said the old man. "Maybe you've

160

been wantin' to get me news that my grandfather's gone and died and left me his million. Ain't that right?"

"What I wanted to talk to you about was junk," said Dave Bates.

"Well, a gent can talk about pretty nigh anything," said the trapper. "I suppose that junk would be good enough to talk about, too."

"It depends on where a gent aims to put the junk," said Bates.

"Where would *you* start the business?" asked the trapper.

"What about Rusty Gulch?" asked Bates.

The trapper loaded a shortstemmed pipe and lighted it carefully and tamped down the flaming coals with a thickskinned forefinger before he squinted at Bates through the cloud of smoke and answered: "Rusty Gulch, eh? Ain't there a junk dealer down in Rusty Gulch already?"

"A junk dealer that knows his business," said Bates, "is always dead ready to take in partners, you know."

"Maybe, maybe," said the trapper, narrowing his eyes more and more. "But how would you go about askin' him?"

"I'd come up the side of Mount Passion and find a heliograph," said Bates.

"Would you find one there?"

"I'd find an old man setting in front of his house," said Bates, "and he'd know how to start my message shooting south to Rusty Gulch."

At this the trapper shrugged one shoulder and made a slight gesture with his hand.

"All right," he said. "You fire away and tell me what you want."

"I'll write it," said Dave Bates.

Being a man of method and some business, he carried a small notebook with him. He sat down with the book on his knee, scribbled a message first in English, and then on another sheet slowly transcribed it into code. When he had finished, he tore out the code message and gave the paper slip to the trapper.

161

"Start shooting that," he ordered.

The trapper looked down at the message with a grin.

"What kind of hell pops after I send this?" he asked.

He went in to the shack and came out with his apparatus, which surprised Bates by its size and weight.

"We gotta have luck," said the trapper. "Sometimes the other gents that had oughta pick me up seem to be asleep most of the day. Yonder on Turner Peak is where I oughta get a flash back if I'm having luck."

Dave Bates, looking across the vast chasm of the Turner Valley, studied the head and side of the opposite mountain through patient minutes. And then a muttered exclamation came from the trapper.

"He's got me!" said the trapper.

It was a moment later before Bates saw a rapid winking of light from near the head of Turner Mountain. But the trapper was satisfied.

"We're goin' to step the message right across the mountains and down to Rusty Gulch," he said. "Sun talk is talk that don't make no noise, but it says a terrible pile. How big a pile is this goin' to say, stranger?"

"This here sun talk," said Bates, pleased by the phrase, "is all about gold and hosses and men."

"Sure," said the trapper. "Gold is always what lies behind the sun talk. So long, then. Give Pop my regards, will you? And tell him that the game is getting sort of scarce on Mount Passion. Tell him I want a change."

CHAPTER 35

It was almost at the time when the sun talk was passing with a silent glittering from mountain to mountain that the Overland Kid came into Rusty Gulch.

The Overland Kid sauntered through the town with an

ample step and a wide smile, but when men caught his eye, they generally became a little uneasy. That was because of a habit that the Overland Kid had fallen into. He looked at a man and printed the picture far back in his brain. It was necessary for him to remember faces in order to recognize trouble as soon as trouble recognized him. And when he looked at a man, he sized the other fellow up and generally found him wanting. That was why strangers were uneasy when they met the Kid's eye. They felt themselves added up and knew that the total was not very big.

The fact that the Kid was so young, so smiling, and so handsome made him seem all the more dangerous. Only the veriest tenderfoot would have been fooled by the Kid's good looks and genial manners, and in these days he found, more and more, that he had to hunt for trouble hard before he could find it.

He always managed to succeed in his search. Before long, he could warm up any community, and then the ground grew so hot underfoot that he had to move on.

Nature was too kind to the Kid. She gave him his height and breadth, and plenty of substance, too, when he was barely fifteen. Then she filled him out with strength, and drew his nerves tight and true, and rigged him with all the power and aptitude that a human could want. The range was his school, and by sixteen he had received his diploma in riding, roping, and shooting. He got better and better in all three, but the Kid realized, it seemed, that this was an age of specialization, and he chose to specialize in guns.

He did not limit himself. Shotgun, rifle, revolver, he was at home with anything. He had three passions, and these were the three. For each he had a peculiar love. The revolver was a fine tool for close work. The rifle had about it a dignity. It conquered distances; it required exquisite precision, and nerves of chilled steel. But always he yearned for a time when a crowd of enemies might assail him and he could turn loose with a sawed-off shotgun and plenty of ammunition.

It will be seen that the Kid was a fellow of parts, and though he was a scant twenty-one, and though his perpetual smiling often made him seem even younger, the hard, bright glint of his inner nature would often peep out at his eyes, and, as has been said, chill the very spinal marrow of other men.

He walked right through the town of Rusty Gulch, and even went by all the saloons without being tempted, and on the outer and farther edge of the town he came in sight of the building that had been described to him—a huge old barn that had been turned into a house, a big, gloomy place with a tall wooden fence surrounding the yard behind it.

The gate was open, and the Overland Kid walked inside. It was all as he had been told it would be. There were the many big piles of junk rising here and there from the ground, some of them partially covered with tarpaulins. And off to the side an old man was sorting a heap of weather-reddened chains.

The Overland Kid stopped in midstride when he saw this man. For his senses were very acute, and in that fellow, who must be Pop Dickerman, he guessed at evil so dark and so profound that a disgust which was almost as cold as fear came over him.

In that moment while he stared at Pop Dickerman, the Overland Kid summed up all the features of that long and down-ward face, the grizzled, ratlike fur which masked it, the eyes which were too close together, too small, and too bright, and the very red and smiling lips. For even as Pop Dickerman worked along, without an audience, he was wearing a smile.

When he saw the Overland Kid, he straightened, looked at him, and nodded. Then he went on with his work, for Pop Dickerman was accustomed to having people come out to his junk yard and look through the piles of rubbish, as the Kid now started to do.

The Overland Kid first found a hand rake; next he discovered an ax handle; and from a big heap he extracted a single tile. He went to the junk dealer and laid the three on the ground. Two

164

or three scrawny cats came out from behind Dickerman and sniffed at the three things, and looked up into the face of the stranger as though they were beginning to understand something about him.

Dickerman said: "Rake—ax handle—tile. Hey?"

"That's it," said the Overland Kid.

"What might that spell?" asked Dickerman.

"You tell me about it, partner."

"R-a-t, it looks like to me," said Dickerman.

"Well, that's a word," said the Kid.

"Sure it is," agreed Dickerman, nodding, and then rubbing his hands together as he looked over the big dimensions of the Overland Kid. "That's a word that might mean a whole lot, depending on where a gent learned how to spell it this way."

"Turk Loomis, he's the hombre that taught me how to write like that."

"You a friend of Turk's?"

"Him?" said the Overland Kid. "I wouldn't be a friend of his. The dirty sneak!"

Dickerman made a light clucking sound and kept right on smiling. "Turk must think a lot of you, or he wouldn't 'a' sent you to me."

"Aw, you know how it is," said the Overland Kid. "The bum got into a jam, and I happened along. I was on the road, d'you see, and I just happened along when Turk needed a happening. That was all. There was three men climbing his frame. I took 'em off, was all."

"Took 'em off or picked 'em off?" asked Dickerman with a greedy little flicker of light in his eyes.

"I picked off the top man," said the Overland Kid, "because it looked like he was ready to prune the head off the tree with his knife. The other two was shaken off in the fall, and started running."

"You didn't know Turk when you seen him in trouble?"

165

"Nope. I never seen his oily mug before."

Dickerman nodded in an understanding of this youth.

"Well, what about it? What happens?" asked the Kid.

"What do you think ought to happen?" asked the junk dealer.

"How would I know? Turk tells me to come up here to you, and I come."

Dickerman grinned. "Come inside and have a snack. You're hungry."

"I'm not so hungry. I'll go with you when I know why."

"Your belt's up two notches," answered Pop Dickerman, "and you haven't eaten since you left Turk Loomis's place. You better come in and have a snack."

"All right," replied the Kid. "I don't mind taking a chance now and then."

This insolence Dickerman did not appear to notice, but as he turned his back to lead the way, his upper lip twitched once and made the fur bristle on his ratty face.

Perhaps it was because he was angry that he glanced up at this moment toward the head of the northern hill that looked down over Rusty Gulch. And he saw there a little rapidly winking point of light.

"Here—quick!" snapped Dickerman. "Come along. I got something to do."

His long stride became almost a run as he led the way through a back door into the kitchen.

"Start up a fire in the stove," he directed. "Bacon and eggs and things in that pantry yonder. Help yourself! I got a job to do right away!"

And he shambled swiftly away, closing all of the doors soundlessly behind him.

It was fifteen or twenty minutes later before Dickerman had finished his work on the roof of the house, and then, sitting in an upper room, decoded the jumbled letters which had been spelled out to him by the heliograph.

The "sun talk," deciphered, read:

166

Reata found us on way and swore he would get the stuff and take it back to Jumping Creek. He stampeded our horses and got away with everything clean. He is traveling hard for Jumping Creek. He has fresh horses. We are trailing him close. Work from that end. His line is from Chester Draw.

When Dickerman had finished this translation, he sat for a moment with his head straining farther and farther back toward his shoulders, and an expression of frightful anguish on his face. Then he went down the stairs toward the kitchen.

The arrival of the Overland Kid at this time was so much to the point that Pop Dickerman was fairly staggered by the good chance.

When he came into the kitchen, the Kid was already taking the coffeepot off the stove; on the table stood a frying pan that held no fewer than eight eggs, and an equal number of strips of bacon, flanked by a loaf of bread.

Said the Kid, glancing toward the junk dealer: "Kind of gripe you to see me spreading out all this chuck?"

"No," said Dickerman instantly, "bums are cheap; but a gent has to pay for the top sawyers. I always pay big!"

CHAPTER 36

There was a burning impatience in Pop Dickerman, but he controlled all the fire of it carefully until his guest had finished the solid food and come down to his third cup of coffee. Then, relaxing in his chair and making for himself a cigarette with a careless flick of the fingers, the Overland Kid began to smoke and sip coffee.

"You keep some eats in this house," he said. "But you look kind of lean and yellow to me. How come that first-rate chuck don't put some red in your skin, Dickerman?"

"Me? I got no stomach," said Dickerman hastily. "A little milk and stale bread. The doctor, he says it's better for me."

"Hey, but why d'you keep all the eats around, then?"

"For my friends," said Pop Dickerman. "I got a lot of friends that have appetites, partner."

"A lot of friends like me, eh?" said the Kid.

"Some of 'em like you," agreed Dickerman. "What might your name be?"

"Any old name would fit me pretty good," said the Kid. "Some call me the Overland Kid, because I travel quite a lot, and sort of fast."

"The Overland Kid," said Dickerman. "Aye, and I've heard of you. Now, how you feel about a job?"

"How does the job feel about me?"

"The job feels good about you."

"Why?"

"Because you shoot straight," said the junk dealer. "And this is a shootin' job."

"How high does it shoot?"

"You ever hear of a fellow by name of Reata?"

"That's a greaser name for a rope."

"Aye, and there's a man that wears the same name because he's got a reata and he knows how to use it. You never heard of Reata?"

"No. Never. What's he like?"

"Like a bullet between the eyes," said Dickerman, softly and thoughtfully, "or the poison in a rattlesnake's tooth, or the point of a flash of lightning."

"Kind of fast and mean, eh?"

"No, he ain't mean," said Dickerman. "He don't look mean. He looks kind of mild. He ain't big. He don't weigh more'n a hundred and fifty pounds, kind of light in the legs and big in the shoulders, but nothing to talk about. But lemme tell you something. While you was setting and saying good morning to him, Reata would pick that gold filling out of that tooth."

The Overland Kid straightened and was about to make an

168

angry denial. He contented himself with saying: "Well, maybe! I've got to see that."

"Wait a minute," said Dickerman. "Maybe I can tell you something more. This Reata, he never carried a gun. But—well, you've heard of Bill Champion?"

"I dunno that I have."

"You keep thinkin' and try to remember."

"Hold on. Yeah. I've heard something about him. He's the gent that can't miss with a rifle or a Colt, and he ties up iron bars like they was twine. Where does he mostly hang out?"

"In hell," said Dickerman cheerfully, "where Reata put him. Him and his size, and his guns, and his big gray stallion, and Reata with his rope—but Reata was the one that did the killing, and Bill Champion was the gent that died!"

"It ain't possible!"

"No? Well, none of the things that Reata does is possible," declared Dickerman. "There ain't hardly a one of them that folks would believe in, but they keep right on happening! And there ain't a man that I know about that I'd send up agin' him —but I'd send three in a set, and I'd pick you for one of the three."

The Kid stared, and then finished his coffee. He felt rather cold of spirit, and hoped that the coffee would give him a greater warmth of heart.

"It sounds dog-gone queer," he said.

"It's queerer than it sounds," said Dickerman. "Will you ride that trail for me, Overland?"

The Kid was frowning as he answered very slowly: "All the days of my life I never turned my back on any kind of a job like this. But gimme another sort of a slant. The Reata gent— suppose that he was bumped off, it's murder, ain't it?"

"He's carryin' stolen goods," said Dickerman.

"*Your* stolen goods, maybe?"

"Stolen goods," repeated Dickerman, "and if the law comes up with you after you put a bullet through him, the law'd thank you mighty big and fine, Overland."

169

"Dickerman," said the Overland Kid, "you look poison mean to me. But I reckon that I need a job. How high do you pay?"

"I ain't a rich man," said Dickerman, "but I'll pay ten thousand dollars for Reata dead!"

"And I am to split that three ways?"

"Your partners on the job, they each get a split. You get a half, and they each get a quarter. That's five thousand for you, son."

The Overland Kid nodded. "I'd be a fool if I didn't take this here job," he said. "Dog-gone if it ain't a big country, Dickerman, for a gent like Reata to be wanderin' around and me never heard of him."

"Nobody much will ever hear about him," answered Dickerman, "because he's smart enough never to brag. He never hunts for no trouble. He waits for it to sneak up behind him. And then he stretches it out cold. I guess he never drew a drop of blood in his life, hardly. But he turns gunmen into wooden soldiers."

"I've heard enough about him," growled the Overland Kid. "When do I start?"

"Finish your coffee; give yourself another cup, and then come outside. I'll have a hoss waitin' for you."

The Overland Kid stepped out into the bright heat of the sun and stood fast, his eyes closed, letting that warmth soak into him. For it seemed to him that a cold shadow had sunk into his very heart. He had been shown a terribly difficult objective; now it would lie in his own discretion to handle the long chance in the best possible manner.

When he looked up again, he saw old Dickerman coming toward him, leading a bay gelding of sixteen hands or a bit more, a powerful and high-blooded brute that kept shouldering against the old fellow, jolting him to a stagger as he bore back as well as he could against the reins.

The sight of the horse instantly lifted the heart of the large young man. There was a mount which would be able to carry even *his* weight with consummate ease. The saddle was new and

170

good. The bridle was plain and strong. There was no show about this outfit, but it was the best of everything, and he saw the butt of a rifle thrusting out at the end of a long saddle holster that extended down the right side of the horse.

"That's a hoss after my own heart," said the Overland Kid. "I'll sure take good care of it for you!"

"Take care of it?" Dickerman chuckled. "No, sir, but use it up like scratch paper. Use it up and throw it away. There's plenty more where that one came from. You use this hoss like it was nothin', and I'll think all the better of you."

The Overland Kid stared. He began to see more clearly that there was indeed a great goal at the end of this trail.

Dickerman went on: "Now write down in your head some things I'm goin' to tell you."

"Blaze away," said the Kid, filled with increasing respect for this strange and evil old man.

"You know the country from the Chester Draw to Jumping Creek?"

"I know it like a book."

"That's the line that Reata is riding. You're goin' to stop him. There's three good men of mine behind him. They're spotting the trail and they're ready to fight hard.

"You ride straight east from Rusty Gulch till you come to Tyndal Creek. You know that place?"

"I know that place."

"Go down Tyndal Creek till you come to the bridge, and a quarter of a mile below the bridge there's a grove of a lot of tall poplars. You come up to that grove, and you come slow. And as you come, you whistle, d'you hear? And the tune you whistle is 'Auld Lang Syne.' And if you whistle it loud enough and long enough, there's two men will come out of that wood, and one of 'em is dark, and he's Blackie, and the other one's short and blond, and his name is Chad. Two good men, and two good hosses, and two good rifles. If you whistle that song, they know you come from me, and you can boss 'em. Tell 'em what I've told you. And that's all."

171

He added suddenly: "Waitin' for anything?"

"No."

"Then get out of here and on the way!" shouted the old man. "Ain't every minute drainin' the blood out of my heart? Reata has seven or eight hundred pounds of gold that belongs to me. Go and get it!"

CHAPTER 37

Tyndal Creek raced its white horses between banks of green, shouting on its way with never a thought that it would leave the mountains and join a sullen, muddy river, and so go down to its destiny. And up the side of Tyndal Creek the Overland Kid rode the bright bay until he came to a bridge, and, beyond the bridge, to a gleaming, tall grove of poplars.

When he was near the wood the Overland Kid, as he had been instructed, began to whistle with all his force, "Auld Lang Syne." He whistled it and he sang it, and he rode his horse up and down within fifty feet of the woods.

Presently he was aware of a tall, dark man with a straight line of black mustache ruled across his face who had appeared on the verge of the wood and was leaning one hand against a tree. He leaned on his left hand. His right hand hung just off a conveniently angled leg holster that carried a revolver. These were small things to notice, but the Kid had the eye for them.

"Seems like a pretty good day for a song, all right," said the stranger. "Kind of clears up your throat, don't it?"

"Blackie," said the Kid, "we've got to ride. Where's Chad?"

"How would I know?" asked Blackie, showing no surprise that his name was known.

"You know Dickerman, and you know he sent me," said the Kid. "We've got no time to waste. There's blood running out of Pop Dickerman's heart every minute you hang back."

172

"Let him bleed for a while," said Blackie. "He'll never bleed his heart white."

The Overland Kid laughed. "All right," he said, "I dunno that I care so much for company. I'll ride alone if I have to."

"Come and take a look at this hombre, will you?" said Blackie, looking calmly over his shoulder.

A shorter and very blond man appeared beside Blackie.

"He looks kind of young to me," said Chad, for it surely was he. "He looks too young to know much, I'd say."

"I'm old enough to know a tramp from a white man," said the Overland Kid readily enough.

"What d'you know here, then?" asked Chad, sticking out his jaw and stepping a pace beyond the verge of the trees.

Then the Overland Kid could see all of him. He was not more than eight inches over five feet high, but there must have been nearly two hundred pounds of him. He was smoothed over, not with fat, but with a deep gloss of muscle. The Overland Kid dropped off the bay horse, threw the reins, and walked up to Chad.

"You look like a big pile of cheese to me," said Chad, and smote the Kid on the nose.

The Kid staggered back. He was, in fact, thrown a little off balance, and his arms flung out wide as he strove to recover himself. But he was by no means as far at sea as he seemed. The lore of a thousand barroom and lumber-camp fights was stored in the back of the Kid's brain, and he shrewdly noted how Chad rushed in with red lust of victory in his eye and his guard down, ready to throw punches with either hand.

The Overland Kid clipped him high across the temple with a damaging left. With the same hand he shifted on Chad's wind as the shorter man came to a halt, and as Chad tried to jump back, the Kid shifted again and brought over his right to the button. The blow sounded like a butcher's cleaver chopping through a bone. Chad dropped flat on his face.

The Kid held out his red hands toward Blackie.

"Come on and get your letter of introduction stamped, partner!" he called.

Blackie had not moved.

"You got brains and you got a pair of hands," he said. "But if it comes to *real* trouble, that dog-gone crow knows more about you than I do."

For a crow, as though alarmed by this fighting, had sailed out of the top of a tree and was flapping heavily just overhead.

The Kid snatched out a gun and put a bullet through the bird. It was a lucky shot even for him, but everything came right, and the first shot did the trick. The crow tumbled heavily, head over heels, and thumped the ground with a good solid thwack.

"There's the crow handy for you," said the Overland Kid. "Now you go and ask him what you want to know."

"Anything that bird told me now would sure be dead right," said Blackie.

His own remark amused him so much that he smiled all on one side of his sour face.

"See if you broke the kid's jaw," said Blackie. "Maybe we're goin' to ride with you, after all."

At this Chad sat up unassisted. He rose and rubbed the side of his face with one hand and his stomach with the other, but his voice was perfectly genial and cheerful.

"A good little man ain't got any business with a good big man," said Chad. "Never did have, and never will have. About this here ride you was talkin' about, partner. When do we start?"

"Now," said the Overland Kid. "But wait a minute, first."

He held out his hand, and Chad, after a bit of a grimace, suddenly took it.

"It ain't the first time I been licked," said Chad, "so you don't need to feel so proud. I thought you had the dust in the brain, or I wouldn't 'a' come in so wide open."

"I got a lot of lickings myself," said the Kid, "before I
174

learned how to fake a beating before I felt it. Come along, Chad. I'll tell you the news on the way."

The pair of them were out with him in five minutes. And the first thing that the Kid noted was that they were mounted almost as well as he. By that he knew instantly that if Dickerman had many men, these were among the most chosen.

"Dickerman hosses, eh?" he said.

"Same as you," answered Chad, whose jaw was swelling fast, but whose spirits seemed much higher than those of Blackie. "Now tell us both a pretty story, partner."

The Overland Kid told them his pretty story, as Dickerman had said that he should do. When he finished, Blackie surprised him by saying: "This hombre, Reata—this one you say don't wear no gun—I never heard of him before. But if Dickerman says that he's poison, poison is what he is. There ain't nobody like Dickerman to know about things like that. If he's riding from the Chester Draw to Jumpin' Creek, he'd likely come through Jericho Pass, wouldn't he?"

"That's the way I've been figgerin' it," answered the Kid.

"Sure, he'll go through Jericho Pass, unless he wants to throw away a whole lot of time," said Blackie. "We'll lay for this hombre there and cook *his* goose."

So they went up into Jericho Pass, where the hills split away and a way was found among them, narrow and straight.

There they lay through the hot, still middle of the afternoon, their horses tethered back among the rocks, and their own positions chosen with skill for cover and the distance they could command. They had their rifles ready, every man. They even had chosen the targets.

The Overland Kid had said: "You shoot for the head, Blackie. Chad, you try for the head of the hoss. I'll try a heart shot on this here Reata. We'll get him, hoss and man."

Afterward, the conscience of the Overland Kid bothered him a little. But he pacified himself by declaring to his soul that a man handling stolen goods did not need a great deal of consid-

175

eration. And yet—well, he felt that it would be much, much better if he could have a chance to get at Reata man to man and take his equal chances.

Remember that the Overland Kid had never yet been beaten by armed men in fair fight, and the sense of invincibility was strong upon him. And his nature, too, was about equally divided between day and night. What the Overland Kid had never learned was that it is really possible for men to be good. Since the days when his stepmother had beaten him; since the days when he first had to fight his way through a grim world, he had known nothing but battle, and treacherous battle, at that.

So he lay there baking in the sun, ready for murder, with the sweat slowly rolling down his face.

A buzzard began to circle high above the place. Another buzzard joined higher up. A third buzzard came, highest of all. They kept wheeling and waiting on.

And then Blackie gasped: "There! He's comin'!"

The Kid saw him a moment later, a man on a tall, thin gray horse with an unsaddled roan scarecrow following without a lead, and three other saddled horses moving as though weary, apparently carrying loads, though nothing in the way of a load could be seen except their empty saddles.

In front of all, at first barely visible, was a true midget of a dog, trotting in the lead.

Now the rider and his horses came close and dipped out of view into the hollow immediately beyond.

The prize was almost in the hand of the Overland Kid. He smiled a little grimly to think that this fellow Reata was so surely riding to perdition.

Well, we never know where we are riding.

The Overland Kid looked back, and a mile down the trail he saw the flimsy little wooden bridge that spanned a deep ravine. When he trotted his horse across that bridge, he had been aware of a small qualm in the bottom of his heart, for the bridge had wavered a little, horribly, under the weight of the horse. A
176

quick thought of death had come to the Kid at that moment. And now Reata—

The little dog came over the rise briskly. He stopped, looked about him, sniffed the air, and suddenly turned back with his tail between his legs.

Well, Reata would not be able to read the air, and Reata would not be able to run for his life. Bullets would attend to that business!

And still no Reata appeared.

Long minutes dragged on.

"I'll tell you what," said Blackie softly from the side. "This here hombre has stopped down there at the run of water in the hollow to let his mustangs drink."

That had to be the explanation, and it smoothed the wrinkles of worry out of the brow of the Overland Kid for a time. But as the minutes lengthened again, he grew very restless.

Even he, however, was shocked by the exclamation of Chad: "Boys, the little dog warned him, and he's gone the long way through the pass!"

At that the Overland Kid leaped to his feet, and saw swinging into the smooth of the trail behind him, already well started for the flimsy little bridge, the rider with the five horses, and the horses galloping furiously for safety!

CHAPTER 38

To an ordinary rider of the wilderness, that retreat of the small dog from the narrows of the pass would have meant little. A snake might have crossed its path, for instance. But to Reata every move of Rags had become eloquent with almost the detail of words. And that roached-up back, that tail between the legs, that stealthy haste meant to him plainly, danger.

So Reata had halted his horses for one instant only, and when no men appeared, he understood that men must be waiting up

177

there among the rocks. For that reason he took no chance. Men who wait in a boiling caldron do not do so for a good purpose. And Reata turned aside and carried his horses and his treasure through the winding way of the second pass.

When he got onto the plain beyond he put his mustangs into a gallop and sped for the bridge. Even so, he was rather desperate, and he was not surprised when a shout rang thin and far through the air behind him.

Looking up and back, he saw three riders racing their horses down the slope from the pass, and they came with a speed that made him groan.

He could cross the bridge safely enough, but horses carrying a dead weight cannot keep pace with horses that bear a smaller burden of living, acting flesh. He ground his teeth as he surveyed mentally the picture that lay on the other side of the ravine, beyond the slight rise of rocky ground.

There was simply a broad and open sweep of rolling ground, with a few patches of trees here and there. He could not find shelter for five horses in such a region, and he could not keep those riders from catching him swiftly and surely.

Behind him he could hear the hurrying rhythm of the hoofbeats. Glancing back, he saw the three riders bending far forward, like jockeys. Something about the recklessness of their going told him the sort of treatment he would have at their hands.

He had heard—he never would forget it—that Pop Dickerman could not be beaten. How word could have traveled to Rusty Gulch as quickly as this he could not guess. But the thing must have been done. These must be men of Dickerman, posted to intercept the line of his retreat!

The bridge was nearer. It was so rickety that, in spite of his haste, he dared not take it at a gallop, so he slowed the horses to a walk that cost him agonies.

And always the rush of horses behind him grew louder and louder, and he heard one devil yelling like mad with excess of exultation.

178

Reata looked up grimly, and it seemed to him that the tall, jagged pillar of rock which stood by the bridge was like an old funeral monument. Battered and worn, the whole top of it sagged outward, as though ready to fall on the bridge.

That mental image gave him his idea. As he reached the end of the bridge, he leaped to the ground and shouted and struck at the gray to send it ahead over the mound of rocks on the other side. There the horses would be safe from rifle fire.

Then he leaped for the stone pillar and went up it like a cat. He was glad, not frightened, when he felt the great shaft of stone quiver slightly beneath him. The whole pillar was in an advanced state of decomposition, the frost cracks sinking deep into the core of the rock.

So he came to that point near the top where a huge bit leaned out above the bridge. He leaned, sprang with his whole weight against the slanting fragment, and felt it go away from before him as though it had been wooden instead of solid stone!

He barely managed to reach back and grapple a ledge of the pillar, and, dangling over nothingness, he saw the two-ton fragment topple and strike the bank beneath.

There it burst in two with a loud report, and into the sound came the dismayed yelling of the three horsemen. The second half of the stone rebounded and struck fairly on the end of the bridge. The timbers gave out a half-screeching and half-groaning sound as they gradually collapsed. Then the entire ruin pitched down into the creek bed, a hundred feet below.

Reata had drawn himself up to safety on the rock by this time. And now he rapidly commenced his descent.

Rifles were crackling before he got to the ground. Yet none of the bullets whirred anywhere near him. Instead, when he looked up, he saw that the gray horse had not led the others clear over the mound. It had paused on the top, as though the better to outline the horses for a target against the sky, and the rifles of the three pursuers were taking advantage of that fact. They had halted their horses not far away when they saw that they could not get across the ravine by this pass, and now Reata

179

saw one of the burden-bearing mustangs rear, plunge, stagger. Another squealed as Reata heard a rifle bullet audibly thump into its body. And the gray suddenly bent its knees and dropped its head.

Then the whole group of horses surged across the mound of rocks, out of sight.

Could Reata reach them?

He tried, running, dodging like a snipe that flies downwind. One bullet kissed the air beside his cheek. Another tipped his hat forward. And then, with a last leap, he was over the rock ridge in the safety of the farther side.

Safety?

Safety for him, no doubt, since he had the roan mare ready to carry him away, refreshed as she had been by traveling this part of the day without carrying even the weight of a saddle.

But the treasure of the Decker and Dillon Bank was gone, it seemed. The tall, thin-sided gray that had gone so gallantly all day long carrying Reata and leading the other mustangs, now lay on its side, dying. Two more were failing fast. The brown sat down in a ludicrous and thoughtful attitude. And another had blood gushing from a hole in its side.

There were three almost dead horses here, and that left two animals sound to carry Reata and seven or eight hundred pounds of gold.

The thing could not be done! There was no way in which he could manage to make headway sufficiently fast, for there was another bridge not so far up the deep trench of that ravine, and he could hear the rattling hoofbeats as the three riders stormed along with their horses in that direction.

And before Reata lay this despair, and a smiling, peaceful landscape, singularly smooth and unbroken except by an occasional grove of young trees. To make all seem more peaceful, there was a rancher roping down a load of hay which he had just pitched onto his two-horse rack at the side of a wide field of standing shocks.

Calmly the rancher went on with his work, an old man,

180

straight enough in the shoulders, but with a shining bit of silver beard on his chin. The wind blew strongly toward the ravine, and he could not have heard the guns.

Reata looked up toward the sky with a quick groan of impatience.

Three horses down—three horses dead. He stood over them with a blind, gathering rage in his heart. Murderers of men, they are black enough, but murderers of poor dumb beasts—

Not for the first time he regretted that he had given up guns forever, never to touch them with his hands if he could avoid it, never to fondle their shining deadliness.

He could save himself, but what did he matter to these scoundrels? They wanted the stolen gold—and they would have it!

Automatically, nevertheless, he loaded the gold onto Sue, the roan mare, and onto the remaining mustang. It made a severe load, and he did not add his own weight, but strode forward, with Sue following him and the other mustang after her.

He went blindly forward. There was nothing to see except the load of hay, and therefore he went toward that, and saw the farmer standing up, hands on hips, staring toward him.

The picture brought another idea to him that made him hurry forward on the run. He waved as he came up.

"Yeah, I been seein' you," said the old man. "Looks like you left some hoss meat behind you over yonder. But maybe you take kindly to the coyotes and wanta leave some food for 'em. You even left some saddles yonder."

The old man was apparently as keen as a hawk when it came to long-sightedness.

Reata panted: "Did you ever hear of the Decker and Dillon gold robbery over yonder in Jumping Creek?"

"Maybe I have," said the rancher. "You got any news about it?"

"I've got seven or eight hundred pounds of that gold loaded on these two horses," said Reata. "I'm trying to get it to Jumping Creek, and there are three devils riding me down. They've shot three of my horses, and I can't make any speed with these.

I broke down the bridge across the ravine there, but they'll come over the second bridge in a minute. What I want to know is this: Will you let me throw the gold into your hay load and take it away? They'll never suspect you!"

The old man took out a plug of tobacco, worried off a corner of it, and deliberately stowed the chew in the center of one cheek.

"Well," he said, "how come you was able to bust down the old bridge short of dynamite?"

At this delay, Reata groaned. But he explained: "I climbed that pillar of rock by the head of the bridge. The top of it was almost broken off. I finished the job, and the fall of that part of the column smashed the bridge to flinders."

"That was to keep them gents from swarmin' right over you?"

"It was," said Reata. "They'll be in sight in a minute, and then it will be too late to do anything. Will you take this stuff or won't you?"

"It ain't no part of my property," said the rancher. And he shook his head.

Sweat poured down the face of Reata.

"You're giving a fortune into the hands of three hounds and a rat-faced devil who set them after me. What's your name?"

"Dan Foster is what my ma called me," said the rancher.

"Foster," said Reata, "I see why it is. You'd take the stuff, but you know that your measly little pair of mules wouldn't be able to pull the hay and that much added weight."

"Hey! Hold on!" said Dan Foster. "I never said no such thing as that! Them mules—"

"It's all right," said Reata. "I know your heart's in the right place, but you know mighty well that the mules couldn't pull that load even with you on top of it, let alone seven or eight hundred extra pounds."

"They can't, hey?" asked Dan Foster. "Well, dog-gone me if I don't show you that this here load of hay ain't no more'n a feather to them mules. Throw up that stuff. Gold or not, it

182

ain't too good for Beck and Bird to haul!"

Reata eagerly took the heavy little forty-pound sacks and swung them up to Dan Foster, who took them and plunged them into the loose fluff of hay.

As he handled them, he complained: "Gold! The stuff that some folks bust their hearts for. But nothing comes out of it, nothing but dead hosses, like them yonder, and dead men, like you and me are apt to be, stranger!"

"Where does that load go?" asked Reata as he swung up the last chamois sack and watched it disappear.

"This here hay goes into Tyndal, to the livery stable," said Dan Foster. "Timmons, he always thought a hoss took more kind to the hay that I cut out here than they take to most fodder. I dunno but maybe it's right, too. Seems to stick to the ribs of a hoss."

"I'll meet you at Tyndal at the livery stable of Timmons this evening," said Reata. "Good luck to you, Foster!"

"The same to you," said Foster. "Wait a minute and see Beck and Bird start this here load like it was a feather!"

"I'd like to stay," said Reata, "but I'm overdue on the other side of the sky line. So long!"

He started the roan mare away with a good, sweeping gallop, and the mustang that remained of the four followed willingly enough now that the heavy weight had been taken from its back.

But always, anxiously, Reata looked to the north and west toward that rock ridge beyond which lay the ravine. And now he saw them coming, the three horsemen bending low to gain a greater speed.

The roan mare would hold them easily enough, but not the mustang, even with an empty saddle. He untied the horse and let it run, and then gave Sue her head.

CHAPTER 39

Once in sight of the prey, the Overland Kid and his two new friends stormed like mad across the rolling ground. They saw the second horse turned loose. But the long, low roan mare skimmed away from them with an amazing and an effortless ease.

Two minutes of that running convinced them that they would never overtake Sue, and Reata in the saddle on her, with the little dog Rags before him. So they turned savagely, and quickly Chad had a rope on the mustang that Reata had cut adrift.

Like three wolves they searched her. But in the saddlebags they found nothing whatever.

"She was loaded, this here," said Chad. "The way all them hosses ran except the roan, they was loaded pretty fair."

"With gold," said the Kid. "He's cut loose from it. It must be somewhere back there near the dead hosses."

"Aye, or in that hay wagon!" said Blackie. "That's a thing I might think of if I was Reata. He knew there was a second bridge up the way. He knew that he didn't have much time, all right!"

They seized on the idea eagerly, and rushed for the wagon of Dan Foster. When Blackie reined his horse across the trail —it could not be called a road—Dan Foster threw forward the long brake lever and the wagon drew screeching to a halt.

"Hello, boys," said Foster. "How comes everything with you young gents? And what is all the hurry with everybody today?"

"The feller yonder started it," said Chad, pointing.

"Yeah? Him that is slidin' over the rim of the hills yonder?" murmured Foster. "Well, I never yet seen a gent in a hurry that there wasn't trouble somewheres around. What's he done?"

"Robbery—murder—dog-gone anything you want to name is what he's done," said Blackie.

"What's he robbed?" asked Foster. "Stage or something?"

"What did he pass up to you here on your wagon?" asked the Kid.

He was guessing. Foster looked him straight in the eye and knew it.

"What would he be passing up to me?" asked Foster with an air of great surprise.

"Stuff that weighs seven or eight hundred pounds," answered the Kid. "You know what it was. Boys, we gotta search that load of hay."

"Come on up and hunt," said Dan Foster. "I got an idea that I speared a field mouse with one of them forkfuls of hay, but I dunno for certain. If you find the mouse, I'll give it to you. You can cook it for supper, the three of you."

"He's kind of talkin' down to us, ain't he?" asked Blackie, looking at the old man with a dangerous eye.

"Foster," said Chad, "if you got anything from that other gent, and we find it when we go through this here load of hay, we're goin' to cut you up the back and pull your skin off over your head! Now's the time to talk up. If he give you something, say the word and you go free—except for the stuff."

"Thanks," said Dan Foster. "I was tellin' you before that maybe there was a dead mouse in this here load of hay. I ain't sure, but I think I heard a kind of a squeal when I was hoistin' up a forkful of the hay."

"Mean old gent, he is," said Blackie. "I got a mind to dump his load of hay off onto the ground for him anyway!"

"Leave the old hound alone," said Chad. "We ain't got the time to waste on him, anyway!"

"Sure, we ain't," agreed the Overland Kid, who had been studying the thin, dry face of the old man all of this time. "Leave him go. Back there where the horses are lying—back there we might find something worth while!"

They left old Dan Foster accordingly, to go on his way, which he did without in the slightest degree rushing the mules. But back by the verge of the ravine, the three riders dismounted and there searched thoroughly.

185

The saddlebags of the dead horses were empty. Perhaps, therefore, Reata had dropped the sacks down among the crevices of the rocks? They searched and they probed for a long hour, and still they found not a sign of the treasure.

Then the Kid sat down on a rock and made a cigarette, which he lighted without haste.

"This hombre is everything that Pop Dickerman claimed for him," he decided. "He comes up right under our noses, and then he slides out and away again. And we kill some of his hosses, and he makes the load disappear. Now, what does it sound like to you?"

"It sounds like he made fools of us," said Chad. "Maybe he dropped the gold into the ravine. There's water down there would cover it."

"He wouldn't do that," argued the Kid. "A gent like him, he'd find a way of makin' that gold walk sort of in the direction that he wanted it to go in. Blackie, you had it the first crack out of the box!"

"The gent with the load of hay?" asked Blackie.

"Him? Sure it's him that's got the stuff, and the old goat, he took and bluffed us out!" shouted the Kid. "Come on, boys. We're behind time, but we can trail the sign those wagon wheels leave on the ground. Come on, and come fast! The more I think about it, the surer I am!"

They remounted silently, and rode grimly on through the end of the day. It was not hard to follow the tracks of the wagon. They wound with leisure across the hollows and up the slight rises of the land until they pointed, straight as a string, toward the glimmering lights of a town.

CHAPTER 40

Not half a mile from the edge of the town, in the midst of a small hollow, where the twilight seemed to be more darkly pooled, the Overland Kid and his two friends came on the hayrack of Dan Foster again. They let the mules trot down the pitch and tug up the farther slope, and then the Kid brought Foster to a stop.

The old farmer was perfectly calm.

"Hello, boys," he said. "Lookin' for more news? Or are you thirsty? There's a dog-gone cool can of water hangin' on the side of the rack where the hay drips down over it."

"Go aboard, partners," commanded the Overland Kid, and was instantly on top of the load to set the good example.

Gold goes to the bottom of lighter stuff, but so did the Kid through that load of light, fluffy hay, and it was he who first closed his hand on a chamois sack. He held it up in the darkening light of the day.

"What's this?" he demanded of Foster.

"I never seen inside of it," answered Foster honestly. "What you think it might be?"

Both Blackie and Chad had, by this time, found other chamois sacks. There was no need to ask what was in them. The weight alone was enough to tell. Chad yelled like an Indian and danced up and down until the hayrack began to rock a bit under him.

"Shut up," said Blackie. "Gold shows a red light that folks can see pretty far, anyway. You have to bring 'em down with a lot of yellin'?"

"What're we goin' to do with this old hound?" asked Chad, pointing to Dan Foster.

The rancher sat half turned on his driver's seat, biting off a fresh chew of tobacco. He remained singularly unconcerned.

"He's gotta stay with us a while," answered the Kid. "Old-timer, you took this stuff off of the hands of Reata, did you?"

187

"I didn't know the name of the gent," answered Foster, "but I seen that he was in a terrible hurry. Why, he reminded me of a time when I was—"

"Be quiet!" said Blackie. "Listen. Hey, you've brought up somebody with your yellin', Chad!"

In the breath of silence that followed, the Overland Kid could hear clearly the drumming hoofs of horses at a slow gallop, and now he could see them coming down the track of the wagon wheels toward the town.

"Three gents bound for Tyndal," said the Overland Kid. "Leave them go by. If they ask why we're here, say that we're restin' the mules a minute before pullin' on toward the town. Foster, your business is to keep your mouth shut."

"Sure," said Dan Foster. "I understand that, all right. They're just some more cow-punchers that've heard about the gypsy show that comes tomorrow."

"What gypsy show?" asked Blackie. "You don't mean Queen Maggie and her gang, do you?"

"Aye, that's the lot of thieves that I mean," answered Foster.

Here the three fresh riders dipped into the hollow and swept up beside the wagon.

"Who's there?" called one of them.

"By thunder, it's Salvio!" said Blackie. "Hey, Gene! Is that you, Harry Quinn? We're Blackie and Chad, and here's the Overland Kid. Glad to see you, boys."

"It's Blackie talkin'," remarked Salvio. "What're you hombres doin' up here?"

"The front part of the trail you been backin'," said Blackie. "And there's another thing—we've got the goods!"

"What goods?" asked Dave Bates. "What goods you talkin' about?"

"In chamois sacks," said Chad.

"Then you've got a dead man in that load of hay!" exclaimed Harry Quinn. "Reata's dead, and dog-goned if I ain't sorry to know it!"

"Reata ain't dead," said the Overland Kid. "We gave him a

brush and killed some of his horses. He passed the stuff on to this old gent. Look here, Blackie. Are these fellows really in on the deal?"

"Pop's right-handers is what they are," said Blackie. "Overland, this is Gene Salvio. Here's Harry Quinn. And this here is—sure, it's Dave Bates. Hello, Dave!"

After these greetings they held a brief consultation. They could transfer the gold from the wagon to their horses, but what could they do with Dan Foster, who would go on to Tyndal and give the alarm to the townspeople?

The Overland Kid said: "We could get the old boy to promise to keep his mouth shut. That would be all right."

"Reata's there in the town, waiting for him. When he shows up without the stuff, Reata's going on the back trail," said Gene Salvio. "The question is, do we want that devil clawing at us, or don't we?"

"Hey, look here," said the Kid. "There's six of us, ain't there? Are you talking scary about one man? '

Salvio turned sharply on him in the twilight, but said nothing.

"He don't know about Reata," said Dave Bates soothingly. "He don't know, or he wouldn't talk so easy."

Harry Quinn put in: "We can cache the wagon in a clump of trees and go on to that old shack up Tyndal Creek. You know the one, Gene. The hosses sure need a night's rest, and tomorrow we can pull out and head along for Pop. Ain't that sense?"

"That's good sense, and that's what we'll do," said Salvio.

"I don't know," interrupted the Kid. "I'm not sure that's the best dodge."

There was a brief and heavy silence.

"Oh," said Salvio, "you don't know, eh?"

"No," answered the Kid. "I don't know. Want me to say it three times, or will twice do?"

He could feel rather than see the rigidity of Salvio, but Blackie broke in: "Wait a minute, Gene. The Kid's a newcomer, but he's sure first rate. Take that straight from me. Overland,

189

you'll know Salvio better after a while. I say that he's Pop's right-hand man, almost. Ain't that good enough to hold your hosses?"

"Pop gave me this job, and I'm going to do it," insisted the Kid, the bulldog in him yearning for a fight.

"Suppose that you and me step aside and have a little talk," suggested Salvio with gentleness.

"Nothing would please me better," said the Kid.

Dave Bates stepped between them and held up both hands.

"You two hombres quit it," he commanded. "We going to spoil this job by brawling with each other? Harry's got the right idea. We go on to that shack up on the creek, and we take the old man along with us till the morning. Ain't that good sense? Now, you two shut up. You can go and claw yourselves to death whenever you please afterward!"

This speech was so extremely to the point that the Overland Kid had to admit the force of it. The whole plan of Quinn was clearly the best. For the horses of Salvio and his two mates were plainly done in. Their heads hung low, and sweat ran down their sides and dropped from their bellies onto the ground.

Quinn got into the driver's seat and ordered Dan Foster to drive his wagon into a clump of trees not far away.

"I'm goin' to spend the night with you boys, eh?" said Foster, as cool as ever. "It'll make the old woman worry a pile, but that won't hurt her none. Giddap, Beck. Hi, Bird! Go on, gals!"

The mules hit the collar; the wagon reeled and then lurched ahead, and the outfit was soon brought to a halt in the midst of a black growth of trees. There they hunted through the hay load for the rest of the treasure. Twenty-one sacks had to be found; they were forced to pitch most of the load to the ground before they got the last of the gold loaded onto the backs of the horses. The mules were unhitched, and with Dan Foster riding aside on one of them, the whole party traveled on until they heard the rushing noise of the waters of the creek.

They passed through more trees, and on the bank of the

190

stream they found a little abandoned squatter's shack—one room and an attic.

Salvio took command and gave orders to Blackie and Chad to unload the horses, to Quinn and Bates to start cooking a supper, and then Salvio himself and the Overland Kid hobbled the horses to graze in the long grass of the clearing.

When they had finished this work, the Kid said: "All right, Salvio; any time you say."

To his surprise, Salvio laughed with a genuine amusement.

"You *like* trouble, don't you, Kid? Well, I'll do what I can for you later on. We've got our hands full now. And maybe we'll have Reata on top of us before morning."

"Any way that suits you suits me," said the Overland Kid regretfully. "But about this here Reata. There's only one of him, ain't there? Is he likely to come with a crowd behind him?"

"He works alone, but one of him is sure plenty," answered Salvio. "Maybe he looks small to you, but when his hands start movin', he's plenty big. Who's the fool that's making that noise?"

For a wild shouting and singing had broken out from the shack, and when the Overland Kid went inside with Salvio, he had sight of Chad leaning over the contents of a whole sack of gold, which he had poured out on the little homemade table in the center of the room. Chad was dipping his hands in the yellow, heavy dust and lifting it up, and letting it stream down, bright as rays of lamplight in the dance and flicker of flames that came from the fire which had been kindled on the open hearth at the side of the room.

"He's drunk," said Salvio calmly. "And a gold drunk is the worst kind of a drunk in the world. We gotta keep our eyes on that gent tonight, or he'll do something crazy. Pass the word around. Chad's going to give us trouble before the morning comes!"

It was not Chad alone. Every man in the place was watching, with a wide, thirsty grin, the colorful sheen of the gold dust

191

under the manipulations of Chad.

Yes, there was apt to be trouble before the morning came. The only man in the shack who seemed indifferent to what was going on was old Dan Foster, who regarded the gold no more than if it had been so much bright dirt.

The Overland Kid felt that there were only two real men in the place. He was one, and Gene Salvio was the other. And they would need their manhood by the morning!

The Kid stepped to the door, and through a cleft in the trees he saw the lights of Tyndal glittering not very far away. Suddenly he was thirsty in body and in soul for the sight of other faces—the faces of honest men who were not maddened by the gold hunger. He would slip away after supper and get his foot on a bar rail for a half hour or so and have a drink or two, and become a different man. That would mean more than sleep to him!

CHAPTER 41

Reata, as he came in toward the town of Tyndal through the dusk of the day, saw a camp of covered wagons and tents just at the side of the town, revealed by the light of a fire in the center. When the flames lifted high, the entire camp could be seen, but at other times the night poured in over most of the circle, and only a bit of it would be illumined. Around the edge of the wagons, hobbled horses were being guarded by small boys, half-naked little barefooted youngsters. And one of them he saw dancing in swift circles to the shrilling music that ceaselessly continued from the camp.

They were gypsies, he knew. He turned a little aside. If there were gypsies in this part of the country, they were almost sure to be Queen Maggie's band; and it was in their hands, of course, that he had left poor Pie Phelps.

But did he dare enter the camp to make inquiries? He knew

the gypsies were quick and fickle, as passionate in their loves as they were in their hates. Perhaps he could tell what the general tone of his reception would be if he spoke first to one of the boys tending the horses. So he rode up closer and sang out to the little fellow who had been dancing to the music.

The answer was a yell of delight. The boy caught hold of his stirrup leather and began to jump up and down, waving his hand and yelling: "Reata! Reata! Reata!"

Others of the horse herds came racing. Their shrilling voices picked up that name and made a chrous of it.

Reata, suddenly assured and confident, came into the wagon circle with a swarming throng about him.

He saw the big fire in the center of the camp, with huge, black pots hanging into the flames, and the unwieldy bulk of Queen Maggie in her man's coat and hat striding about it, the cigar at its usual angle in her mouth, and the famous iron spoon like a scepter in her hand. She was turning from the fire now, shouting out in the gypsy jargon, and waving the spoon while she nodded at Reata.

"What trouble are you bringin' me now?" she asked.

"A question or two," said Reata. "And I want to see Pie Phelps. Is he here? Is Miriam here?"

"Over yonder in that tent, likely fixin' herself up a little brighter," said Queen Maggie. "Set yourself down. The rest of you—whoosh!"

She waved her iron spoon. The whole gang of the gypsies, big and little, scattered, laughing. Only Georg remained to grip the hands of Reata and exclaim: "Ah, brother!" Then he, too, was gone with the rest.

"Phelps is all right," said Queen Maggie. "He's gotta keep his arm still for a while. Are you hungry, Reata? Set down in that chair of mine. I'll make you a sandwich."

She took up a loaf of bread, slashed it in two lengthwise with a stroke of a great butcher knife which she pulled out of a carving block, and then, out of one of the black pots, she ladled a dipperful of chicken and tomato stew, which she

193

heaped along the length of the bread.

"Sink a tooth in that," she commanded. "Here's some coffee."

She ladled him out a great iron cup of the black coffee, and Reata sat down to eat like a wolf.

The smoke and the heat blew about him. A vast relaxation spread through his body. He was instantly rested, as though he had slept for hours. That was what it meant to feel the gypsy circle spread around him like a guard after his recent adventures in the land of danger.

"Trailin' trouble up and down the country!" said Queen Maggie. "There ain't nobody else like you, Reata. I've tried to get your throat cut before, but now I'm glad to see you ag'in. I'd put a red silk sash around your head, Reata, and make a gray-eyed gypsy of you, son. My man didn't give me no children, Reata." She sighed, and then swore. "But I reckon you wouldn't be happy here with us. Romany, even, ain't wild enough for you. The tribe can't travel as free and as fast as Reata rides on the roan mare. Well, here's where I'm ending my talk, because Miriam's comin'. Look at her how she's slicked herself up for you."

The girl came into the firelight, smiling a little. She was as bright as the fire flames in a yellow dress, with an orange silken shawl over her shoulders, and the stones that hung from her ears were as blue as her eyes. He felt the old shock that never failed to go through him when he saw the blue of the eyes under that black, glistening hair.

She took his hand as he stood up, and smiled silently at him.

"Why wouldn't you kiss him, Miriam, you fool?" asked Queen Maggie. "A man likes to be made over."

"Nobody minds you, Maggie," said the girl. "Why do you keep talking? But now that the tribe is all one friend of yours, are you going to be long with us, Reata?"

"Only till I finish the heel of this loaf and that cup of coffee," he answered. "I have to go on into town. But can I see Pie Phelps?"

"He's asleep," said the girl. "I'll call him."

"Let him sleep. Just tell him I was here. Maggie says that he's coming on well. What's in Tyndal that I ought to know about?"

"Steve Balen's there. I suppose that's why you've come?" she asked.

"Steve Balen?" he repeated. "No, I didn't know that he was in Tyndal."

"He," said the girl, "and Lester. Colonel Lester is there. They've given up the Reata trail, folks say. Wayland is with 'em. It's only ten miles from here to Jumping Creek, and the colonel's pretty daughter has ridden over to see her father and go back with them all tomorrow." She looked narrowly at his face.

He had winced a little.

Into Tyndal he certainly must go to meet old Dan Foster and get from him the gold that was sunk in the load of hay. And, once in the town, he could turn over the gold to the custody of Colonel Lester and Steve Balen. But the thought irked him. It was his plan to carry the stolen treasure clear back to Jumping Creek and deliver it there at the doors of the bank.

These things were in his mind, far back, when he heard Miriam talk, but that image which he saw, coming in a bright flash between him and the gypsy, was the face of Agnes Lester. He could not say that it was more lovely, but it brightened in his mind and made him thoughtful.

"Aye," said Miriam quietly. "She's the one, then?"

He stood up.

"Lester, Wayland, Balen—why, the town is full of the devil for me, Miriam. But I have to go in. And I'm coming back one of these days, if you'll want to see me."

Her eyebrows lifted a little. She shrugged her shoulders.

"Why," she said, "there's never a time when I'm not glad to see a friend."

He was gone a moment after that, with the small dog in the crook of his arm, and the roan mare carrying him, and the gypsies clamoring after him, pleading with him to stay.

195

Queen Maggie said, around her cigar, the force of her speaking driving out the smoke in ragged puffs: "Ah, and what a fool *you* are, Miriam! Go on after him. Be nacheral and knock that fool smile off your face. You'll be in your tent in a minute more, cryin' like a baby, and I'll go and drag him to see you. I'll shame you. I'll let him see that you're eatin' your heart out."

"Aye, but what would I do?" said the girl. "Suppose that I kept him here—suppose I were able to—wouldn't it be like tying a pigeon to the ground so that the hawks could start stopping at it? I'd have a happy man for a month with me, and a dead man in my heart the rest of my days. Georg! Georg!"

That slender youth came with a leap and a bound.

"Go after him, Georg," said the girl. "Shadow him. There's going to be danger enough looking him in the face, but you can guard his back, maybe!"

✗

CHAPTER 42

When Reata found out where Timmon's livery stable was, he went straight to it.

In spite of his delay at the gypsy camp, Dan Foster, with his wagon load of hay, had not yet come to the stable. Perhaps it would be a risky thing to put up the mare inside a building when he might need her speed at any moment, but it was too great a temptation to bed her down in softness and warmth and give her a proper feed of cured hay and oats. So he put her up in a corner stall with only this peculiarity in his treatment of her: The lead rope was not tied into the manger rail. She would stand there, untied, until he came for her or called for her later on.

After that he went to the front of the stable, where big, rawboned Timmons himself was impatiently waiting for the arrival of Foster.

"Here I'm late for supper," said Timmons. "The wife's goin'

to have corn bread, too, and it ain't the same after it's been out of the oven for a spell and started to get cold. But, dog-gone me, I gotta wait here for an old gent and his load of hay to fork it off into the mow for him."

"I've got to wait here for a friend," said Reata. "I'll tell him when he comes that you'll be back in just a minute."

"Sure! Do that, and thanks," said Timmons. "You'll know him by the white jag of beard on his chin and the twinkle in his eyes. So long."

Timmons went out, and he had hardly dissolved into the darkness when a splendid young man on a big horse flashed at a gallop out of the night and knocked a hollow thunder out of the floor boards of the stable. He pulled up his horse with a suddenness that made the gelding skid a dozen feet over a wet place where a buggy had been washed not long before. But even while the horse was sliding, the rider was reaching for a gun!

He had recognized Reata, and Reata had recognized in him the big leader of the trio who had blocked him in the pass and shot down his horses later on in the day. They had seen each other only at a considerable distance, but the eyes are sharp when they look at enemies.

And even before the Colt came into the hand of the Overland Kid, the lariat of Reata shot out like a loaded whiplash.

The Kid ducked flat across the pommel of his saddle; the noose rapped the back of his neck with its thin, heavy coil, and he pulled his gun to make the kill then and there.

In that fraction of a second he had a chance to think—to remember what Pop Dickerman and Salvio had said to him of Reata; to consider how their eyes would be opened when they learned how Reata had gone down.

He thought of that, and also that he would send the bullet smashing home into the middle of that brown, cheerful, intelligent face. And with that the flash of the drawn gun was whipping across the saddle horn, ready for the shot.

Certainly there had not been time for Reata to gather in his lariat and make a second cast. There had not been a tenth part

197

of the time necessary for that, but as the rope slid down to the ground, it dropped near the prancing, dancing, nervous front feet of the gelding, and Reata made the most of that good chance.

He put a flying noose over one of those hoofs, and then over the other, and jerked back with a suddenness that did not give the lariat a chance to loosen and pull away. The gelding, at the very moment when the Overland Kid was ready to shoot, lurched forward on its knees and then pitched on its side.

That would have thrown the ordinary rider. The Kid managed to fling himself loose in the very nick of time, and landed staggering, with not one, but two guns now in his hands. Reata used the hand end of his lariat, where, for a better grip, the rawhide was swelled with an insert of heavy lead. It was not a great weight, in fact, but great things could be done with it by Reata. He snapped that butt end like the accurate lash of a black snake in the hands of a mule skinner, one who can, when he will, cut the horsefly away without touching the skin of the mule, or who can make the whip bite out a solid chunk of the hide. That was how the last eight feet of the line curled outward from the hand of Reata, and the loaded butt end snapped solidly on the skull of the Kid.

A flick of a finger armed with a thimble can hurt a very hard head. And the snapping of Reata's line nearly broke the skull of the Kid.

He had not even seen the thing coming. He had barely hit the floor, ready to shoot, when something invisible whished in the air and knocked him to his knees.

The guns were snatched from his hands while his wits were still whirling. He made a vague effort to struggle, but had his wrists roughly jerked back and lashed together behind his back. Then a hard hand twisted into the collar of his shirt and thrust him forward into the darkness of the aisle between the horse stalls.

One step more and Reata would have had his man securely away into the dimness of that aisle, but at the last instant, while
198

he was on the edge of the dim lantern light, that man who of all the world detested him most had to step across the entrance to the stable and look in on him.

It was Tom Wayland who paused in mid-step, struck by a vision, a nightmare—for he had seen the unforgettable face of Reata himself in the dimness of the stable interior! Big, handsome Tom Wayland pulled a gun, but he did not rush at once into the place. He had no intention of rushing. Before this, on occasion, he had charged against Reata, and the memories were not encouraging. The pulling of the gun had been an instinctive gesture of defense.

Then, turning, he raced with all his might down the street. He wanted to stop and call to every man he passed, but he realized that only experts in battle could ever handle Reata. So he made for the hotel, where he ought to find Steve Balen and some of Steve's chosen posse men.

Into the lobby of the old frame hotel Tom Wayland burst, therefore, and saw before him not only Steve Balen and his posse about him like savage cubs about an old wolf, but also there was the pompous figure of Colonel Lester himself, in the middle of a declamation of some sort, making his heavy jowls quiver with the indignation of his speech. And, drawn by the gleam of golden hair, Tom Wayland's eye found the colonel's daughter sitting back in a shadowy corner.

He was sorry that she had to be here now. She might not think a great deal of a fellow who brought information to a small army about where they could find a hunted criminal.

However, this news was too important to be withheld for an instant.

He rushed to Steve Balen and exclaimed to him: "I've found Reata—I've found him—"

His lack of breath stopped him. Balen did not even rise or lift his head, which he merely canted a bit to one side with an air of great attention.

But Colonel Lester sprang up and exclaimed: "Good! Tom, you're worth a thousand! Ten thousand! Agnes, pay attention!

199

Tom Wayland has found the vicious rat of a Reata when we were about to give up hope!"

"Down the street—right down the street!" gasped Tom Wayland. "I saw him walking back toward the stalls. Pushing another man before him. A big man—hands tied behind his back. It was Reata who shoved him along! I know it was Reata! I know he was the man!"

CHAPTER 43

Reata had marched his captive straight back through the aisle between the stalls, and out through the rear door of the barn, and so into the gloom of a group of trees that grew in a dense cluster in the middle of the big corral behind the livery stable.

In the narrow clearing in the center of the trees, he tied the Overland Kid to a tree and then faced him close, for there were only a few gleams of starlight that entered the blackness.

Reata said: "I was expecting somebody at that stable; you came in his place. What's your name?"

"I dunno," said the Kid. "Maybe I might as well tell you a name. But what's the good to me?"

"You're going to hold out, are you?" said Reata.

"Yeah, and why not?"

"Stranger," said Reata, "out there in the open, this side of the creek, there was an old man with a load of hay. What did you do with him?"

"I dunno."

"You cut his throat!" said Reata. "You've had your teeth in his throat—but I'll have mine in your heart! If you touched the poor old fellow, if you even lifted a hand to him, I'll knock—"

Passion strangled him. And the Overland Kid heard that irregularly drawn breath and knew that he was inches only from death.

There was one great mystery. The gold seemed to come

second to Reata. The welfare of the old fellow was what he spoke of first and last. And this could not be a sham.

A queer suspicion came to the Overland Kid that he was confronting a new kind of a man, different in his thinking as he had been from others in the catlike speed and surety of his hand. He could remember how Salvio and the rest had talked. They were fighting men, all of them, but they had talked of Reata as of the devil himself.

This devil now was standing close to him, breathing deeply with a savage rage. And fear leaped suddenly into the strong soul of the Kid.

"But there are others of you!" said Reata. "There are enough of the rest of Dickerman's rats to pay. What I want out of you is talk. You hear me?"

The Overland Kid said nothing.

"You're going to talk. You're going to say everything you know," insisted Reata. "Don't think you're not. I'll—I'll burn the face off you, stranger, if I have to—but you'll talk!"

The Kid said nothing, and in response he heard a savage little whine of rage. Then a match was scratched and held close to him. He could see by the light of it the gray eyes of Reata, now swimming with yellow fury; and Reata could see the strained, set face of the Kid, with a certain dullness and immobility about the eyes, as though already he were striving with all the might of his will to forget his body and thrust its concerns off into nothingness.

Reata said: "I start at the chin, stranger. That'll toast for a while, and then I shift up to the ears. After that a bit of flame up the nose doesn't do any harm. Mind you—I'll burn the face off your skull!"

Terror and horror came up in the Kid's eyes for an instant. "Then talk!" said Reata.

The Overland Kid said absolutely nothing.

The match went out and dropped down into darkness.

"I've given you your last chance," said Reata. "Now I'm going to do what I said I'd do. And if you yell, if you make a noise, I'll drive a slug out of your own gun into your own heart!"

He scratched another match. His glaring face, strained, terrible, drew close to his captive, and then the Overland Kid made that face disappear from before his mind. He forgot it. All that obsessed his brain was that he must not be untrue to his partners.

They were a pretty bad lot, those fellows who worked, like him, for that king of the rats Pop Dickerman. But no matter what they were, they were his companions, and he could not betray them.

Well, if he breathed the flame when it was put under his nose —if a fellow could take one deep breath of flame, it was the end, he had heard. There would be endless agony before that, but he would keep the hope of putting out his life like a light.

Then he was aware that something had happened to Reata. The head of the man jerked back as though he had been stabbed. He gasped: "I can't do it! I can't do it!"

And the second match dropped out of his hand.

The Overland Kid heard a faint, groaning sound of curses, and those words again.

And he said, in a voice that shook a great deal: "Listen, they call me the Overland Kid. The old man—nothing happened to him. There wasn't a hair of him touched."

What was he saying? Well, admitting, by inference, that they *had* put their hands on the old man, or on his wagon load of hay—and of gold. And yet he could not feel that he had been treacherous in speaking like this. He had merely made a fair exchange for something that Reata had spared him, and for something else—a new idea at which he was still vaguely grasping.

"Old Dan is all right?" said Reata. "Thank God for that. I half thought—"

He hushed himself again, and then, after a moment, he added: "I know you're one of Dickerman's rats, and I ought to tear you to bits. But there's something right about you, Over-
202

land. I don't know what, but it's in you. I ought to leave you tied here and gagged all night. But how long would it be before you were found?"

The Overland Kid waited, silent. It seemed to him that through the darkness he could feel the pulse of Reata's struggle. Then Reata was saying: "I'm a fool. I'm the biggest fool that ever lived. But suppose you got loose from this, would you forget that you'd seen me here in town?"

The Kid answered: "I've got to be square with my partners, but I could forget that I'd seen you here. Sure. I could forget that. I *want* to forget it!"

"Will you get out of town and go back to wherever you're headed, and not use the knowledge that you've seen me?"

"I'll do that."

"Then—well, there you are."

Suddenly the Overland Kid was free. He heard a slight, rapid clicking sound.

"Here's your guns back, so no questions will have to be asked. You can load 'em later on out of your belt. So long, Overland."

"Wait a minute," gasped the Kid. "I'd like to—well, I'd like to shake hands on all of this."

"Shake hands?" said Reata, his voice rising a shade and hardening to scorn. "You would have shot me. You came half an inch from doing it. You're one of Dickerman's rats. Shake hands with you? I'd rather shake hands with a slimy water moccasin!"

And Reata was gone, and behind him he left on the soul of the Overland Kid such a burden as never had oppressed it before.

Slowly the Overland Kid went back toward the barn, his head hanging. And as he reached the rear door of the barn, hands suddenly grasped him, and guns glimmered dimly about him in the starlight.

"We've got him!" breathed a voice. "Hey, Balen, we've got him!"

203

"You fool!" exclaimed another. "He's twice the size of Reata! Leave him go. Sorry, partner. Took you for another gent!"

The Overland Kid said nothing in answer. He walked on down the aisle of the barn. There were scores of men on the watch for Reata. Why? Because the world hates a man if he simply chooses to go his own way?

He took his saddled horse and went out of the town of Tyndal, deep in thought

CHAPTER 44

Reata went into the first saloon. He knew there was danger, but he wanted a drink. He needed a drink, a deep drink of rank, stupefying whisky. So he went into a saloon and stood in the corner at the bar, and ordered the stuff like medicine.

There were a dozen other fellows in the place, all men off the range, noisy, their faces covered with the red-brown varnish of long exposure to the sun. Their hands were dirty with the sort of black that harness oil works into the very tissues of the skin. Reata liked standing there among them. They were honest. Aye, hard as nails, but straight as a string, every man, It was like standing in sunshine in the open air after long confinement in a sick room to be back among such fellows as these.

He thought then of the days when he had been building the cabin where he and Miriam were to start life together up there in the mountains alone. He could let his memory wander from day to day, and almost from hour to hour, up to the moment when Miriam had told him that she could not go through with the thing, that she was already bored with him.

Aye, a gypsy girl, and he had wanted to close her up in one spot for the rest of her life. He was a fool! And yet it had been a beautiful folly.

Some one said behind him: "Hey, here's one of the gypsies. Goin' to do some stunts for us to get the drinks."

"Nope, he'll pass the hat afterward. Go ahead, Jimmy. Show us your stuff!"

It was Georg, the new wild rider of horses for the gypsies. He had come into the saloon, and was bowing to all the men assembled. Then he was throwing three knives into the air, one after the other, making the steel blades spin into flashes of fire, like bodiless flames that hung in the air. When a fourth one joined the rest and walked up higher than the other three, almost to the ceiling, turning in a slower cadence, the cowpunchers gave the juggler a good, hearty hand.

The four knives seemed to be enough to keep the gypsy worried, however. And one of them dropped. He collected the rest from the air with a sudden, embarrassed gesture, and scooped up the fallen blade where it was lying on the floor at Reata's feet.

As he leaned over, he was saying, softly: "On guard, Reata!"

And as he rose: "They're after you. Front door and back door."

Then again he was at work, spinning the knives in the air.

His performance ceased to exist for Reata.

"They" were after him, and that must mean Colonel Lester and the rest. "They" had spotted him, then? Well, if they had the front door and the back door blocked, if they were about ready to burst in on him, there was another exit.

He hopped over the bar, while the barman yelled out in surprise. And right through the open window behind the end of the bar Reata dived from a handspring, feet-first, shooting out into the darkness as though into water.

It was not water that received him, however. But heavy bodies flung down on him, crushing the breath out of his lungs, and powerful hands grasped him as though they were striving to tear the flesh from his bones.

"Hold him! Hold him!" gasped the voice of Colonel Lester. "You were right, Balen! The window was his trick! A light, here!"

A lantern was unshuttered, and it flashed with dazzling

brightness into the eyes of Reata. He lay still, without a struggle. The fools were after him again! The half-wits were blocking his way and keeping him from working at *their* real problem! And he had to lie still and submit.

They made a great parade of their achievement. That was the colonel's fault, not Steve Balen's. The colonel had Reata's hands tied behind him, and an armed man at each shoulder of the prisoner, and a lantern before, and a lantern behind. Just in front of the second lantern strode the colonel, sticking out his chest and pulling in his chin, with a long rifle carried at the ready in his hands. It was a good parade all the way to the colonel's hotel, and the people of Tyndal turned out to gape at the spectacle.

When they came to the hotel there was a dash of trouble that made the colonel purple, and Tom Wayland white, for as the parade crossed the lobby of the hotel, Agnes Lester came out of nowhere and ran up to Reata, crying out: "It's an outrage and a crime—and I know that you didn't steal the Jumping Creek money, Reata!"

The colonel got his breath to shout her down and send her to her room. Then he marched Reata upstairs. In the colonel's mind there was a vivid picture of that other occasion when he had had Reata securely confined in a room from which, in all seeming, it was impossible for anything but a bird to escape. And yet Reata *had* gone free, and left Steve Balen tied up in his place!

This time the colonel would not make any mistakes. He would take the matter into his own consideration and be himself responsible for what happened! So he had a seven-foot two-by-four scantling brought to his room, and to this Reata was lashed, not by the hands and feet alone, but with sixty feet of strong rope wound around and around him. And his hands, those formidable and dexterous hands, were held straight down at his sides by the strong twist of the rope.

When Reata was well secured in this fashion, the colonel said to Steve Balen: "Now, you tell me, Balen. Is there any way at
206

all for this scoundrel to get out of my grasp this time?"

"Not that I know of," said Steve. "Not unless help flies in at the window or walks in through the door."

The colonel sat down in a comfortable chair and took a shotgun across his knees.

"I lock the door on the inside," he said. "You and the rest keep guard under the window. I lock that door on the inside. Now tell me how help can come to Reata?"

Balen shook his head. "I dunno that I can tell you," he said. "Nobody can tell you, because there ain't any way that Reata can get loose unless he can break that rope with his breathin'."

The colonel laughed very cheerfully. "Go out, then," he commanded. "I'll take charge of this man and be responsible for him!"

It was at about this time that Blackie, out there in the shack on Tyndal Creek, waked rather suddenly in the middle of the night. They were standing watch, two hours a turn, through the night, and, having finished his session, Blackie had fallen sound asleep while Chad took his turn. Something pulled at the subconscious mind of Blackie, and, waking with a start, he saw with his first glance—by the last glimmering from the fire on the hearth—that the heap of chamois sacks of gold, in the corner of the room, had seriously diminished.

Blackie sat up agape, and reached for his Colt. He heard from a corner the snoring of Harry Quinn. The Overland Kid was asleep near the fire, having come in late from town in a silent mood. And overhead in the attic, old Dan Foster was snoring, also, keeping a soft accompaniment to the noise that Harry Quinn made.

But where was Chad, the man on guard?

At that moment he came in, hastily squinted once around the room, and then picked up two bags of the gold and turned stealthily toward the door.

Blackie could understand what that meant. He jerked up his revolver and shouted: "Murder!" And then he followed his own word by driving a bullet right through the back of Chad.

207

The thunder of the gun instantly filled the room with echoes and with upleaping forms.

"Chad! He's stealin' the gold!" yelled Blackie, springing to his feet.

Chad, knocked flat by the impact of the bullet, had struck the side of the door in his fall, twisted, and gone down with a crash in a sitting posture facing Blackie.

There was a great, stretching smile on the face of Chad, or something that looked like a smile. Even as the heavy slug smote him, he had dropped the two bags of the gold that he was purloining and snatched out a gun. That big Colt now lay on the floor beside him, and he picked it up with a slow hand and raised it.

"Get him!" yelled Blackie, and made a stride forward, shooting. He smashed his first bullet into the jamb above Chad's head. He saw the second crush into Chad's breast. But death would not come to the man. The revolver which he was lifting came to a level with Blackie's breast, and then spat fire. Blackie fell on his face, and Chad lowered his gun and leaned slowly to the side, still grinning.

They were both dead. A bit of dry wood thrown on the fire by the Overland Kid soon showed what had happened, and before the two bodies could be laid out side by side and covered with a blanket, old Dan Foster looked down through the attic trapdoor and drawled: "Now we got a little blood on the gold, eh? Maybe there'll be a mite more before the wind-up!"

Back in the hotel room of the colonel, Reata, giving up hope, had closed his eyes and gone to sleep. He was wakened once by a sharp sound of voices beneath the window; he heard the stern words of Steve Balen, commanding some one to get away and keep away, and then the soft, musical voice of Georg making answer.

The gypsy was trying to make a rescue, but he had failed. Every other agency would fail, also. Help had to come from himself. And what could that help be?

He went to sleep again, and when he wakened, he had a sense

that he was between the brightness of two suns. Then he saw that the sun had, in fact, risen, and was high enough to shine brightly through the eastern window. But to the right of Reata there was another glittering fire, and this, he saw, came from the colonel's concave shaving mirror which he had carelessly placed on a low stool. It was standing up, and the broad face of it fully collected the rays of the sun and focused on the carpet a dazzling patch of yellow-white light so strong in heat that a very thin smoke was rising.

That sight gave a thought to Reata. Knives are not the only thing to sever ropes; flame will do it, also. He glanced toward the colonel and saw him fast asleep, his body sagging far to one side in his chair, and the shotgun appearing in the very act of sliding off his lap. If the gun fell, the noise of it would rouse the colonel and wreck Reata's plan. Or perhaps other noises from the wakening town would rouse him.

Slowly, with infinite effort, Reata rolled himself over until he could adjust his body so that the fine, full focus of the light gathered by the shaving glass dropped exactly on a turn of the rope across his chest, where he could watch it.

The heat began to bite the fabric of the rope at once. The focus with which it had fallen on the rug of the room had been quite inexact; this perfect pinhead focus was hotter than fire, and instantly smoke began to rise, then the surface of the rope commenced to glow.

He could blow down on that glowing point and increase the burning. If only it would flame, the rope would soon part. But there were two difficulties. The sun was rising, and therefore the focus of the light from the glass was altering slowly, so that Reata had to keep shifting his body closer to the mirror, an infinitesimal bit at a time. Besides, as the heat grew greater, it burned not only the rope, but also Reata's shirt, and then his flesh. The pain seemed to him to be drilling straight through his body.

He could not help remembering how he had threatened the Overland Kid the night before. Now the same agony he had promised was being given to him.

Would the smell of the burning rope rouse the colonel? For the drifting smoke filled the room with thin wreaths, and some of these passed right before the face of the colonel.

He groaned. He stirred. He half lifted a hand, and the shotgun slid a little farther forward to the edge of his knees.

Then, with a very light, dull, popping sound, the rope parted across the breast of Reata.

The pain continued, for the cloth of his shirt was now in a glow that was spreading fast. But two or three wriggles caused the rope to loosen in all its length, and a moment later he was free to sit up, to clutch at his shirt and put out the spot of fire, and then to rise to his feet.

CHAPTER 45

He picked up the coils of rope which had bound him. Then he lifted the shotgun from Lester's lap, and the removal of the weight caused the colonel to rouse with a slight start. His great, vague eyes blinked for an instant before he could appreciate that picture of his own shotgun being pointed at him by the hands of Reata.

"Steady, partner," said Reata. "We've both had a good sleep, but now it's time for me to go. I think you'd better have another nap, though. So I'm going to fix you so that you won't slide out of your chair. If you budge," he added sternly, "or if you try to yell, I'll lift off your head with what's inside this shotgun!"

The colonel opened his mouth, but no sound issued from it, while Reata tied him with a cruel firmness into that big, comfortable chair. He wadded the colonel's own handkerchief into a knot and thrust it between his teeth as a gag.

"What a fool you are, Lester!" said Reata. "What a fat-faced fool! And what keeps me from rapping you over your hollow

210

head except that you happen to have Agnes for a daughter? Adios, colonel!"

He unlocked the door and stepped into the hall.

It was empty. So were the stairs, and the lobby below. By the back door, Reata stepped out into the young morning and went around to the livery stable. Through the rear door of that he entered, and little Rags was instantly jumping about his feet in a silent frenzy of joy. And then the roan mare was pricking her ears and wriggling her nostrils in a silent whinny of greeting.

On the edge of the manger, Reata laid a little heap of gold dust taken from his money pouch, enough to pay the livery bill five times over. After that he saddled the mare at his leisure, and rode out behind the town and around it toward the open country.

He struck out in a shallow semi-circle until he came to the trail of the wagon; on that he dropped Rags, and the little dog led him straight on toward the town, across a hollow, and finally off to the right toward a group of trees.

Inside that grove, Reata found the wagon, with most of the hay thrown off it. Beyond the trees there was a very dim trail over hard ground, on which he dropped Rags again, and so it was that he came within calling distance of the waters of the creek, and still Rags went scurrying on toward the trees that screened the banks. Just before them a horse whinnied, short and soft.

So Reata called in Rags with a wave of his arm. With the little dog sniffing the way before him, on foot Reata penetrated the wood, with Sue gliding noiselessly behind him, and presently he came on a semicircular clearing about a shack which stood on the very bank of the stream, with a pair of mules in harness before the house, and six saddle horses.

He had come in the very nick of time, if anything were to be done, for he saw Gene Salvio and Harry Quinn and Dave Bates, in turn, carrying out those familiar little chamois bags and loading them onto three of the horses.

When that was ended, Bates remained with the horses, calling over his shoulder: "You gents figger out what's going to be done with the two stiffs. Dump 'em in the creek, is my idea!"

"Your idea's all wrong," said the voice of the Overland Kid, sounding dimly from inside the shack. "We ought to burn down the shack. That'll rub away any identification marks. And unless those are wiped out, the law's goin' to be down on us for a double killing one of these days."

A warm argument started inside the shanty at this. But Dave Bates shrugged his shoulders at the noise and began to roll a cigarette. He was in the act of sealing the wheat-straw paper when a wisp of shadow struck down across his eyes. Then the thin line of Reata's rope jerked his arms to a helpless rigidity against his sides, and before he could cry out, a flying loop of the rope fastened with strangling force around his throat.

He was not allowed to strangle, however. The flying hands of Reata loosed that lariat from its grip, and, snatching a rope from the nearest saddle, he instantly gagged and made Bates helpless.

And then, still on one knee, Reata looked up to see the Overland Kid in the doorway of the shack, looking straight at him, and in the act of drawing a gun.

He was finished, he knew. For a fellow like the Kid would not miss at such a point-blank distance. Yet it was strange that the movement of whipping out the gun was not completed. For a terrible half second the two men stared at one another, and then the Kid turned his back on the outdoors, and, blocking the doorway with his heavy shoulders and big body, began to say: "Burning is the only way. You can see that, Salvio."

"Aye," Salvio was answering. "Maybe burning is the only way. But maybe we oughta put the bodies up there in the attic, and besides, here's old Dan Foster that can talk about us all."

"Dan's give his word not to talk, and I'll take his promise," said the Overland Kid.

Reata, stunned, bewildered, was catching up the lead ropes of the horses. Then, drawing them away after him, on the verge

212

of the clearing, one gesture brought the roan mare to him, and, mounting her, he fastened to her saddle the end of the last lead rope. Six horses were now strung out to the side and behind him.

Every step was taking them out of sight among the trees when he heard a screaming voice behind him: "The horses! The horses! Hi, it's Reata! Rifles! Salvio, look!"

It seemed to Reata that he could never get the led horses into a gallop. They walked, they trotted, at last they were in an easy canter.

They left the woods. They stretched their legs in a longer and a longer stride, widened the distance between them and the edge of the woods—and then the rifles began.

Salvio, Harry Quinn, and the Overland Kid had run out from the trees, and, lying flat, they opened fire with their guns.

But the distance was great, and now the ground dropped away into a dry-bottomed draw which sheltered Reata and his horses completely.

The firing had ended. Only, out of the distance, he heard the savage, despairing yells of Salvio and Harry Quinn.

CHAPTER 46

Decker, round-faced and empty-eyed, and Dillon, white-headed and tiny and stern, faced one another across the mahogany sheen of the long table in the president's office of the Decker and Dillon Bank. Six other men sat with them, men with a grim and determined look which they shared in common. For the Decker and Dillon Bank was passing into the hands of the receivers.

Decker was silent. His life was wiped out. He was too close to sixty to begin again. He felt that he had the form and the look of a man, but that there was nothing whatever inside him.

As for Dillon, he was closer to seventy than to sixty. It was not the end of life for him. It was actual death and burial when he walked out of this bank and stepped onto the street. But he made a little speech.

"It goes to show," he said, "that men are fools when they work a big thing on a small margin. We needed a hundred thousand to meet everything outstanding. We had twice that much in the vaults in pure gold, and you know it.

"We had a business running, too, that would bring us in sufficient profits, inside of two years, to meet every debt we owe. But you fellows don't want us to have that chance. You want the business for yourselves, and you're going to get it. But what I tell you is that you take over the bank and the curse I put on it. ·

"If a life of honest labor—"

A man at the foot of the table said: "Dillon, you know that we've made up our minds. There's no use gabbling and being sentimental. Matter of fact, we would have acted before this if Colonel Lester hadn't been gadding about the country, chasing a will-o'-the-wisp. Now we've determined on action. Lester himself will be back here before long, but we have the power and the authority to act without him. If you'll finish your speech, we'll get down to details!"

"You see, George?" said Dillon, looking with a strange smile at Decker.

"I knew what it would be," answered Decker. "We might as well wind things up. I'll sign where I'm told to—and there's the end."

It was at this time that a stir came in the outer rooms of the bank, and then a murmur, and suddenly a shouting of people all along the street.

One word came clearly through the thick walls to the ears of the listeners.

"Reata!"

"What's that?" asked one of the bank's creditors, jumping up from his chair. "Reata? That's the name of the rascal that

214

Lester has been wild-goose chasing all over the range. Don't tell me that he's managed to bring the fellow in."

Here a hand knocked heavily on the door, and when it was unlocked and opened, the cashier stood on the threshold, babbling vague sounds, brandishing his two hands.

"The gold? Returned?" shouted Decker.

He managed to get out of his chair, but his knees were bending so that he could not budge. It was little old Dillon who got out of the room into the corridor beyond and found shouting men who were carrying into the bank small chamois sacks, the leather curiously streaked and stained with green.

Twenty-one of those sacks were piled on the floor of the bank. Old Dillon stood over them, with his arms folded tightly across his breast, for he felt that otherwise his heart would break with swelling joy. He ran his glittering eyes over the faces of his mute, gaping creditors.

At last he was able to point to the door.

"The gold has come back," he said; "you'll all have your bills paid. But now—get out of my sight and get out of my bank!"

Afterward, as the crowds thickened in the street, they were able to find out who had brought the stuff back—Reata!

But where had he gone?

No man could tell. And while the search for him went on, Colonel Lester and tall Steve Balen rode with their men into the main street of Jumping Creek. Agnes Lester was with them, high-headed, and very strangely smiling, so that her father could not endure to look into her pretty face.

Before they had gone two blocks they had heard the story. The lost gold had been returned. And the very man they had been pursuing as the thief had brought it back!

The colonel, when he heard this, looked about him wildly, as though all sense, all truth, all logic had vanished from the world.

"But this is not possible!" he shouted at last. "An infernal thief—a criminal—a scoundrel who has actually dared to defy

215

—who has escaped twice from—But his profession is stealing, and he *can't* return the goods he has taken away! It isn't sense. It means nothing. It—"

Steve Balen ventured to interrupt him.

"He's made fools of us all," said Balen. "He's slapped our faces for us, dog-gone it, and now we can like it or lump it. And I reckon that your daughter knew he was a straight-shooter all the time!"

"She? How could she know? Agnes, I have half a mind—I feel as though I'd go mad! Agnes, what *do* you know about this fellow—this Reata—this sneak thief and juggler and—what do you know about him?"

"I haven't talked an hour to him in my entire life," said the girl. "How could I know anything about him?"

But she began to laugh, and she kept on laughing from time to time, as though there were a ceaseless supply of bright happiness in her that could not be exhausted by words, or even by laughter itself.

There was a greater chance for the colonel to be outraged and infuriated when, late in the day, he left Jumping Creek, where all men were still vainly searching for Reata, and went out to his big house beyond the town. There, as he sat beneath the trees, with his daughter beside him, and Tom Wayland, also—big Tom Wayland pretending that he did not notice the looks of scorn which the girl freely gave him whenever he glanced her way—there, into the midst of the peaceful family circle, as it were, Reata suddenly appeared.

At one moment there had been nothing near, and suddenly Reata had stepped out from behind a tree and was saying: "Good evening, Colonel. I've come to speak to Miss Lester, with your permission."

"My permission?" exclaimed the colonel. "I've a good mind to—My permission, you say, you impertinent young scoundrel? Speak to Agnes? Why, I'll have you—"

Agnes Lester walked right by her father and stood between him and the other.

216

"What is it, Reata?" she said.

And the colonel grew dizzy, and almost fainted when he saw how close she stood to this man, and, with her head tilted back, smiled up at him.

This weakness prevented Lester from interrupting, and that was why he was able to hear Reata saying:

"I've come to say good-by. I thought I could say something else, but I can't. The man who wants my scalp is pretty apt to get it, unless I move fast and keep on moving. I've been traveling in a pretty shifty way recently, for that matter, but he's made men and horses grow up in my way before and behind. So I've got to run and keep on running. He'll chase me still the way he's chased me before. But one day I'll shake clear of him and have a chance to see you again, far off, safely."

The colonel, having made out this speech, was even willing to be still; but he almost had an apoplectic stroke when he saw his daughter deliberately turn with Reata and walk away with him through the trees toward the front of the house. At this, Colonel Lester gasped, and he would have lurched in pursuit had not white-faced Tom Wayland gripped and held him.

"It's best to leave them alone," said Wayland. "Anything that speaks against him just now—anything that tries to come between them—why, it would make Agnes leave home and go barefoot after him around the world. Be quiet, please—she'll be back here soon enough."

And while the colonel was still gasping and wheezing, she did, in fact, come slowly back through the trees, her head bowed, and so she went silently up into the house.

Even Colonel Lester, who could not see many things, could understand that Tom Wayland had been right.

As for Reata, he went over the first hill as swiftly as Sue could streak it in order to put one landmark between him and the girl. And in the hollow beneath that hill he was stopped by a rider with a raised arm.

It was the Overland Kid, who said to him tersely: "Reata, I'm busting away from Dickerman. I wanta quit the job with

217

him, and there ain't a thing in the world that I'd rather do than go along with you, if you'll have me!"

Bewilderment closed the lips of Reata.

"You're a better man, and a bigger man, and a righter man than me," said the Overland Kid, "but it seems to me I might be useful to you; I'd try to be square. Would you give me a chance?"

Reata swung the mare close to the Overland Kid and gripped his hand hard; he was still holding it as he said:

"Partner, I'd rather have you along than any man I know in the world. But it's no good. You and I were two little rats trying to scamper away from the king of the rats. If we run together, we'll both sure be found. They say that no man ever gets away from Pop Dickerman, but I'm going to try. Later on you'll hear whether I'm dead or living. Then you can make your own try to get free. But the two of us together would be ten times as easy for him to catch as one man alone. But, if you ever get far enough away from him, come and find me, and I'll be mighty dog-gone happy to be your partner, Overland."

"Do you mean it?"

"Aye, and I mean it, too."

"All right, then," said the Kid. "I can wait, then, and take my own turn."

Afterward he sat his horse and watched the roan mare canter smoothly up the hollow, and then over the next rise, where the image showed for a moment like a little black morsel being drawn into a vast conflagration, for the sky was on fire.